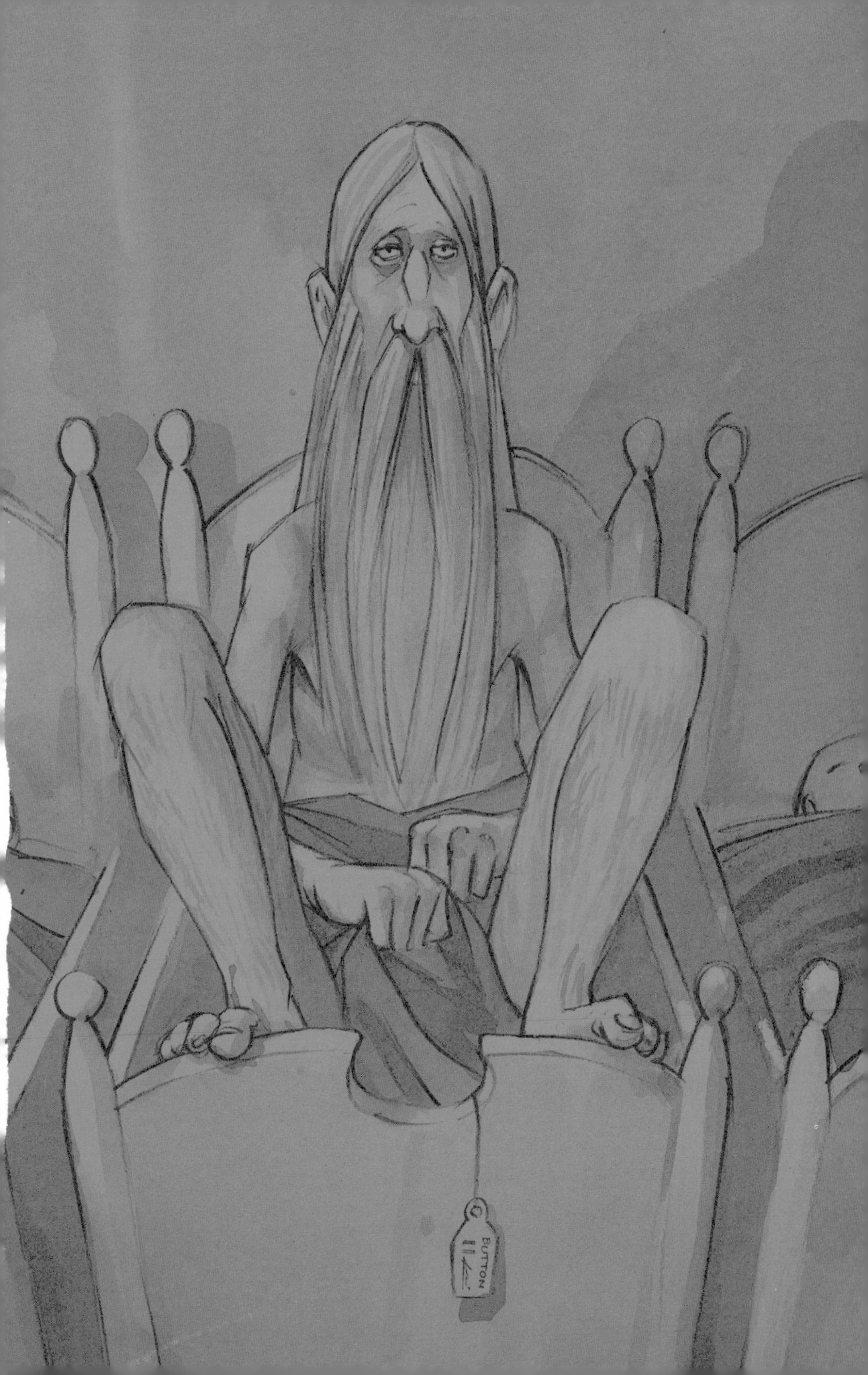
BUTTON

Copyright © 2008 by Quirk Productions, Inc.

Library of Congress Cataloging in Publication Number:
2008923680

ISBN: 978-1-59474-281-1

Printed in China

Typeset in Caslon

Illustrated by Kevin Cornell
Designed by Bryn Ashburn

Distributed in North America by Chronicle Books
680 Second Street
San Francisco, CA 94107

10 9 8 7 6 5 4 3 2 1

Quirk Books
215 Church Street
Philadelphia, PA 19106
www.quirkbooks.com

THE CURIOUS CASE OF

BENJAMIN

BUTTON

A GRAPHIC NOVEL

F. Scott Fitzgerald

ADAPTED BY NUNZIO DEFILIPPIS & CHRISTINA WEIR
ILLUSTRATED BY KEVIN CORNELL

QUIRK BOOKS
PHILADELPHIA

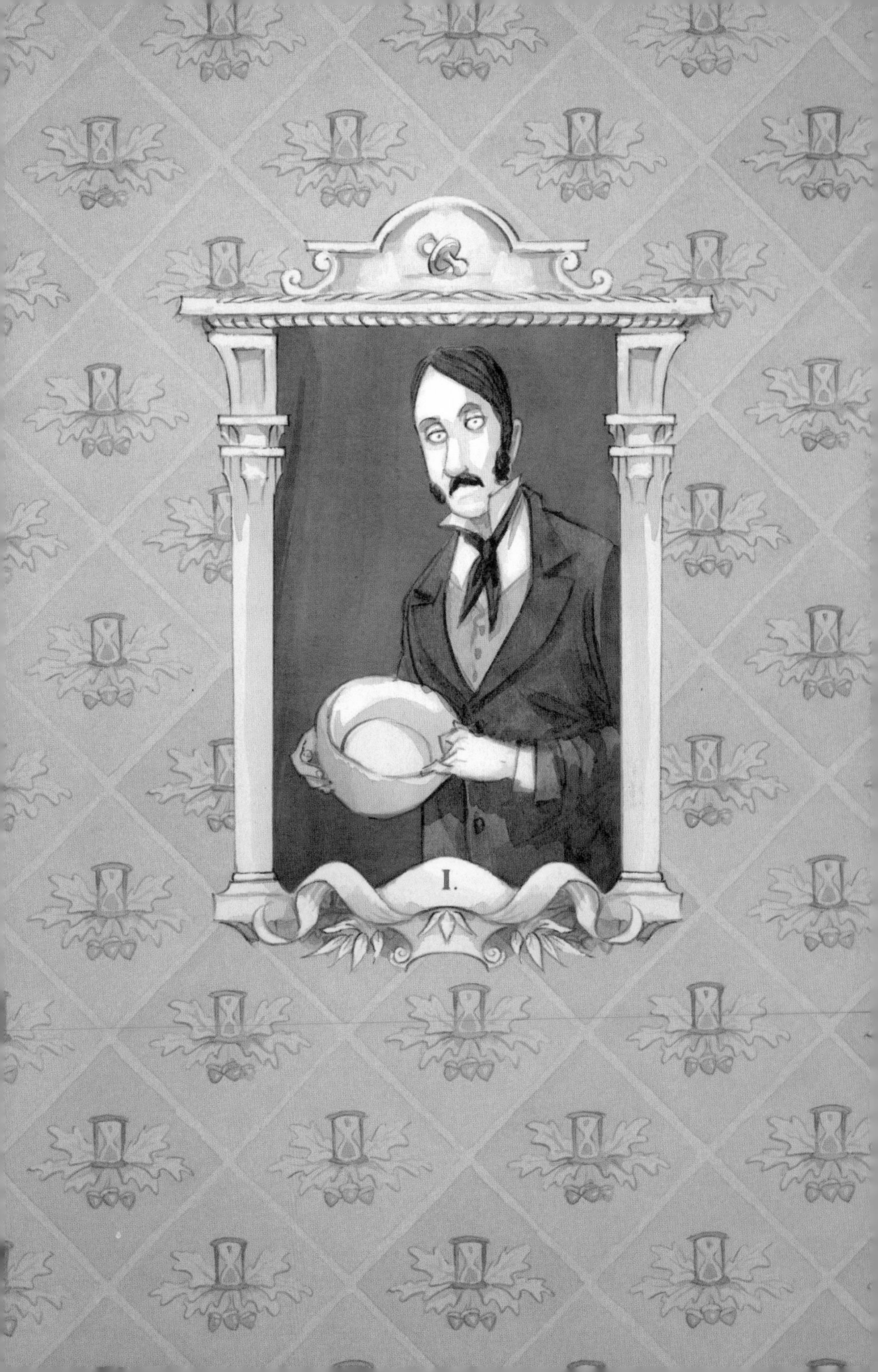
I.

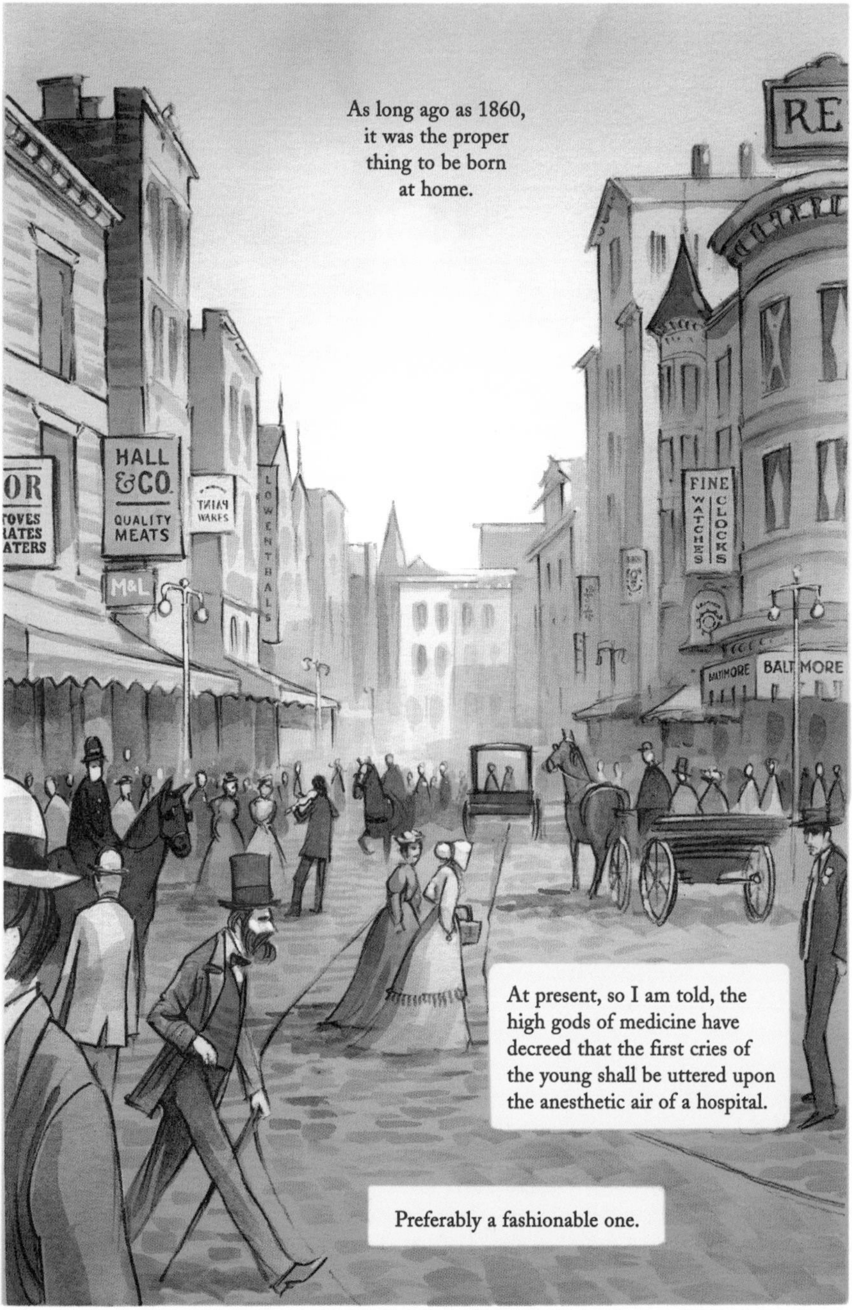
As long ago as 1860, it was the proper thing to be born at home.
HALL &CO. QUALITY MEATS
M&L
PAINT WARES
LOWENTHALS
FINE WATCHES CLOCKS
BALTIMORE
BALTIMORE
At present, so I am told, the high gods of medicine have decreed that the first cries of the young shall be uttered upon the anesthetic air of a hospital.
Preferably a fashionable one.

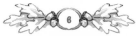

So, young Mr. and Mrs. Roger Button were ahead of style when they decided, one day in the summer of 1860, that their first baby should be born in a hospital.

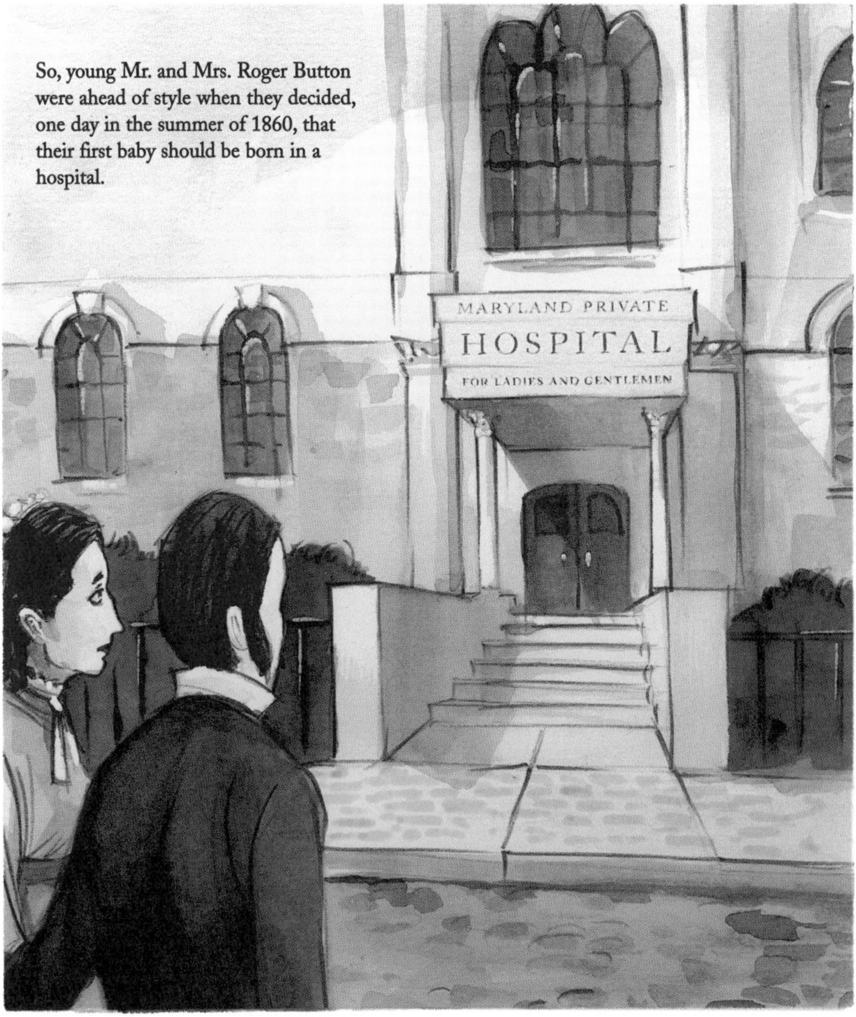
MARYLAND PRIVATE
HOSPITAL
FOR LADIES AND GENTLEMEN

Whether this anachronism had any bearing upon the astonishing history I am about to set down will never be known.

I shall tell you what occurred and let you judge for yourself.

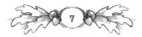

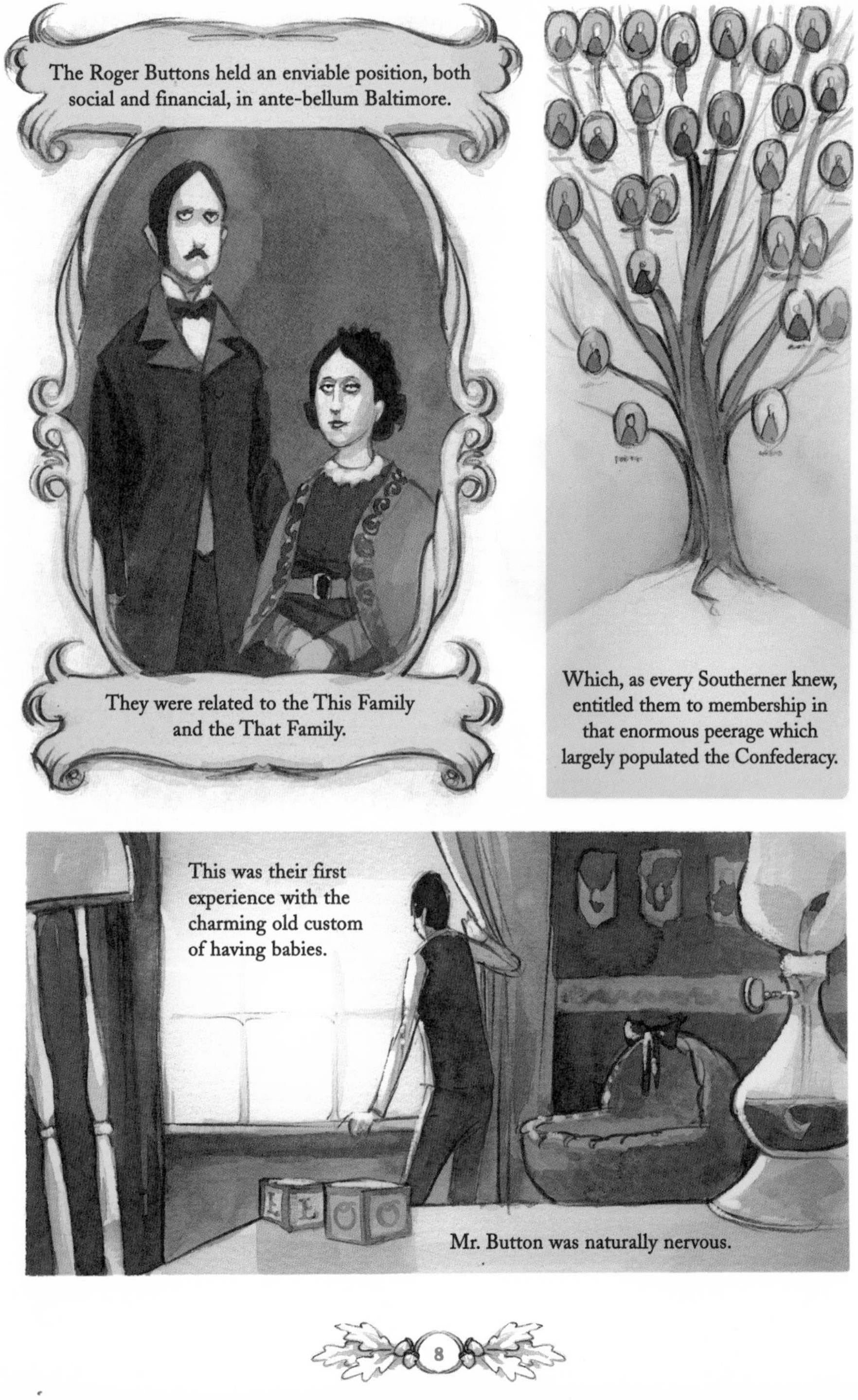
The Roger Buttons held an enviable position, both social and financial, in ante-bellum Baltimore.
They were related to the This Family and the That Family.
Which, as every Southerner knew, entitled them to membership in that enormous peerage which largely populated the Confederacy.
This was their first experience with the charming old custom of having babies.
Mr. Button was naturally nervous.

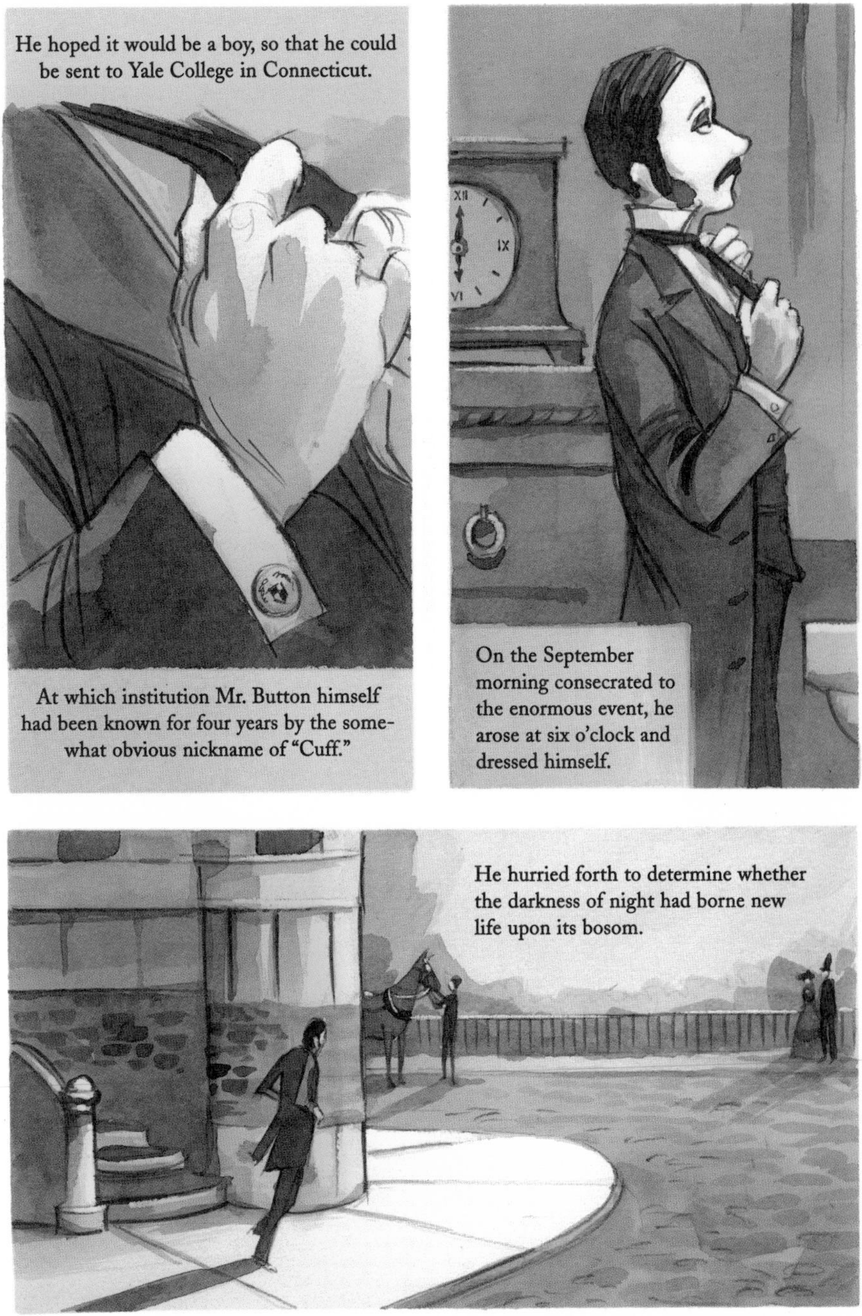
He hoped it would be a boy, so that he could be sent to Yale College in Connecticut.
At which institution Mr. Button himself had been known for four years by the somewhat obvious nickname of "Cuff."
On the September morning consecrated to the enormous event, he arose at six o'clock and dressed himself.
He hurried forth to determine whether the darkness of night had borne new life upon its bosom.

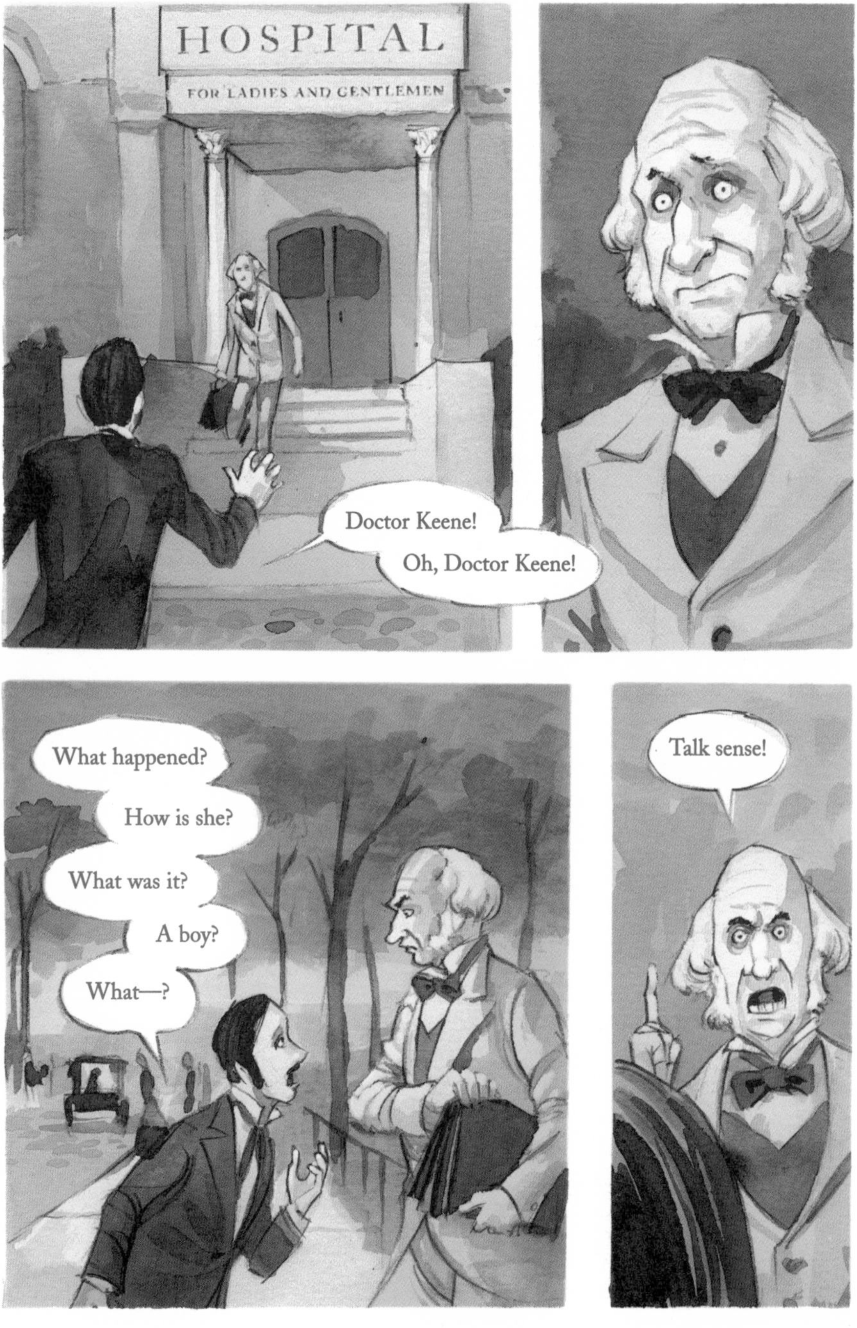

HOSPITAL
FOR LADIES AND GENTLEMEN
Doctor Keene!
Oh, Doctor Keene!
What happened?
How is she?
What was it?
A boy?
What—?
Talk sense!

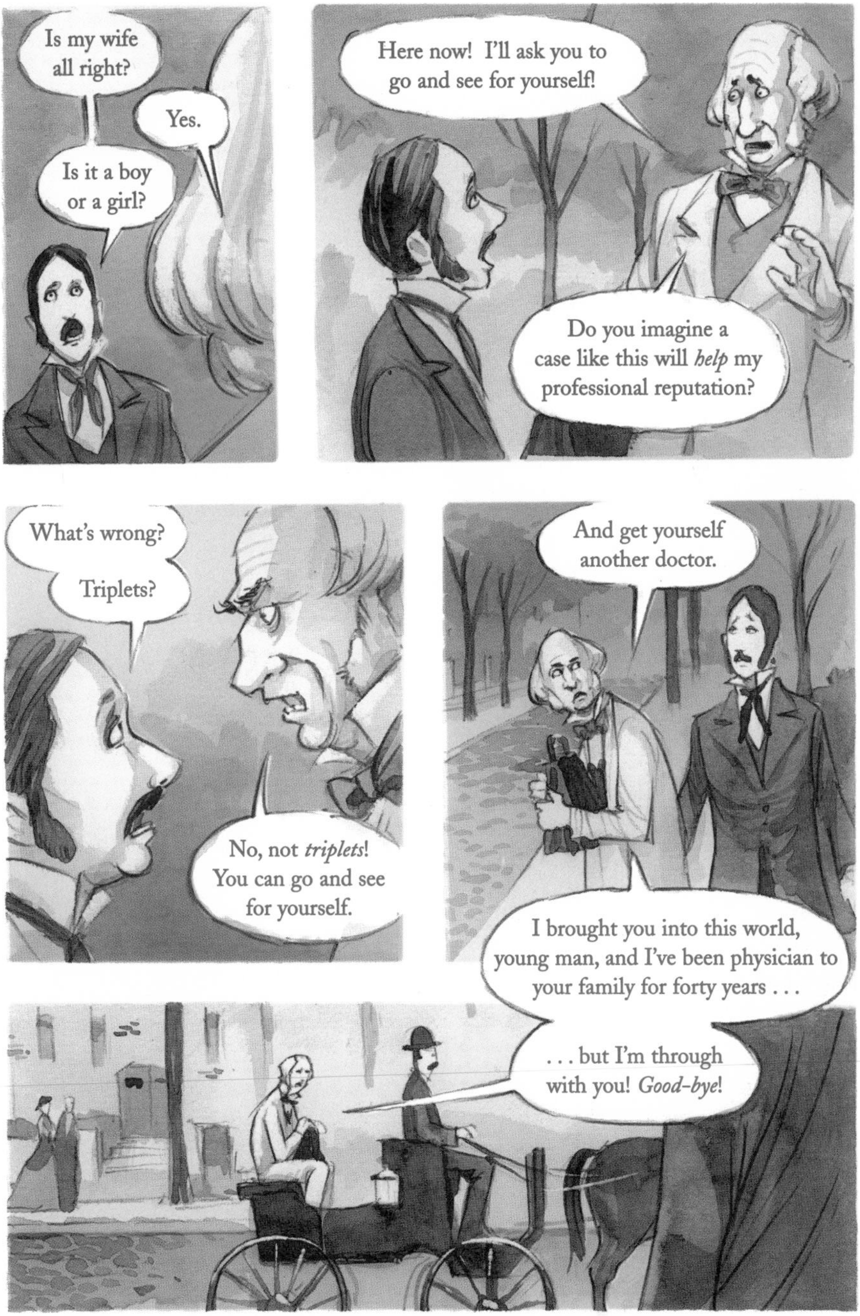
Is my wife all right?
Yes.
Is it a boy or a girl?
Here now! I'll ask you to go and see for yourself!
Do you imagine a case like this will *help* my professional reputation?
What's wrong?
Triplets?
No, not *triplets*! You can go and see for yourself.
And get yourself another doctor.
I brought you into this world, young man, and I've been physician to your family for forty years . . .
. . . but I'm through with you! *Good-bye*!

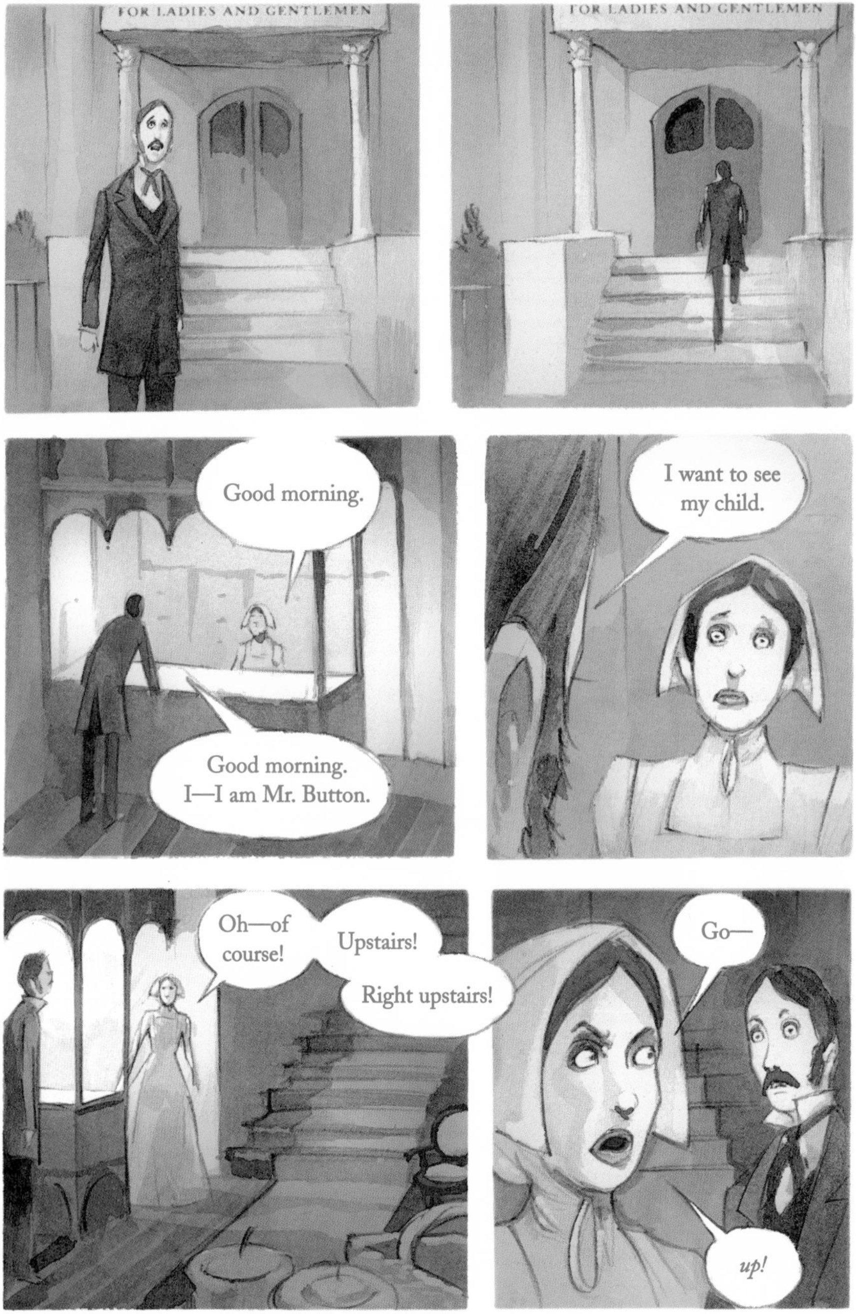
FOR LADIES AND GENTLEMEN
FOR LADIES AND GENTLEMEN
Good morning.
Good morning.
I—I am Mr. Button.
I want to see my child.
Oh—of course!
Upstairs!
Right upstairs!
Go—
up!

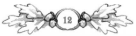

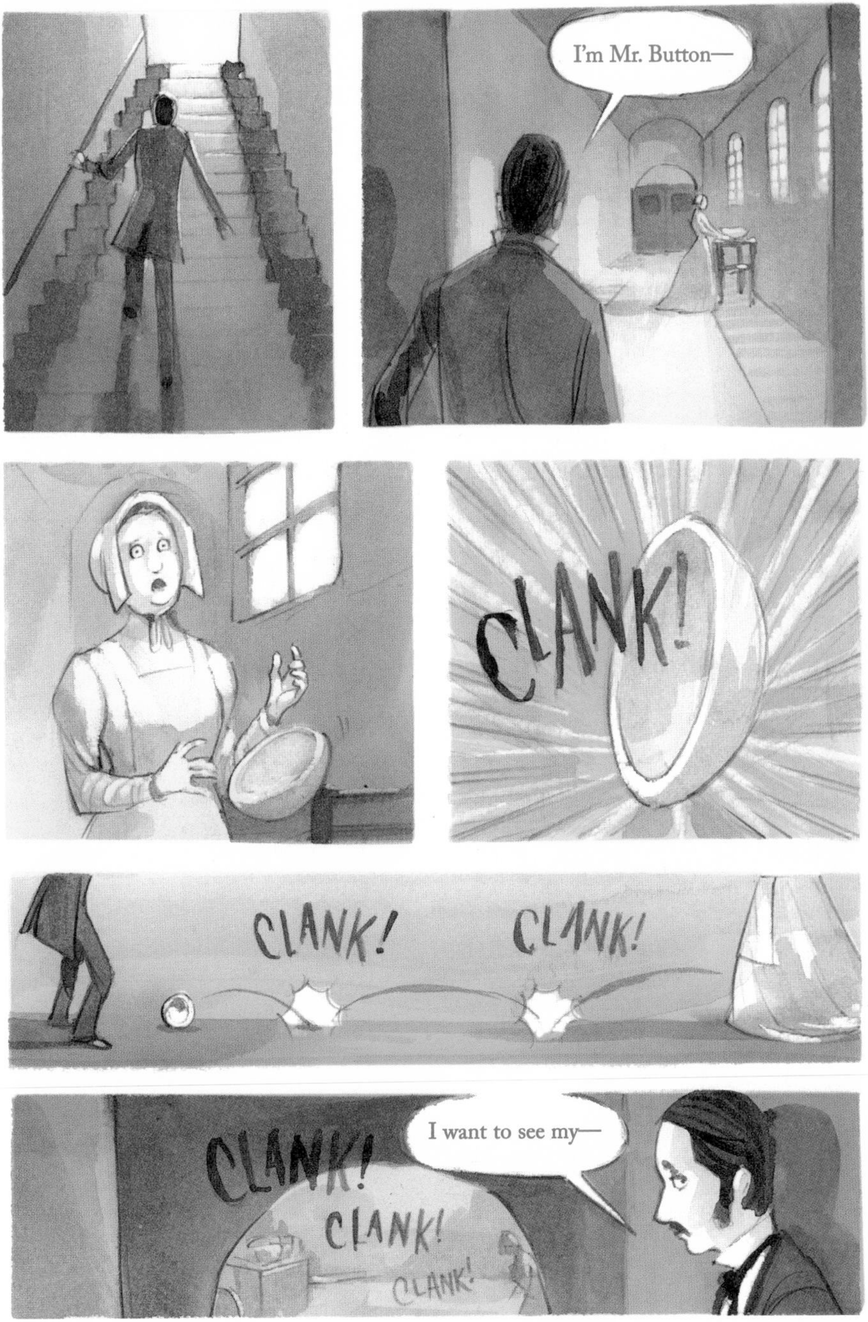
I'm Mr. Button—
CLANK!
CLANK!
CLANK!
CLANK!
I want to see my—
CLANK!
CLANK!

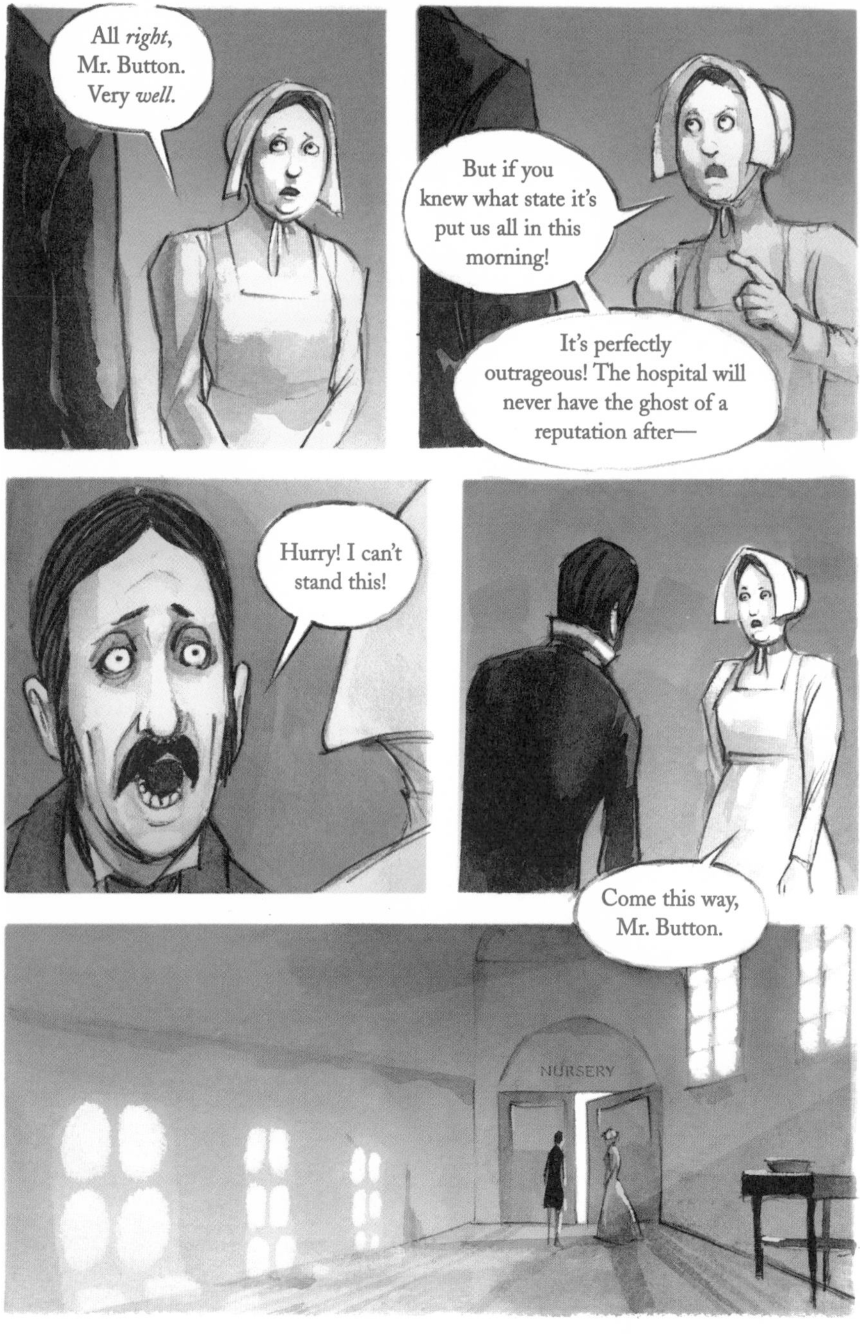
All *right*, Mr. Button. Very *well*.
But if you knew what state it's put us all in this morning!
It's perfectly outrageous! The hospital will never have the ghost of a reputation after—
Hurry! I can't stand this!
Come this way, Mr. Button.
NURSERY

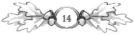

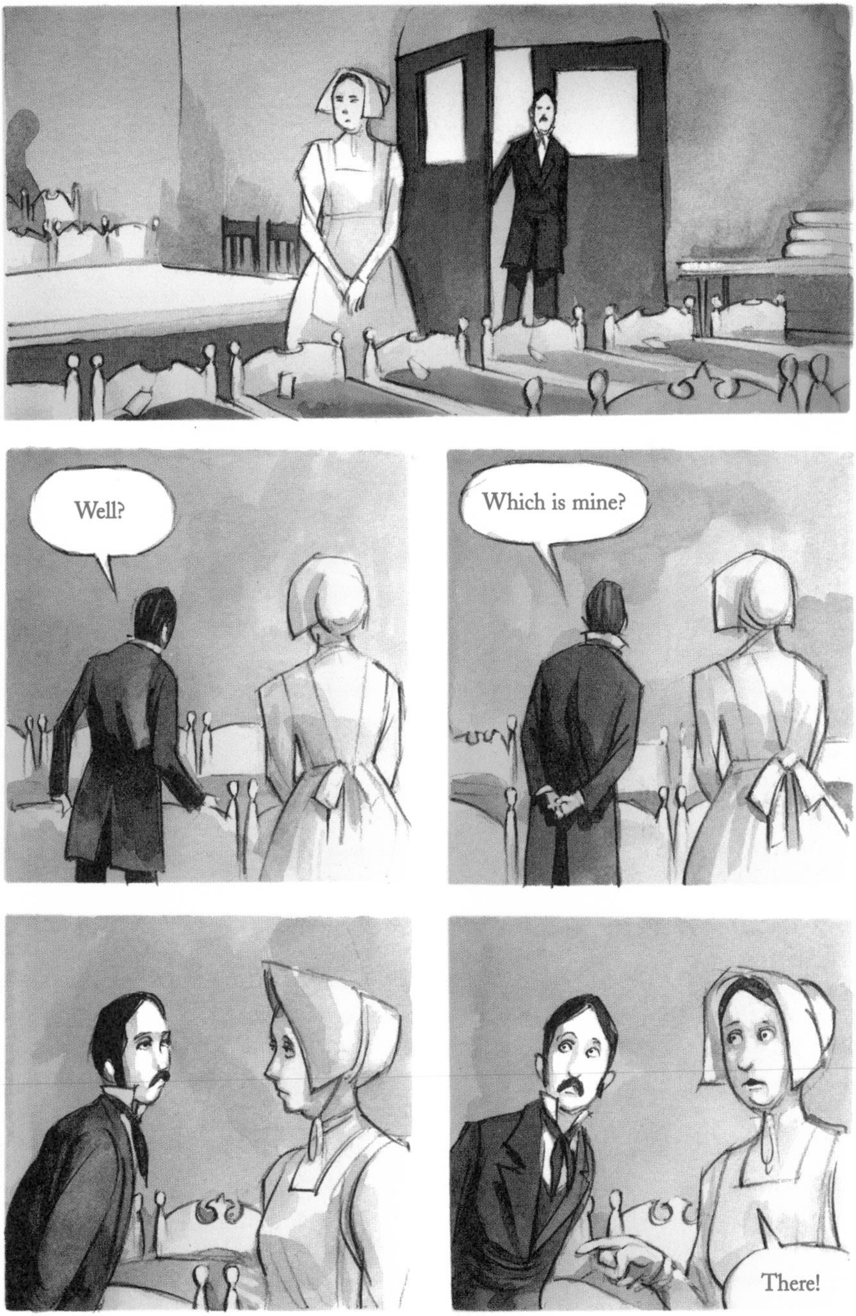
Well?
Which is mine?
There!

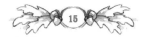

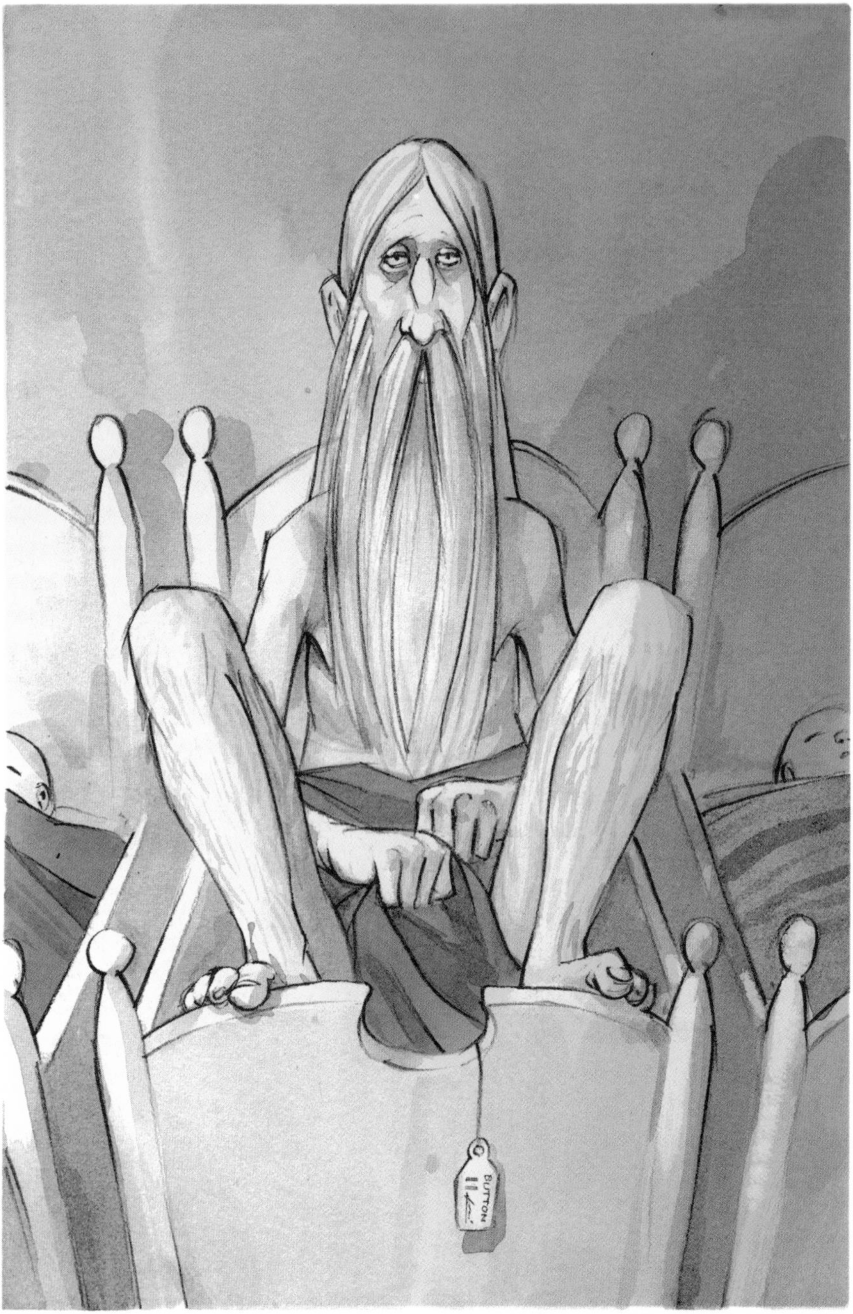
BUTTON

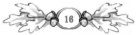

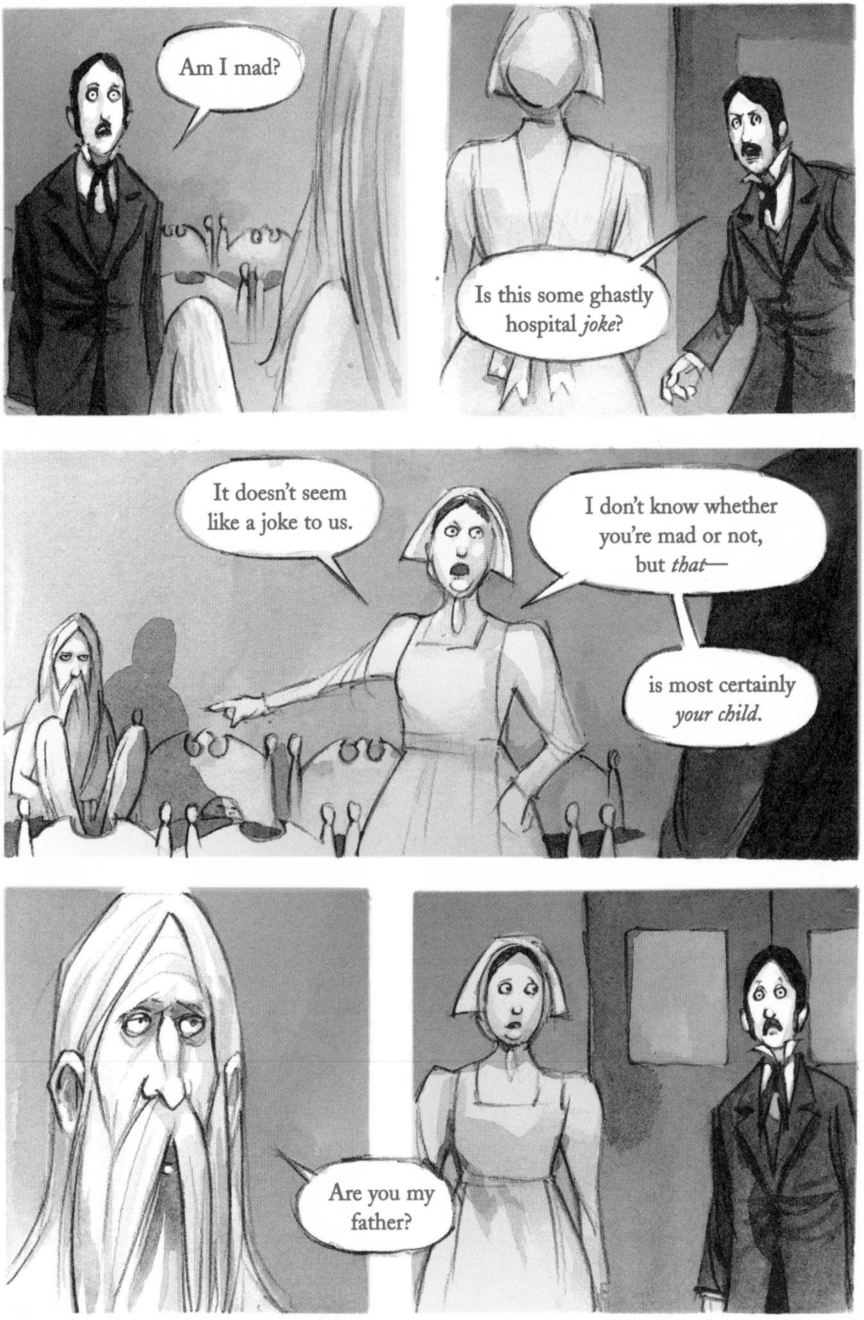
Am I mad?
Is this some ghastly hospital *joke*?
It doesn't seem like a joke to us.
I don't know whether you're mad or not, but *that*—
is most certainly *your child*.
Are you my father?

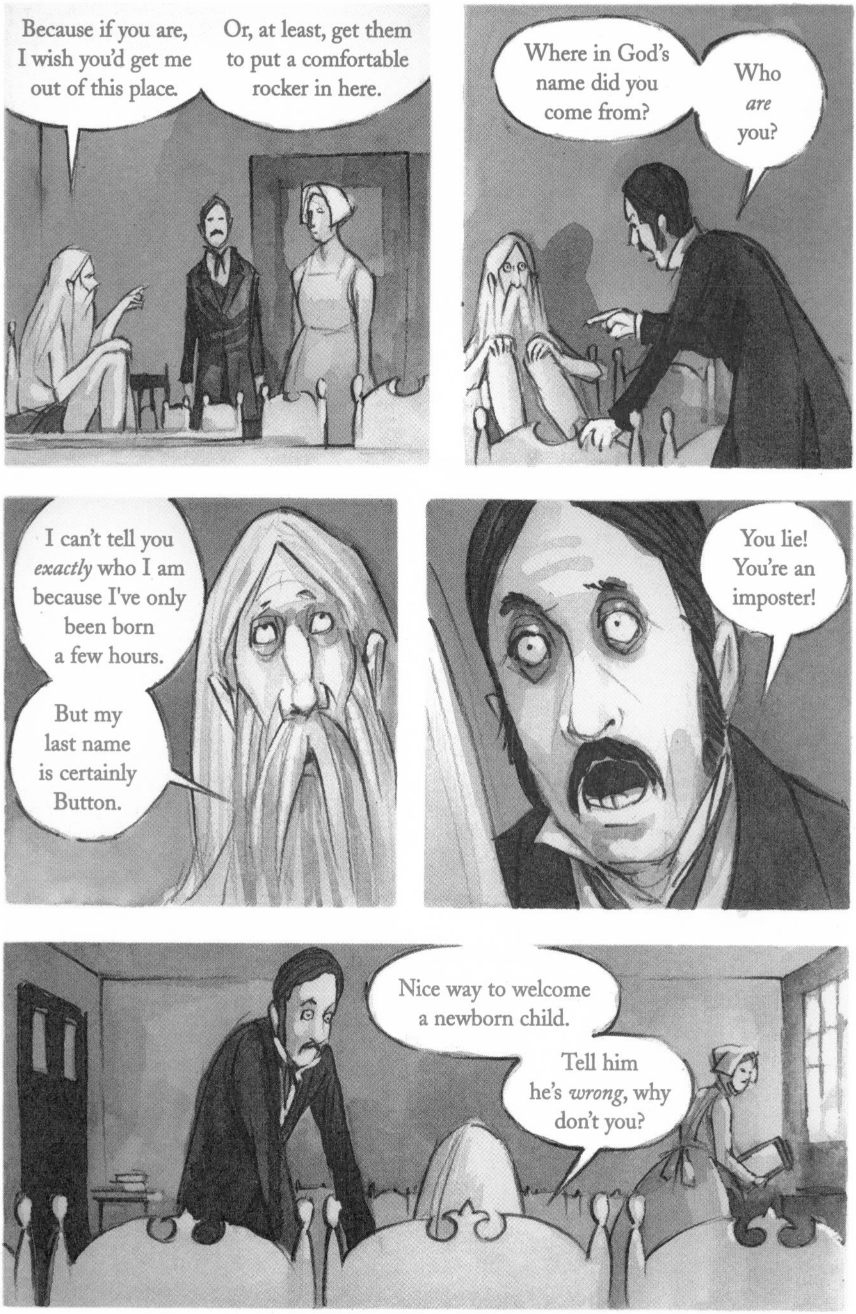
Because if you are, I wish you'd get me out of this place.
Or, at least, get them to put a comfortable rocker in here.
Where in God's name did you come from?
Who *are* you?
I can't tell you *exactly* who I am because I've only been born a few hours.
But my last name is certainly Button.
You lie! You're an imposter!
Nice way to welcome a newborn child.
Tell him he's *wrong*, why don't you?

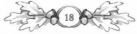

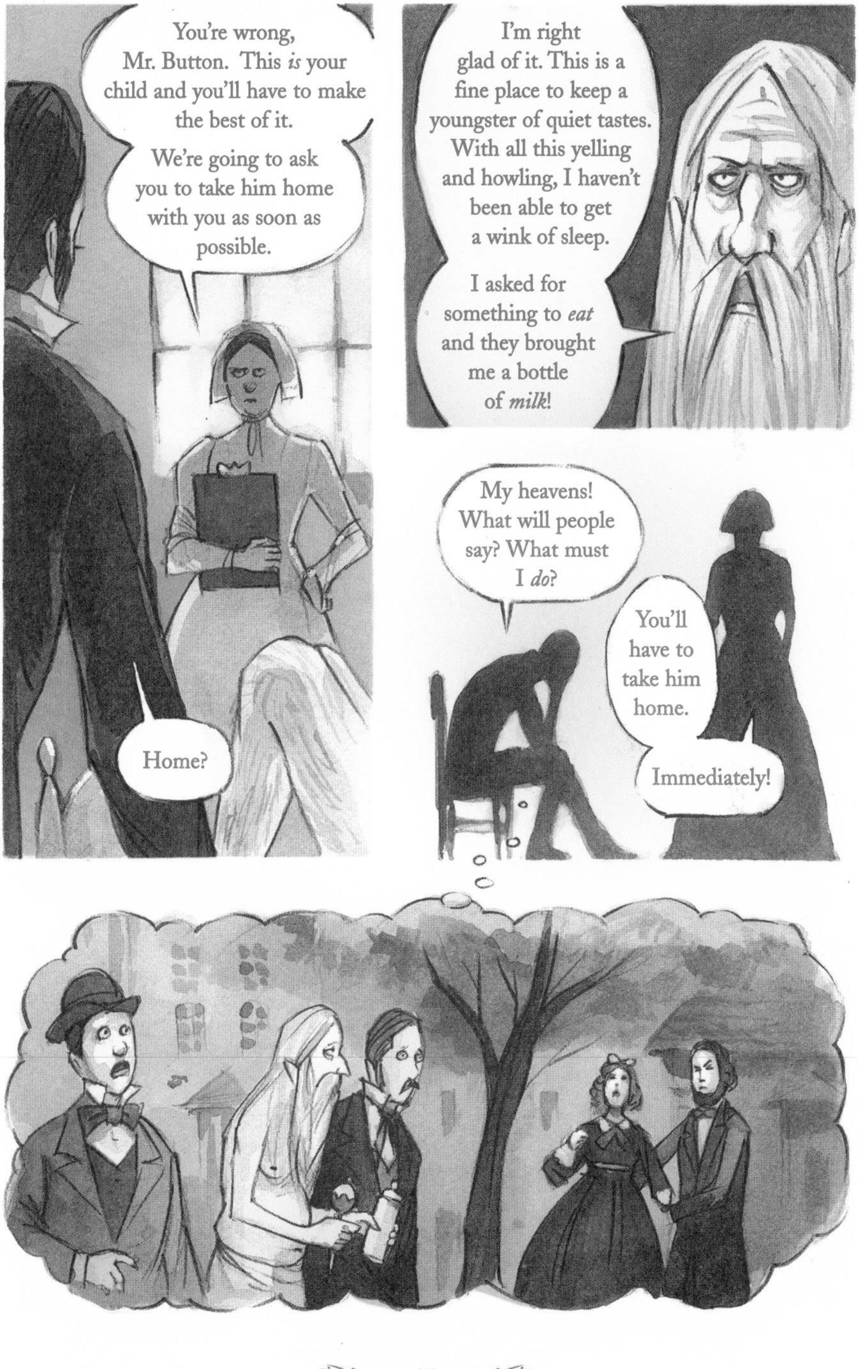
You're wrong, Mr. Button. This *is* your child and you'll have to make the best of it.
We're going to ask you to take him home with you as soon as possible.
Home?
I'm right glad of it. This is a fine place to keep a youngster of quiet tastes. With all this yelling and howling, I haven't been able to get a wink of sleep.
I asked for something to *eat* and they brought me a bottle of *milk*!
My heavens! What will people say? What must I *do*?
You'll have to take him home.
Immediately!

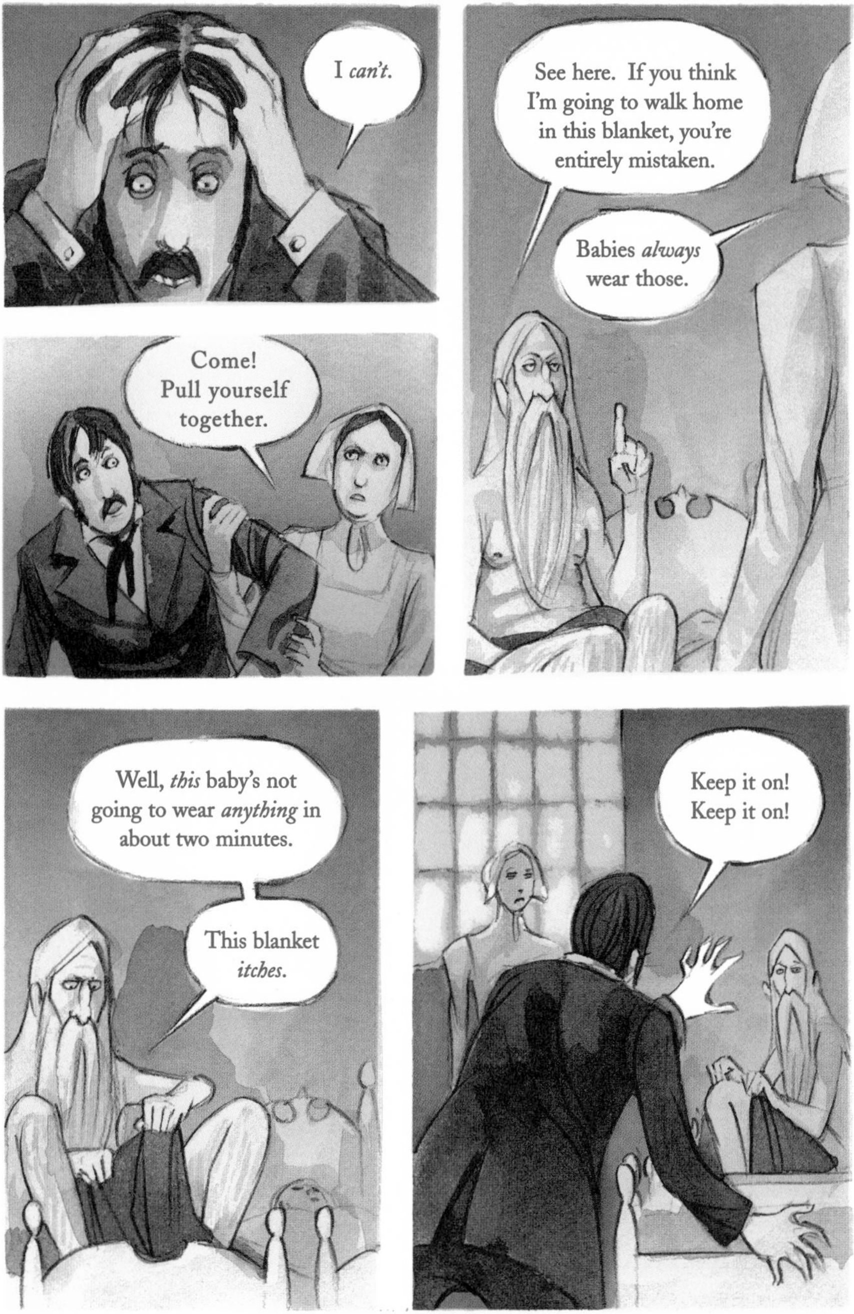
I *can't*.
Come! Pull yourself together.
See here. If you think I'm going to walk home in this blanket, you're entirely mistaken.
Babies *always* wear those.
Well, *this* baby's not going to wear *anything* in about two minutes.
This blanket *itches*.
Keep it on! Keep it on!

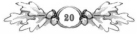

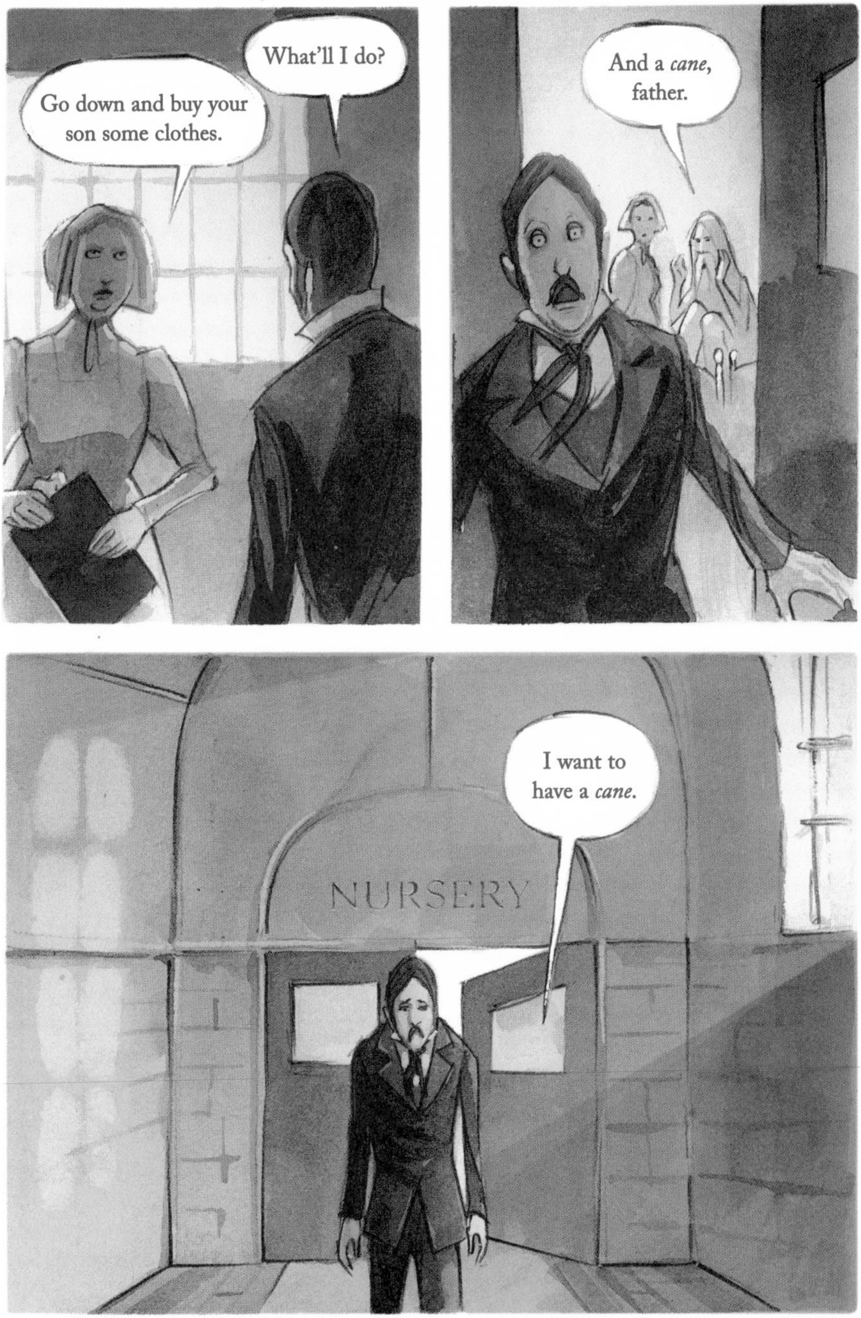
What'll I do?
Go down and buy your son some clothes.
And a *cane*, father.
NURSERY
I want to have a *cane*.

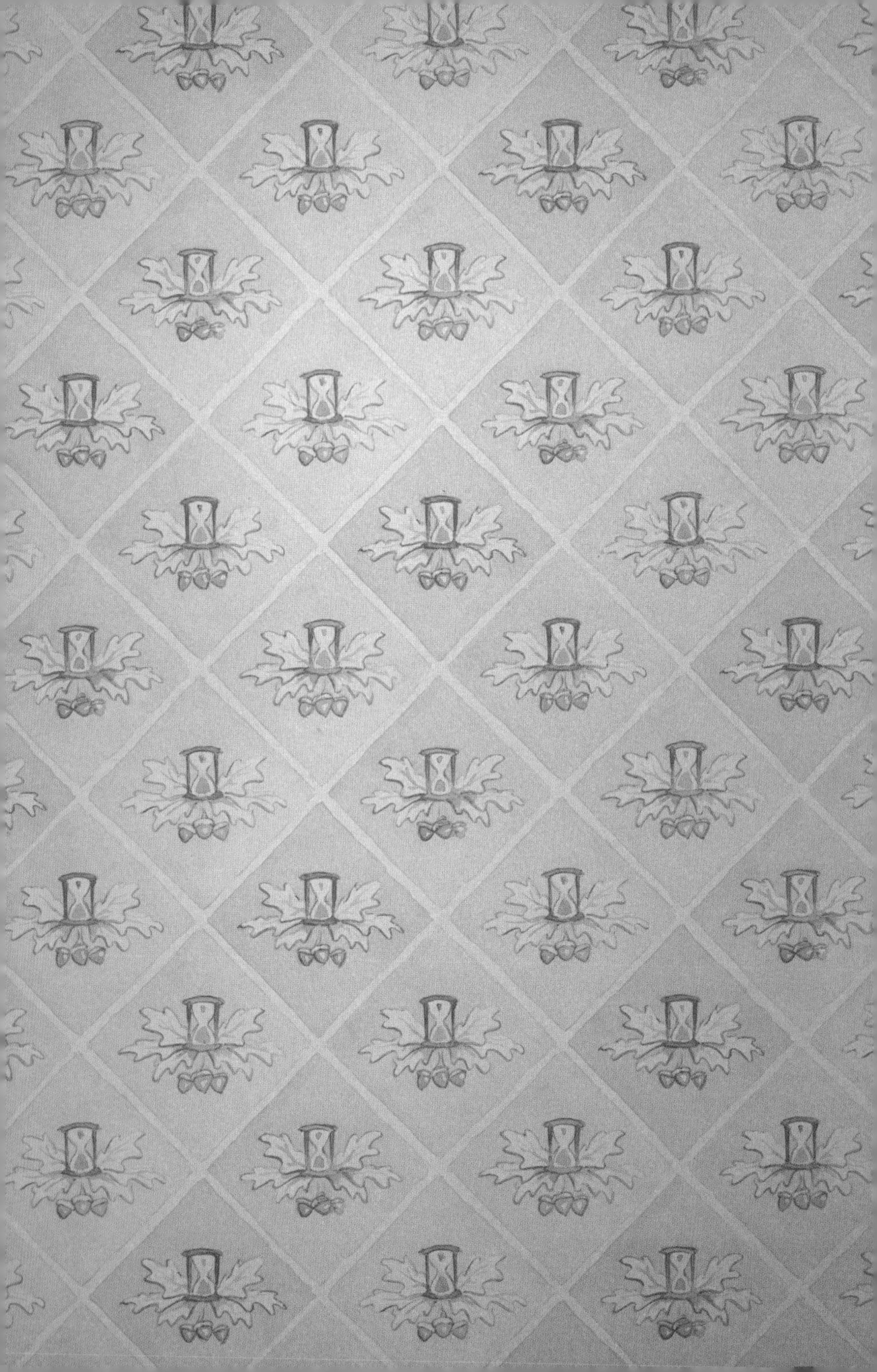

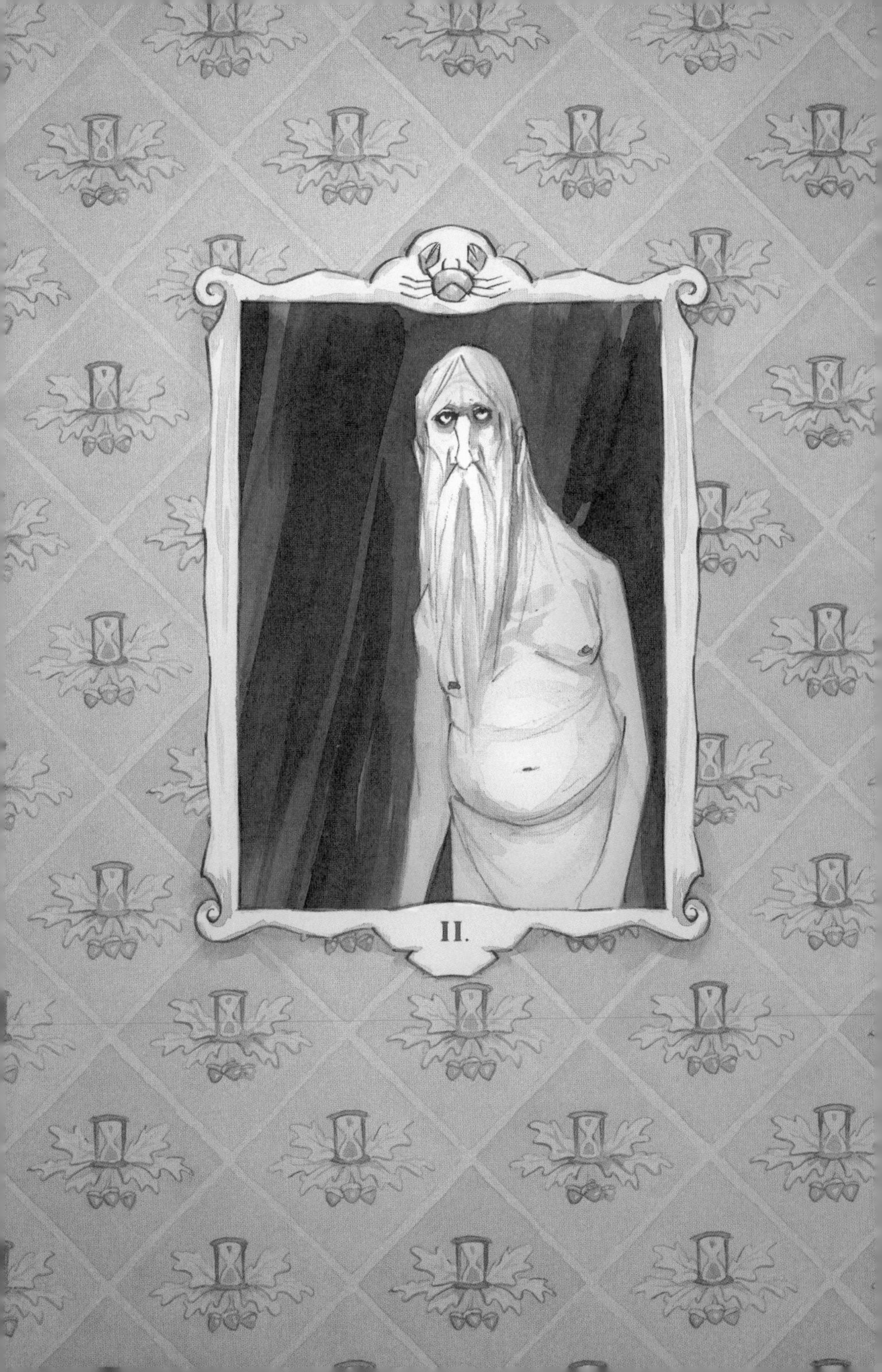
II.

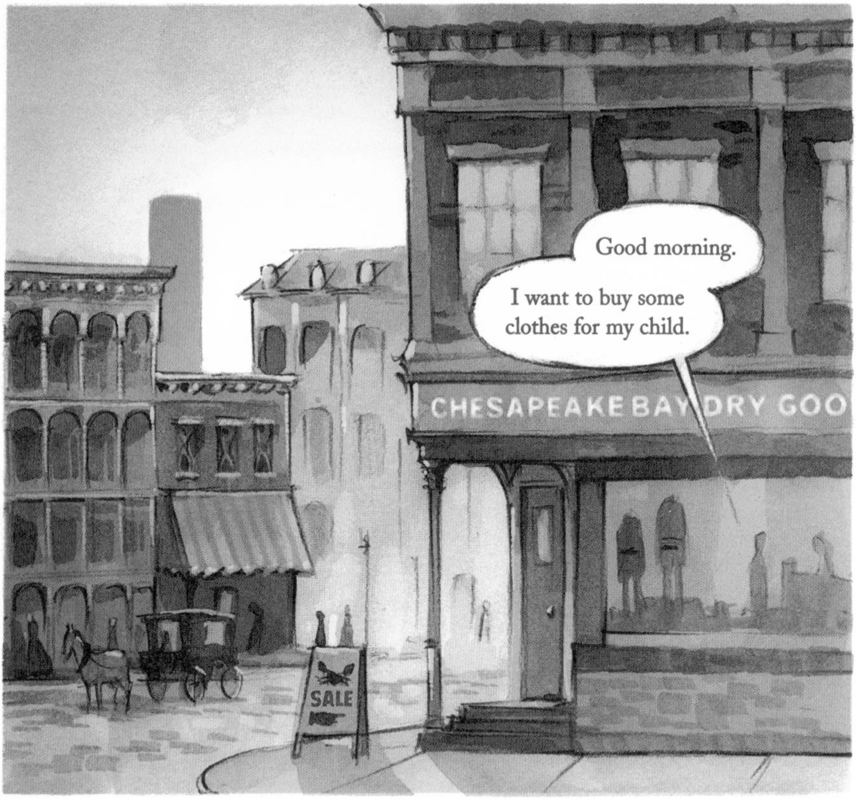
Good morning.
I want to buy some clothes for my child.
CHESAPEAKE BAY DRY GOO
SALE

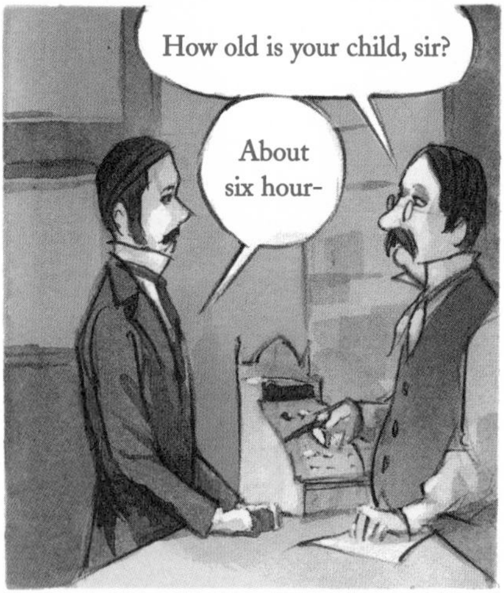
How old is your child, sir?
About six hour-

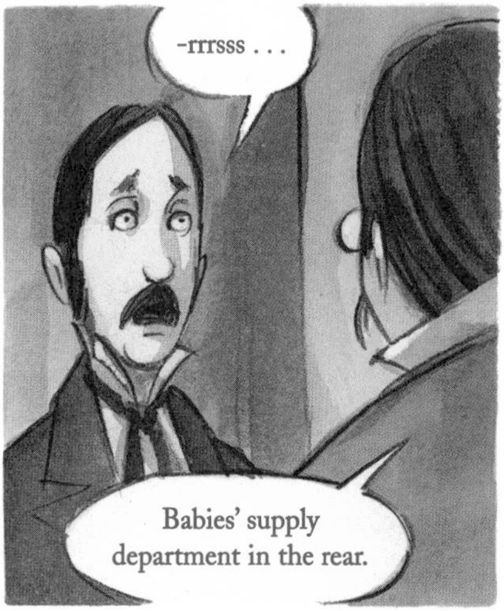
-rrrsss . . .
Babies' supply department in the rear.

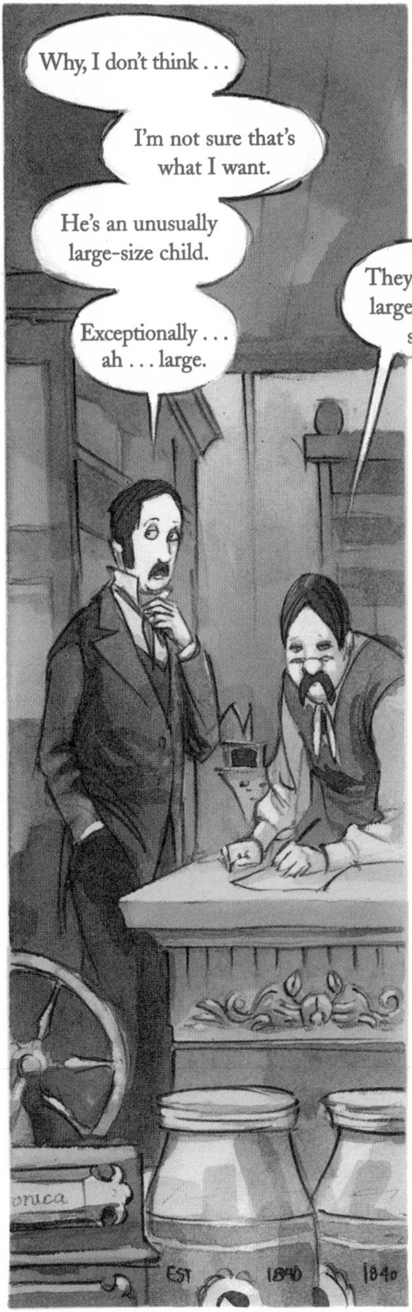
Why, I don't think . . .
I'm not sure that's what I want.
He's an unusually large-size child.
Exceptionally . . . ah . . . large.
They have the largest child's sizes.
EST 1840 1840

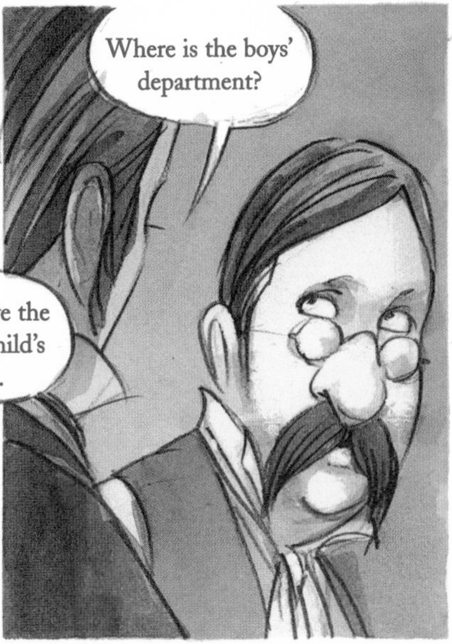
Where is the boys' department?

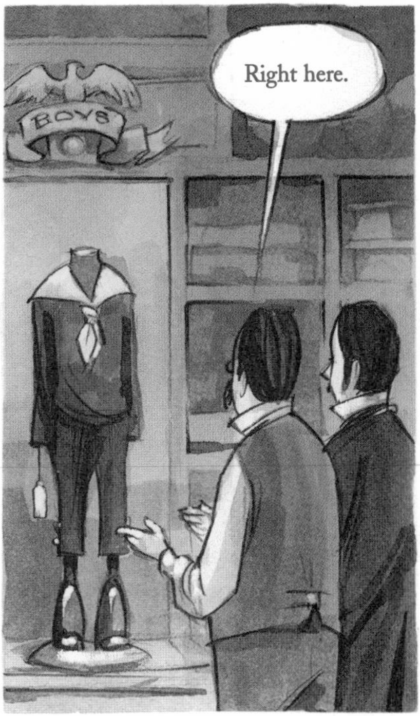
BOYS
Right here.

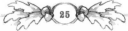

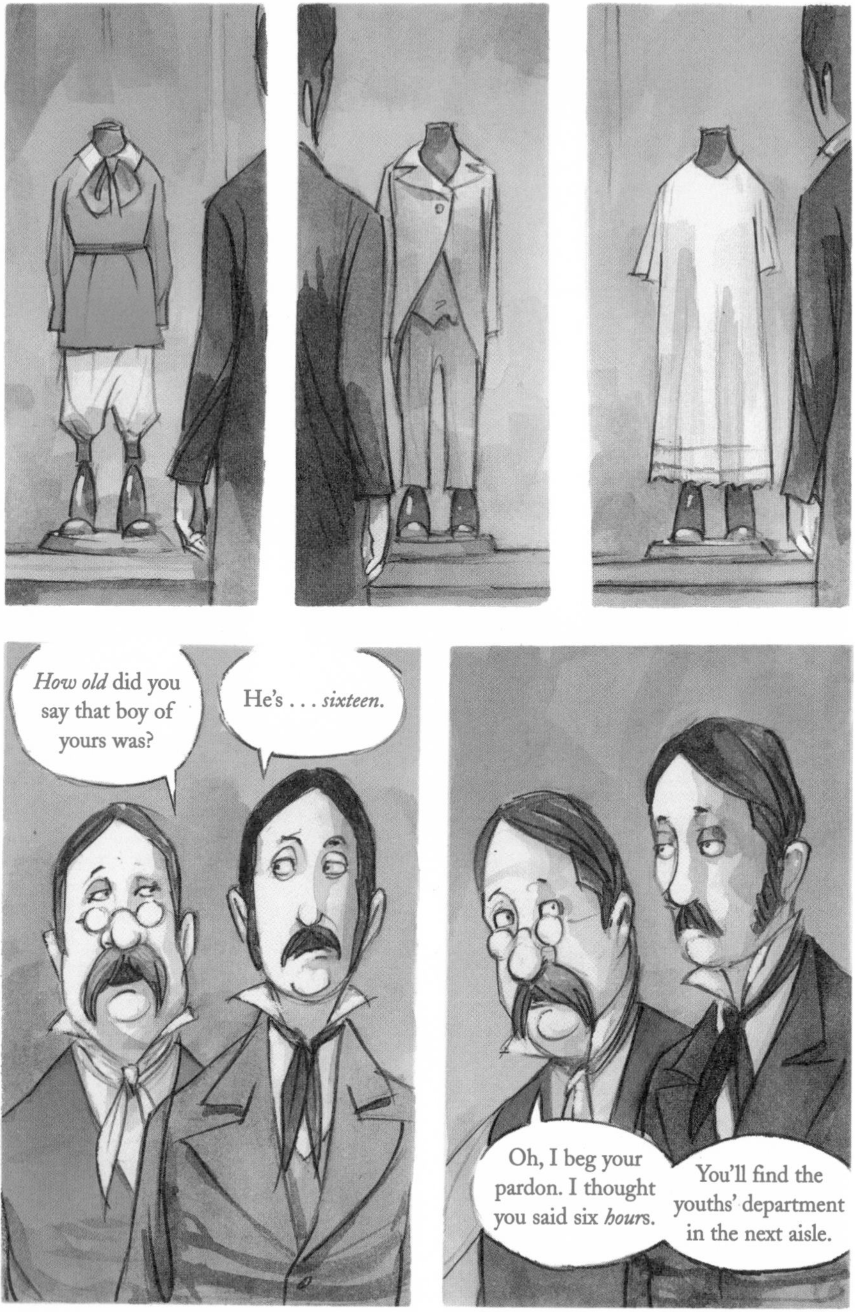
How old did you say that boy of yours was?
He's . . . *sixteen.*
Oh, I beg your pardon. I thought you said six *hour*s.
You'll find the youths' department in the next aisle.

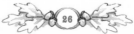

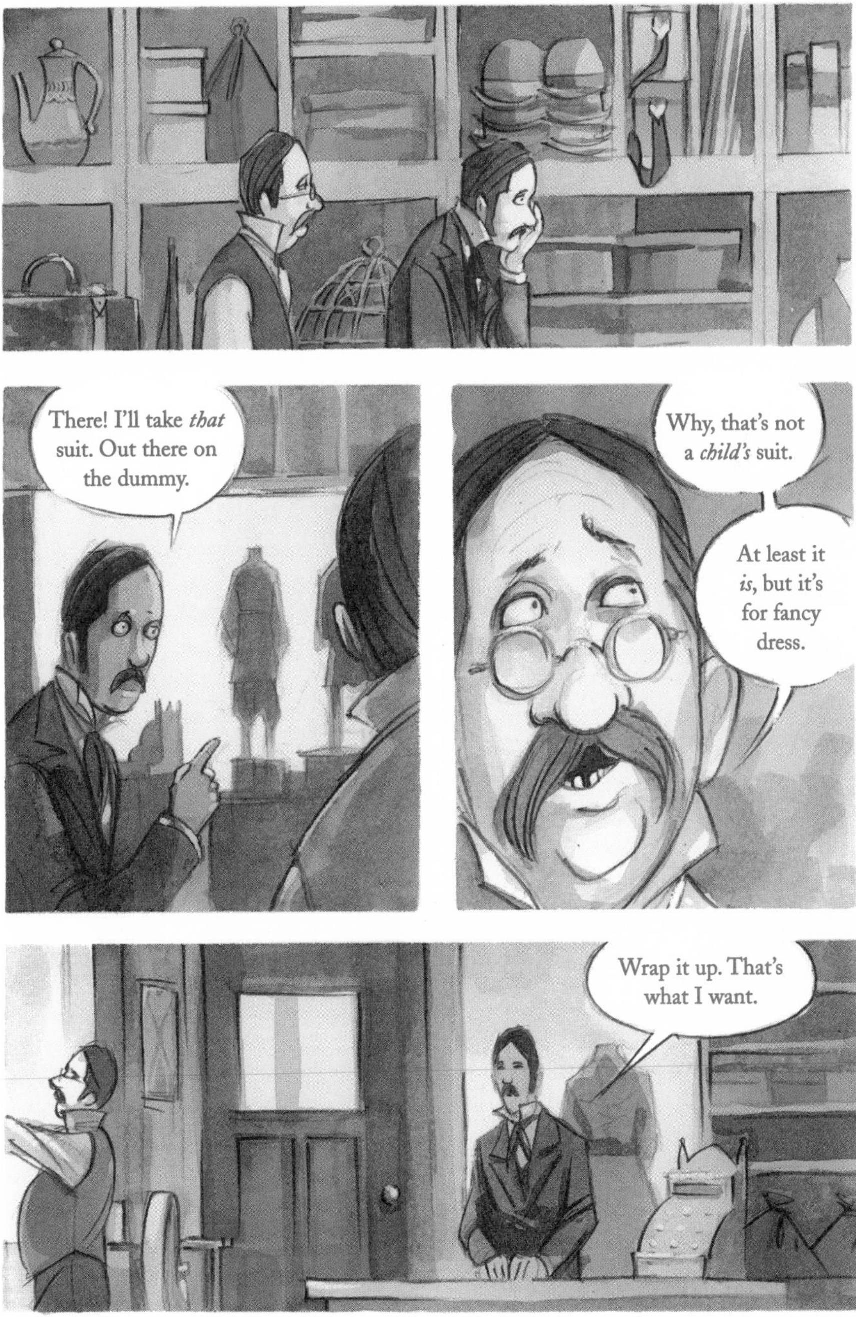
There! I'll take *that* suit. Out there on the dummy.
Why, that's not a *child's* suit.
At least it *is*, but it's for fancy dress.
Wrap it up. That's what I want.

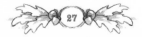

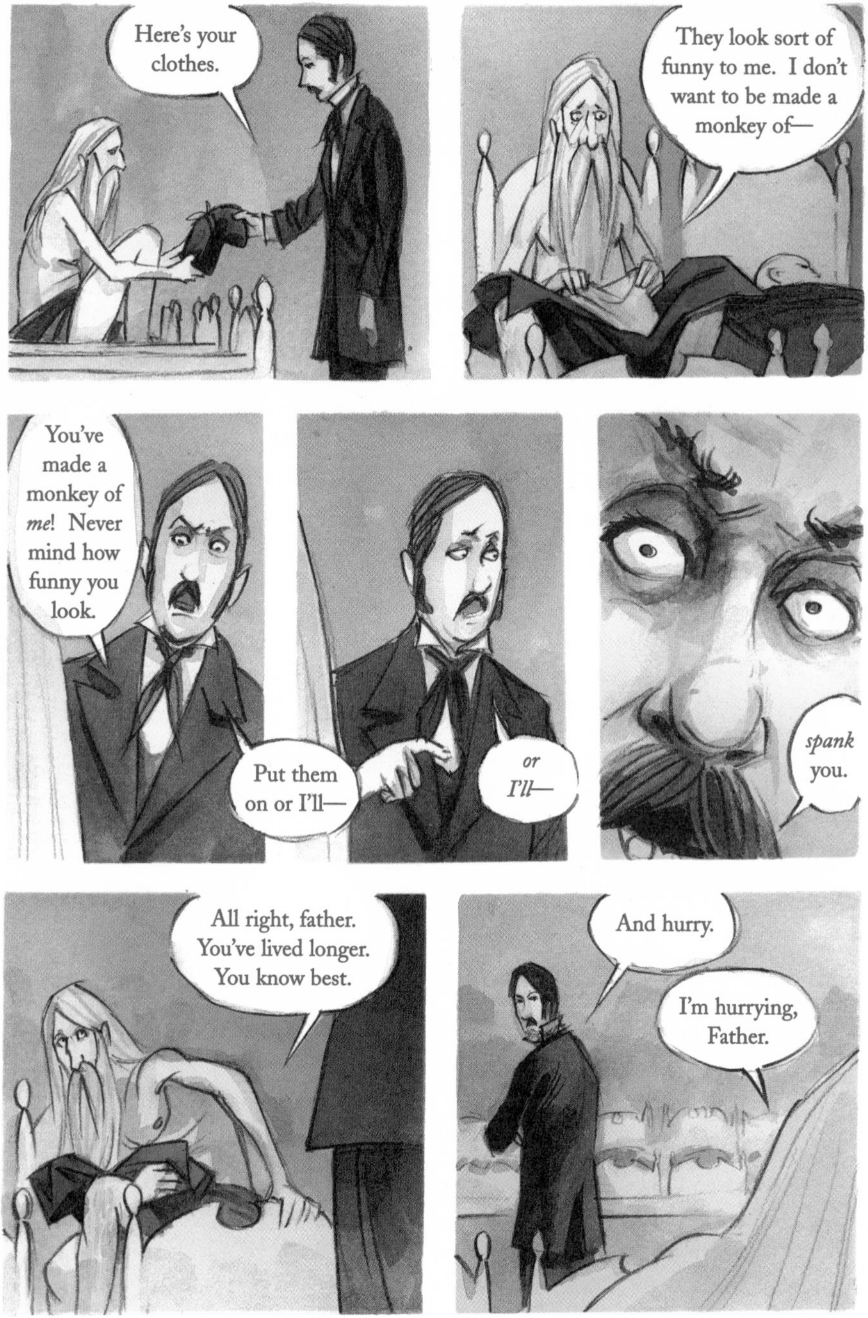
Here's your clothes.
They look sort of funny to me. I don't want to be made a monkey of—
You've made a monkey of *me*! Never mind how funny you look.
Put them on or I'll—
or I'll—
spank you.
All right, father. You've lived longer. You know best.
And hurry.
I'm hurrying, Father.

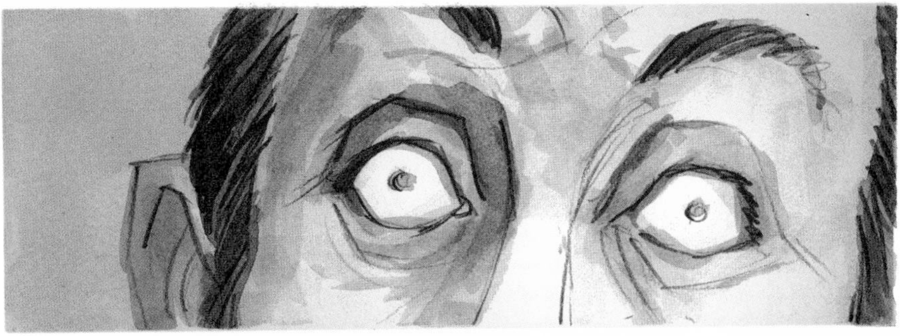

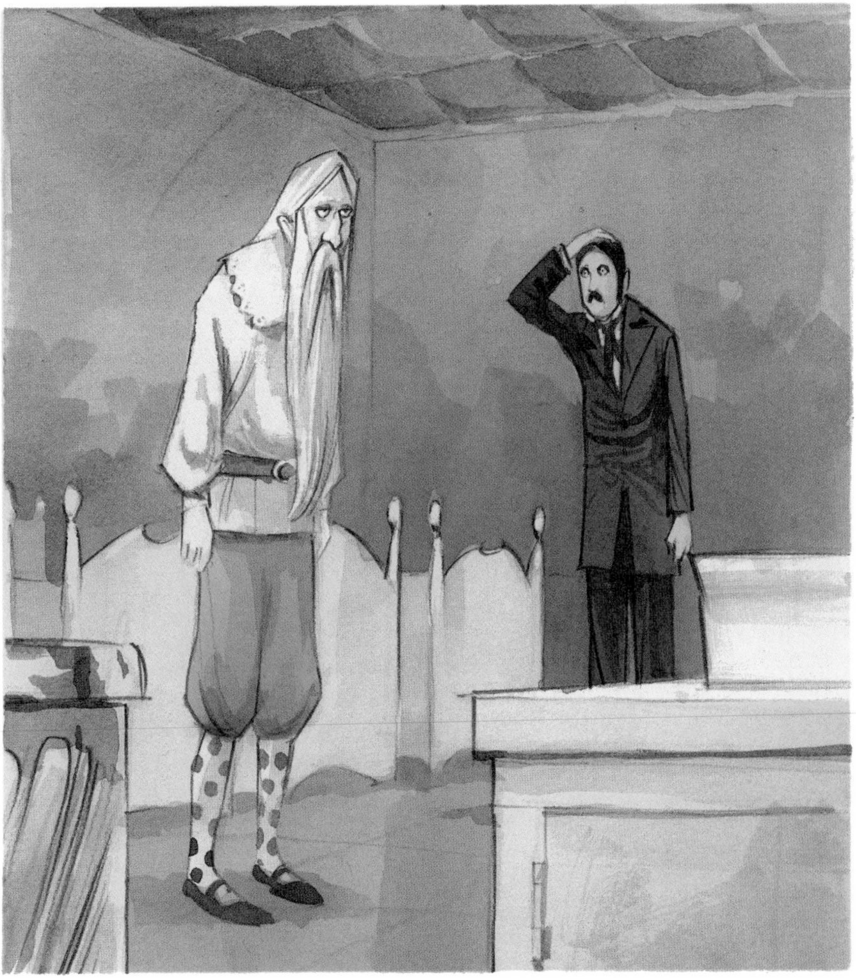

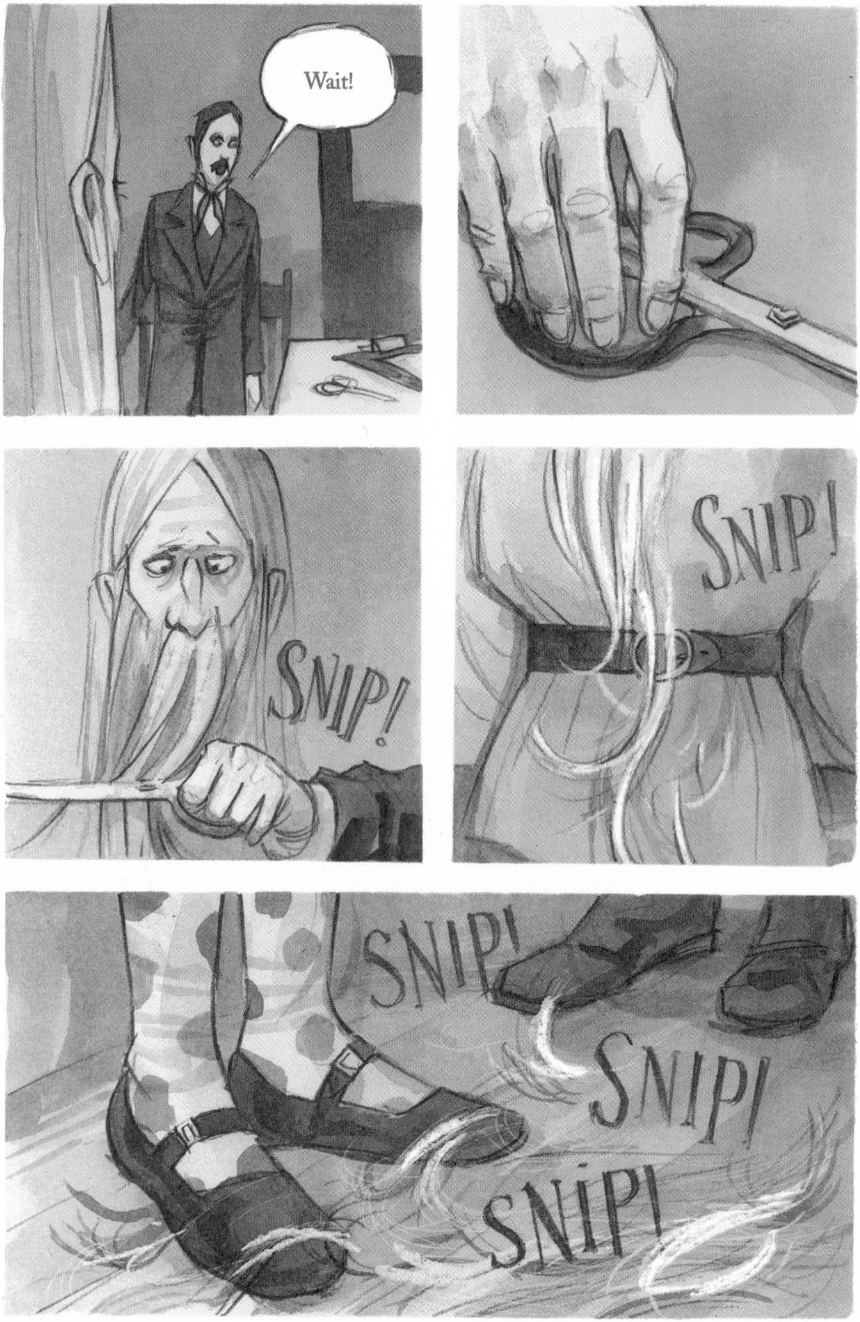
Wait!
SNIP!
SNIP!
SNIP!
SNIP!
SNIP!

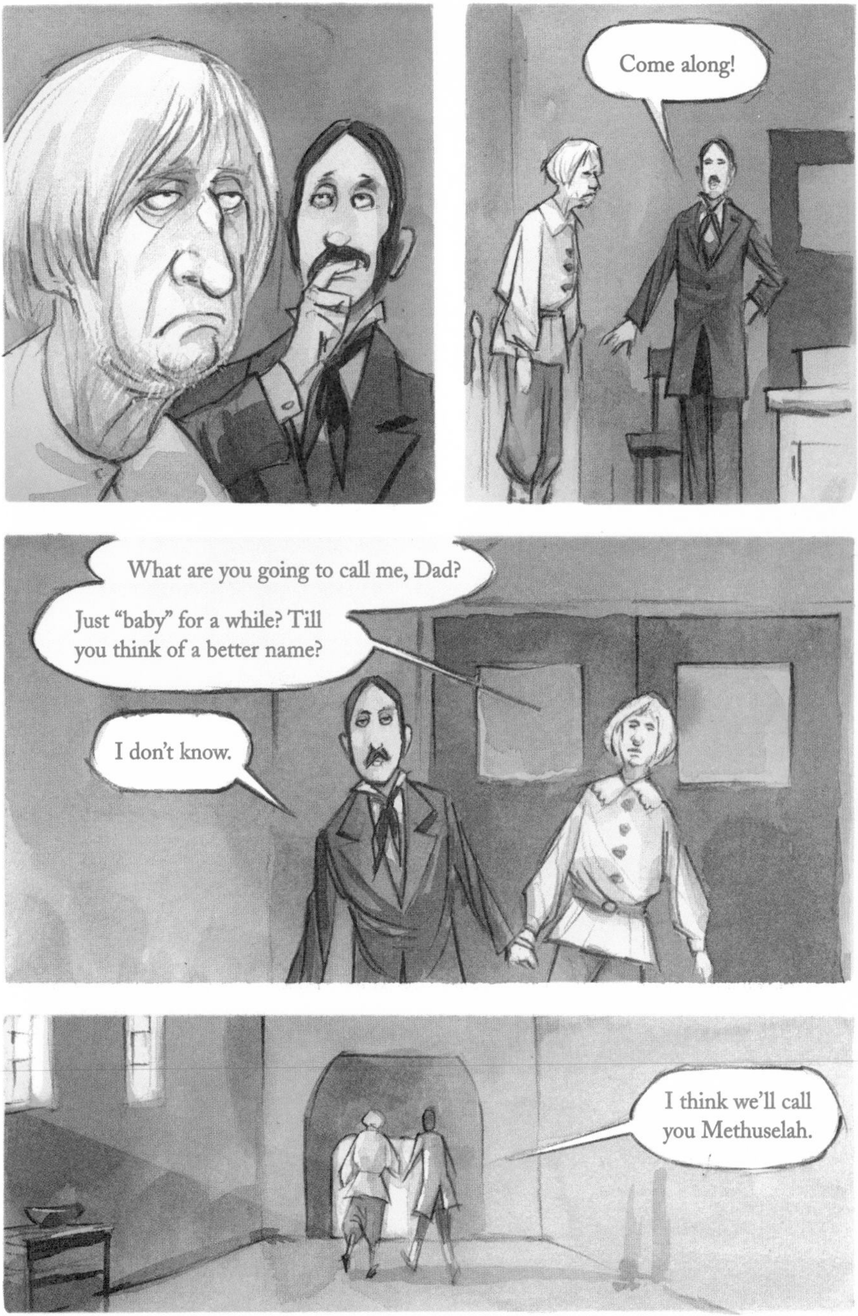
Come along!
What are you going to call me, Dad?
Just "baby" for a while? Till you think of a better name?
I don't know.
I think we'll call you Methuselah.

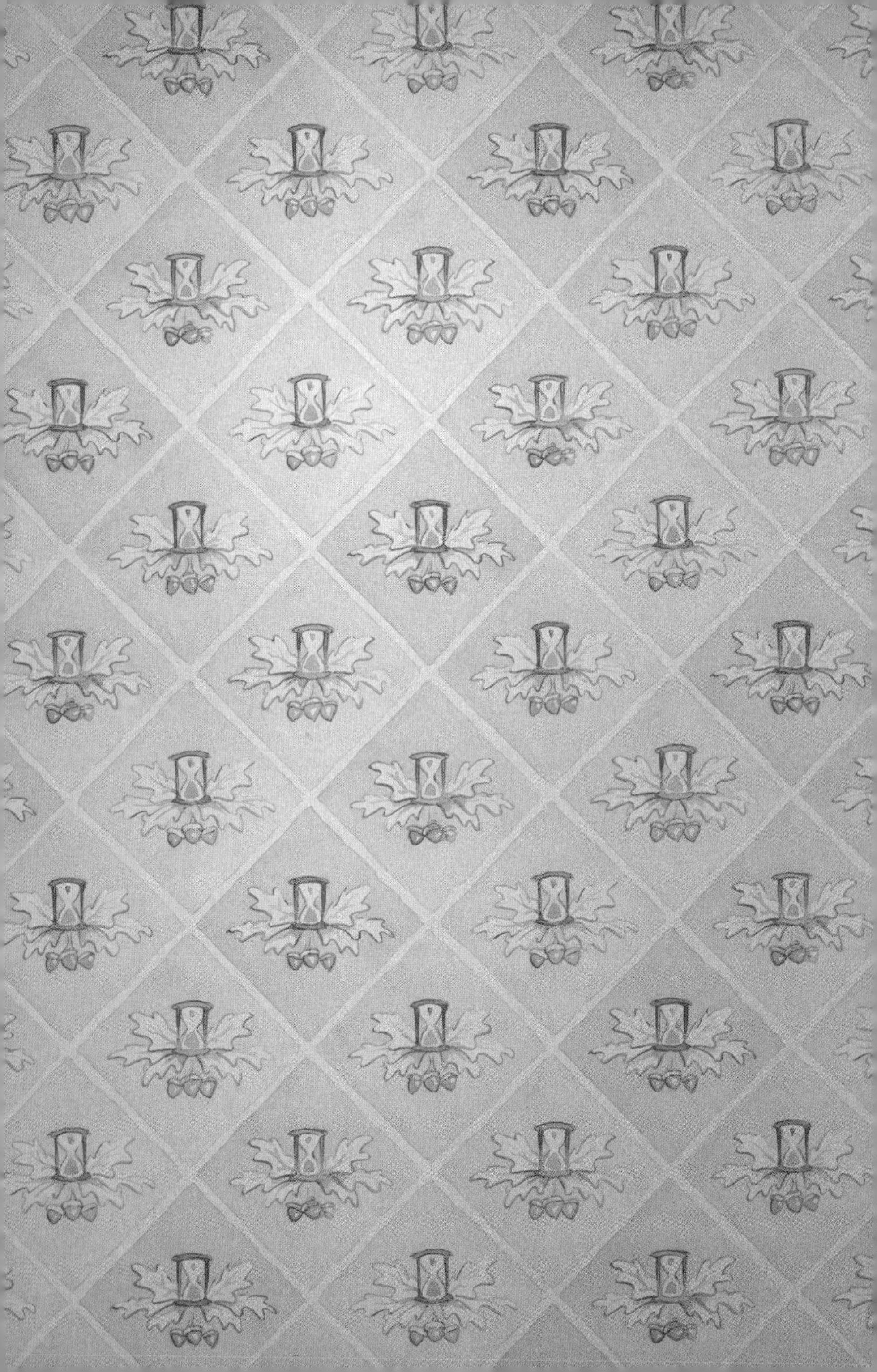

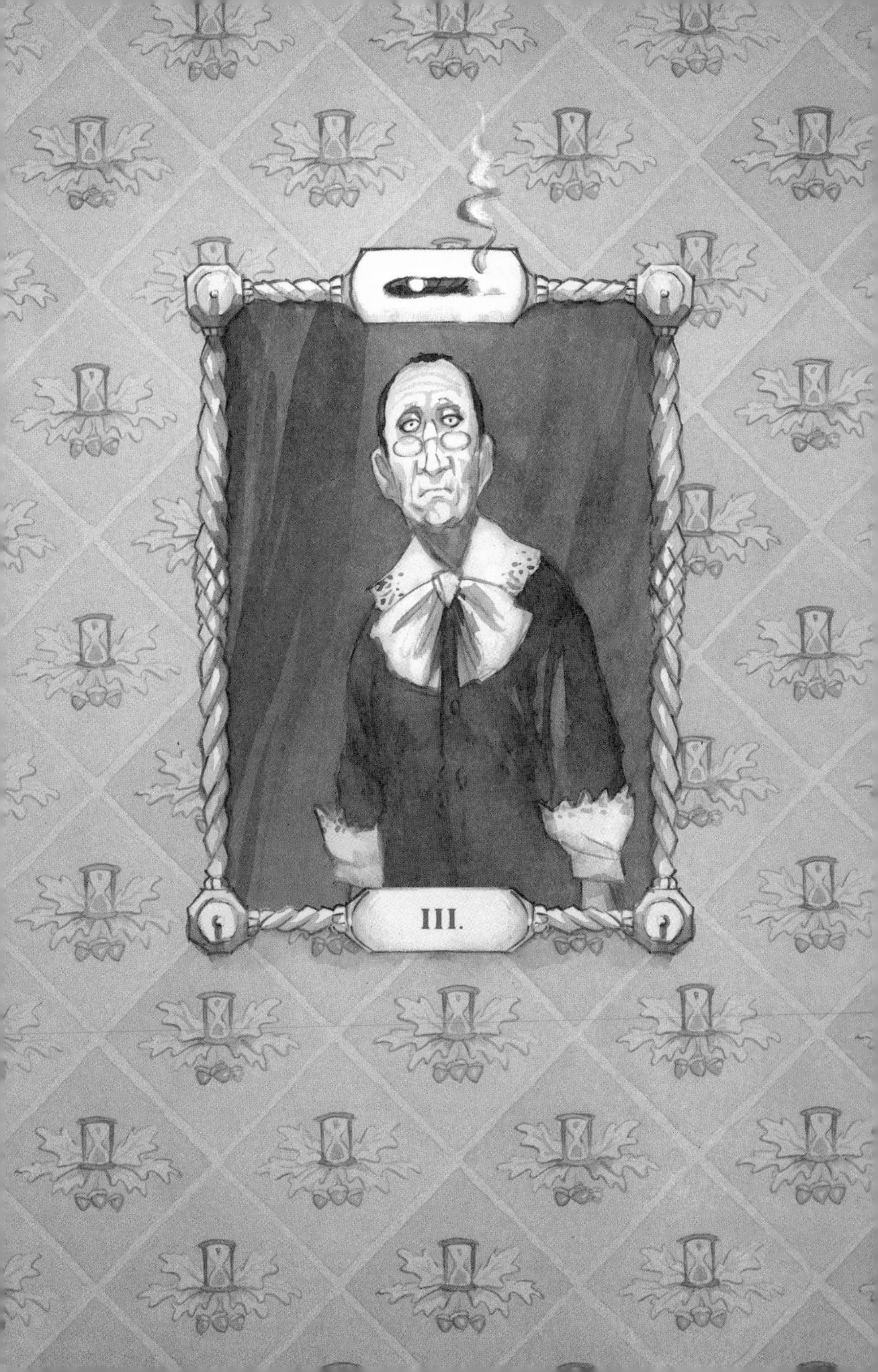
III.

Even after the new addition to the Button family had his hair cut short and then dyed to a sparse unnatural black . . .

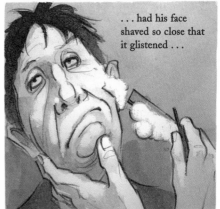

. . . had his face shaved so close that it glistened . . .

And had been attired in small-boy clothes made to order by a flabbergasted tailor . . .

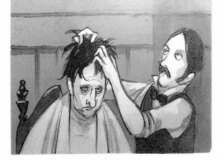

It was impossible for Mr. Button to ignore the fact that his son was a poor excuse for a first family baby.

Despite his aged stoop, Benjamin Button (for it was by this name they called him instead of Methuselah) was five-feet-eight inches tall.

In fact, the baby-nurse who had been engaged in advance left the house after one look, in a state of considerable indignation.

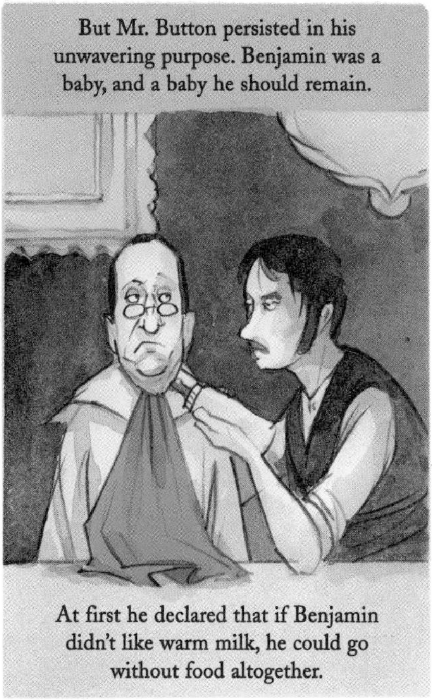
But Mr. Button persisted in his unwavering purpose. Benjamin was a baby, and a baby he should remain.
At first he declared that if Benjamin didn't like warm milk, he could go without food altogether.

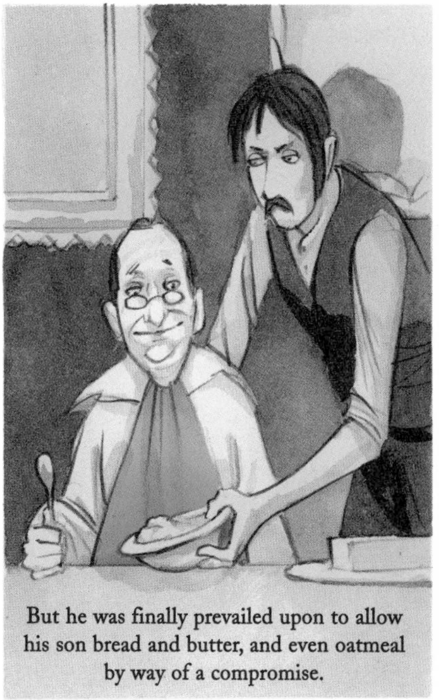
But he was finally prevailed upon to allow his son bread and butter, and even oatmeal by way of a compromise.

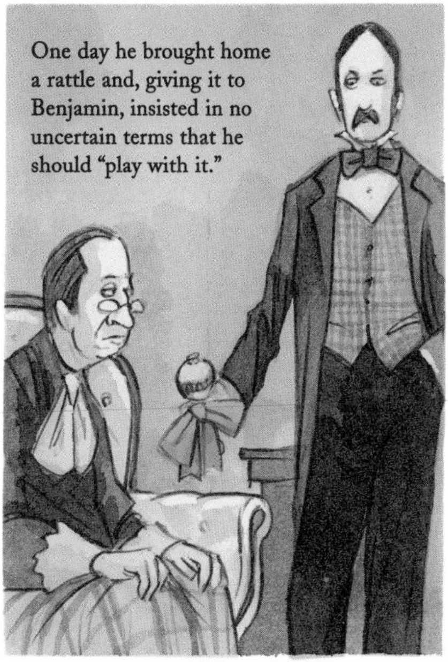
One day he brought home a rattle and, giving it to Benjamin, insisted in no uncertain terms that he should "play with it."

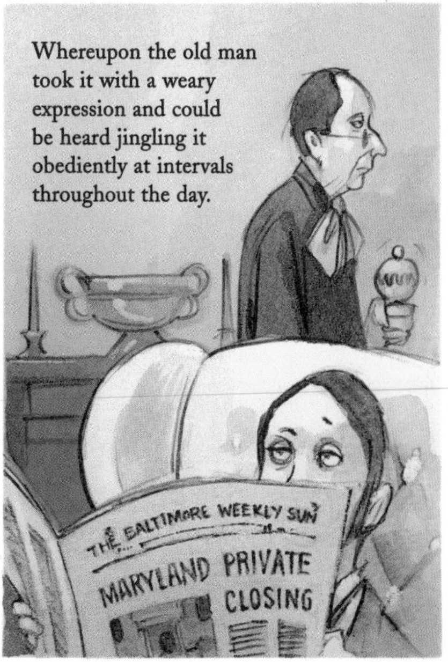
Whereupon the old man took it with a weary expression and could be heard jingling it obediently at intervals throughout the day.
THE BALTIMORE WEEKLY SUN
MARYLAND PRIVATE
CLOSING

There can be no doubt, though, that the rattle bored him and that he found other and more soothing amusements when he was left alone.

For instance, Mr. Button discovered one day that during the preceding week he had smoked more cigars than ever before.

A phenomenon which was explained a few days later when, entering the nursery unexpectedly, he found the room full of faint blue haze. And Benjamin, with a guilty expression on his face, trying to conceal the butt of a dark Havana.

This, of course, called for a severe spanking, but Mr. Button found that he could not bring himself to administer it.

He merely warned his son that he would "stunt his growth."

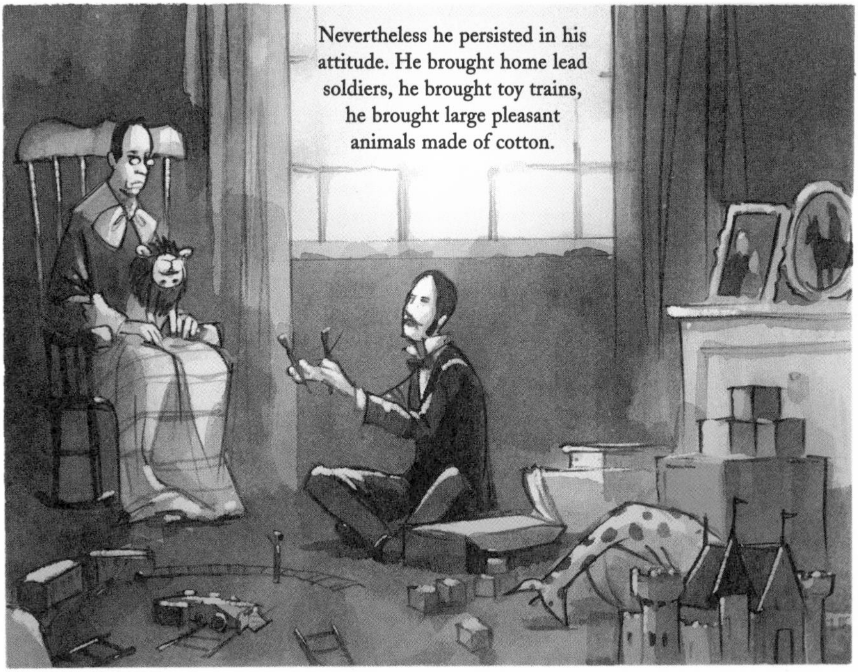
Nevertheless he persisted in his attitude. He brought home lead soldiers, he brought toy trains, he brought large pleasant animals made of cotton.

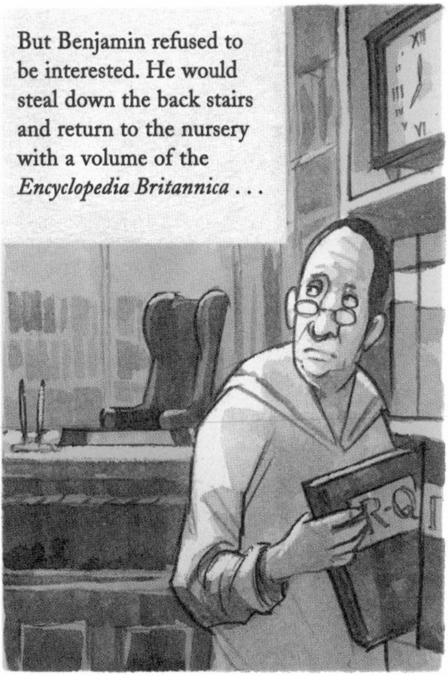
But Benjamin refused to be interested. He would steal down the back stairs and return to the nursery with a volume of the *Encyclopedia Britannica* . . .

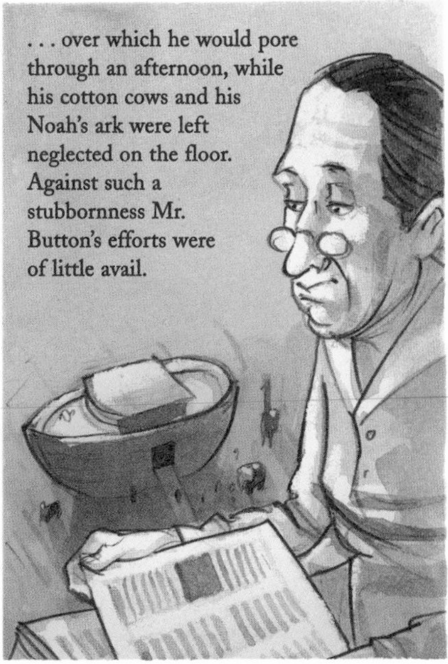
. . . over which he would pore through an afternoon, while his cotton cows and his Noah's ark were left neglected on the floor. Against such a stubbornness Mr. Button's efforts were of little avail.

The sensation created in Baltimore was, at first, prodigious. What the mishap would have cost the Buttons and their kinsfolk socially cannot be determined, for the outbreak of the Civil War drew the city's attention to other things.

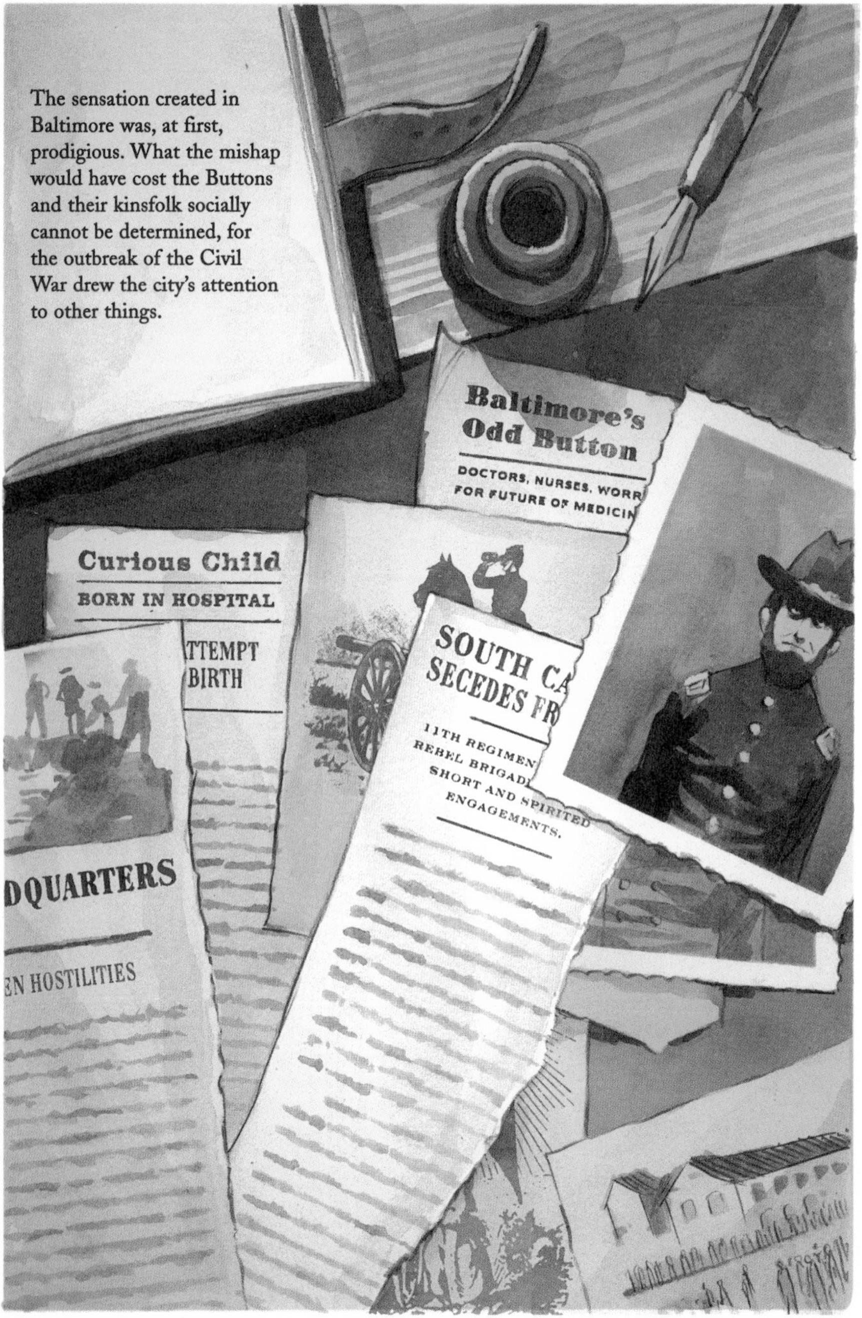

Baltimore's Odd Button
DOCTORS, NURSES, WORR
FOR FUTURE OF MEDICIN
Curious Child
BORN IN HOSPITAL
TTEMPT
BIRTH
SOUTH CA
SECEDES FR
11TH REGIMEN
REBEL BRIGADI
SHORT AND SPIRITED
ENGAGEMENTS.
DQUARTERS
EN HOSTILITIES

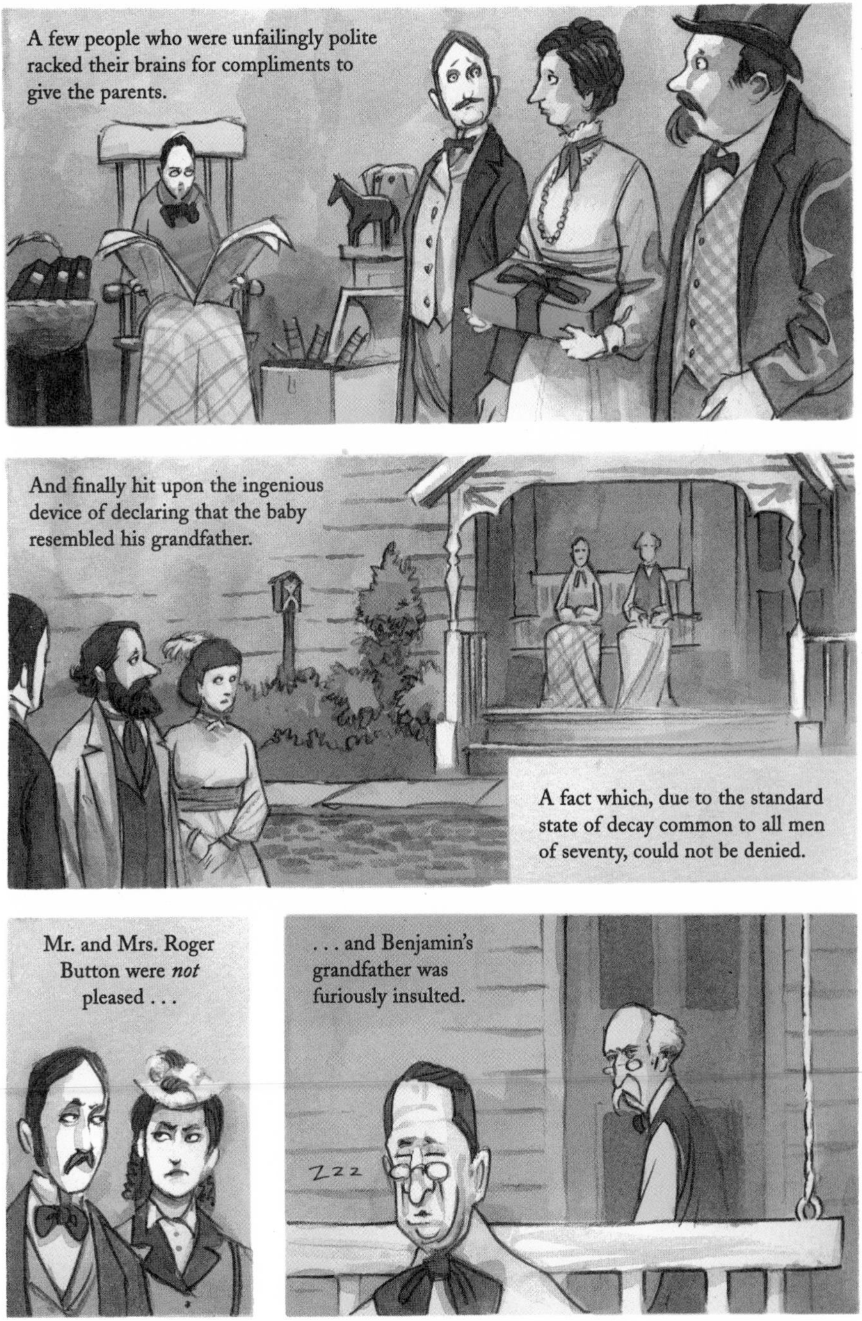
A few people who were unfailingly polite racked their brains for compliments to give the parents.
And finally hit upon the ingenious device of declaring that the baby resembled his grandfather.
A fact which, due to the standard state of decay common to all men of seventy, could not be denied.
Mr. and Mrs. Roger Button were *not* pleased . . .
. . . and Benjamin's grandfather was furiously insulted.
Z z z

Benjamin, once he left the hospital, took life as he found it.

Several small boys were brought to see him.

And he spent a stiff-jointed afternoon trying to work up an interest in tops and marbles.

He even managed, quite accidentally, to break a kitchen window with a stone from a sling shot. A feat which secretly delighted his father.

Thereafter Benjamin contrived to break something every day.

But he did these things only because they were expected of him, and because he was by nature obliging.

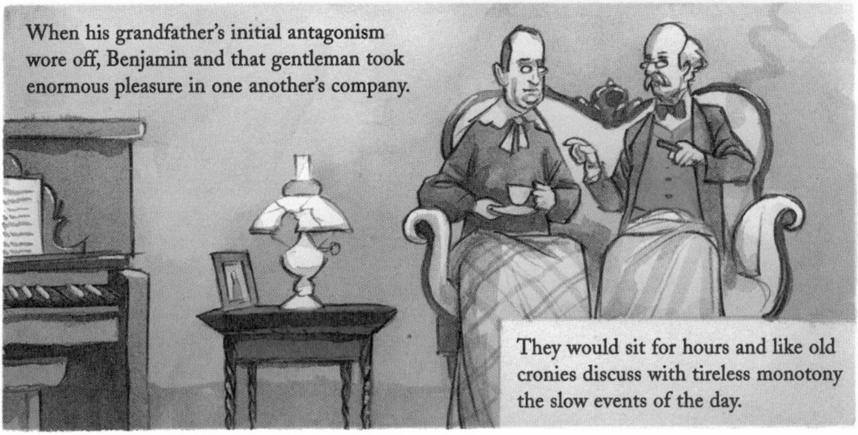
When his grandfather's initial antagonism wore off, Benjamin and that gentleman took enormous pleasure in one another's company.
They would sit for hours and like old cronies discuss with tireless monotony the slow events of the day.

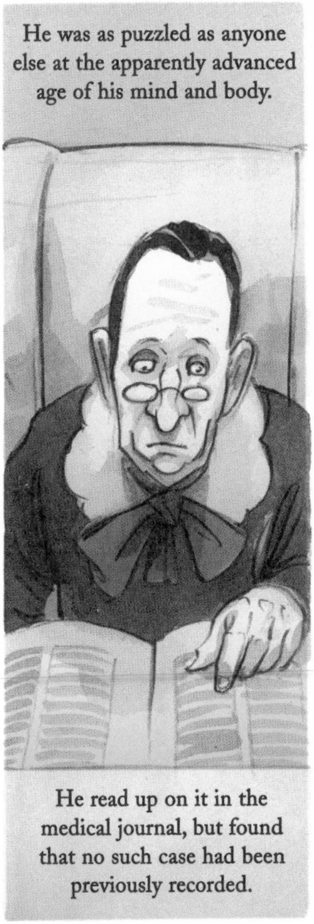
He was as puzzled as anyone else at the apparently advanced age of his mind and body.
He read up on it in the medical journal, but found that no such case had been previously recorded.

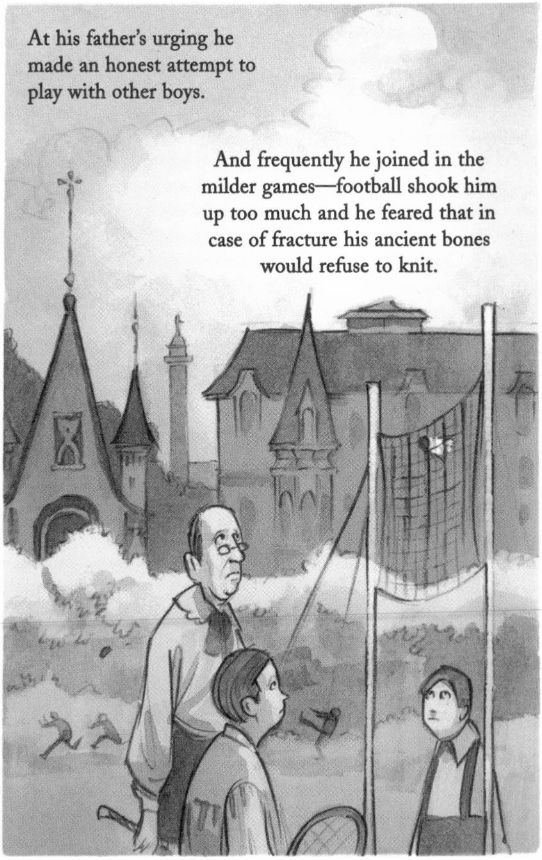
At his father's urging he made an honest attempt to play with other boys.
And frequently he joined in the milder games—football shook him up too much and he feared that in case of fracture his ancient bones would refuse to knit.

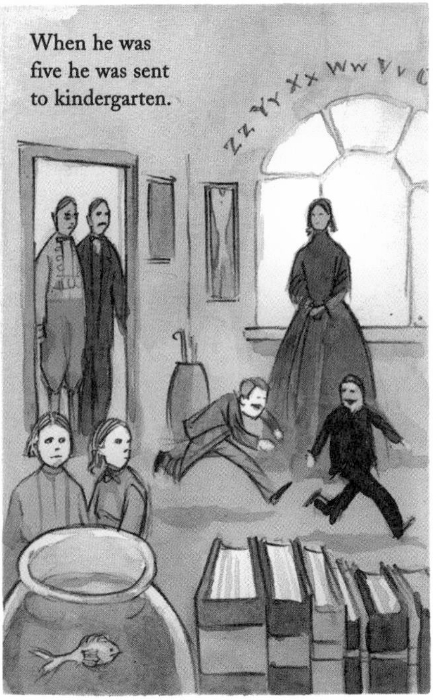
When he was five he was sent to kindergarten.

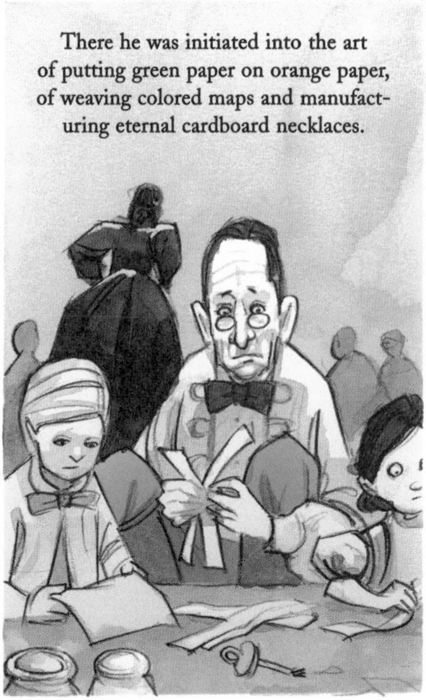
There he was initiated into the art of putting green paper on orange paper, of weaving colored maps and manufacturing eternal cardboard necklaces.

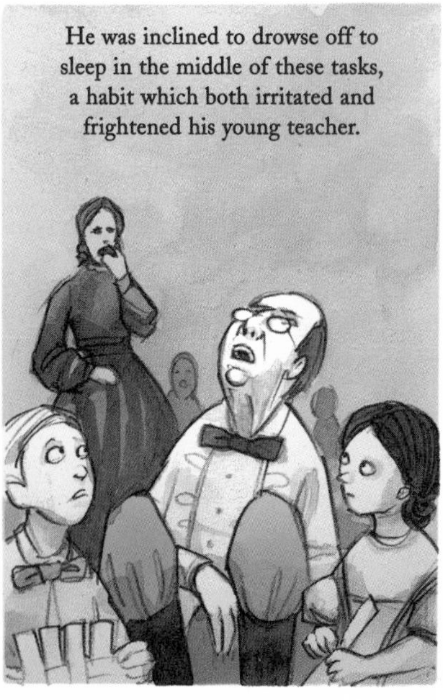
He was inclined to drowse off to sleep in the middle of these tasks, a habit which both irritated and frightened his young teacher.

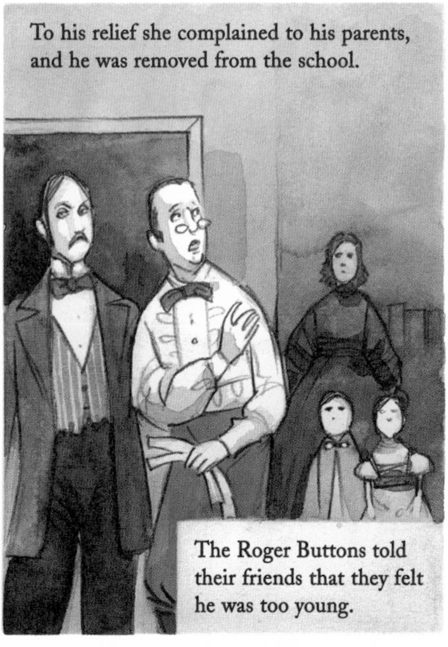
To his relief she complained to his parents, and he was removed from the school.
The Roger Buttons told their friends that they felt he was too young.

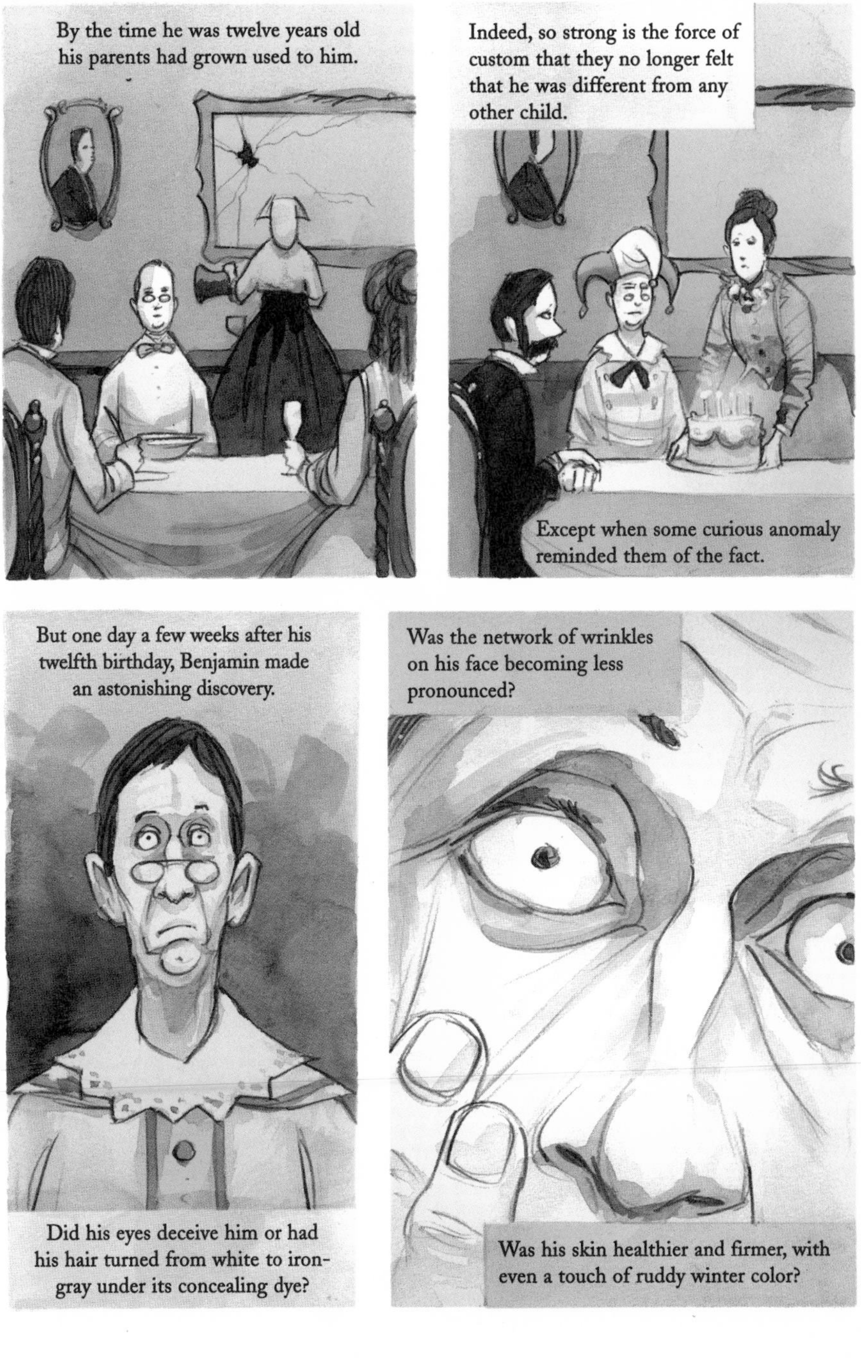
By the time he was twelve years old his parents had grown used to him.
Indeed, so strong is the force of custom that they no longer felt that he was different from any other child.
Except when some curious anomaly reminded them of the fact.
But one day a few weeks after his twelfth birthday, Benjamin made an astonishing discovery.
Did his eyes deceive him or had his hair turned from white to iron-gray under its concealing dye?
Was the network of wrinkles on his face becoming less pronounced?
Was his skin healthier and firmer, with even a touch of ruddy winter color?

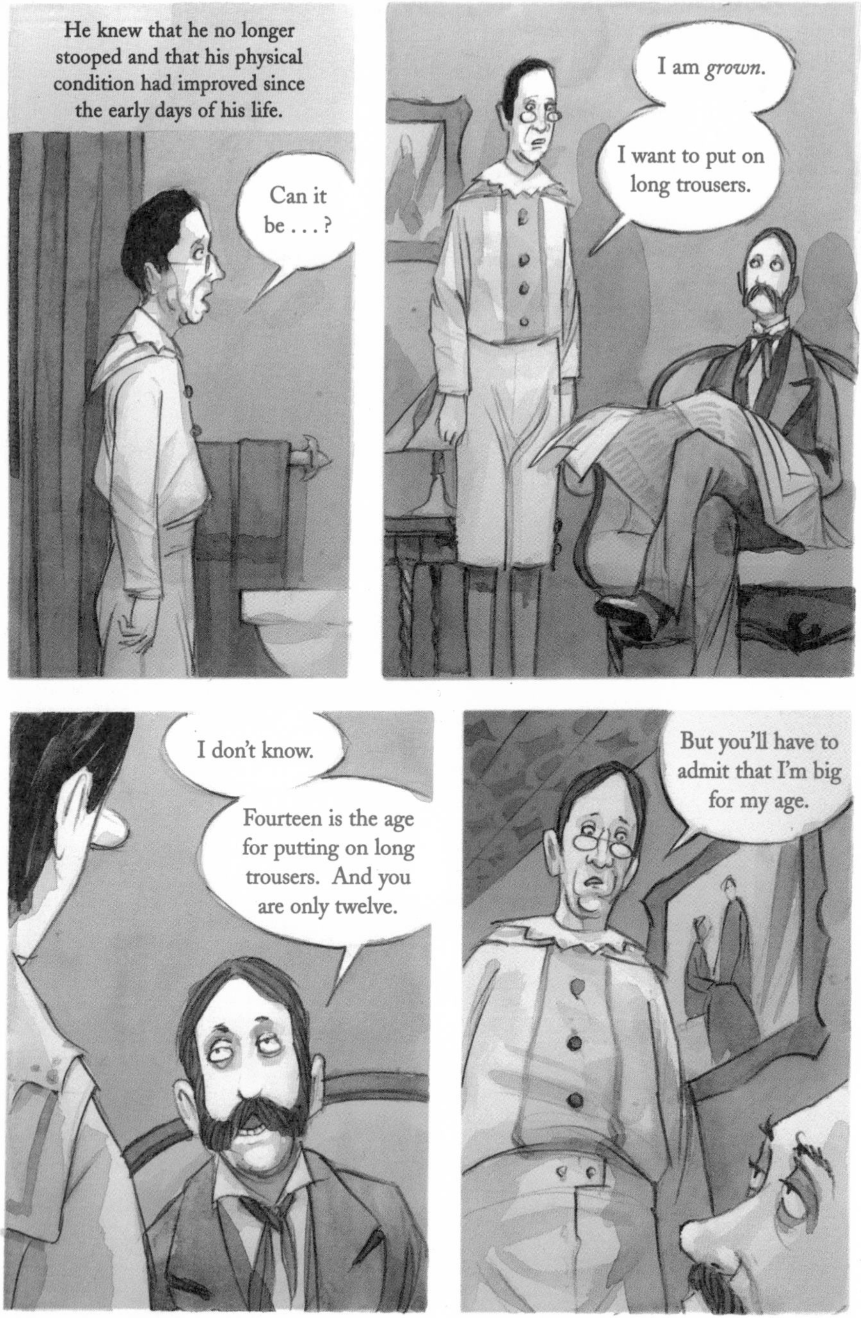
He knew that he no longer stooped and that his physical condition had improved since the early days of his life.
Can it be . . . ?
I am *grown*.
I want to put on long trousers.
I don't know.
Fourteen is the age for putting on long trousers. And you are only twelve.
But you'll have to admit that I'm big for my age.

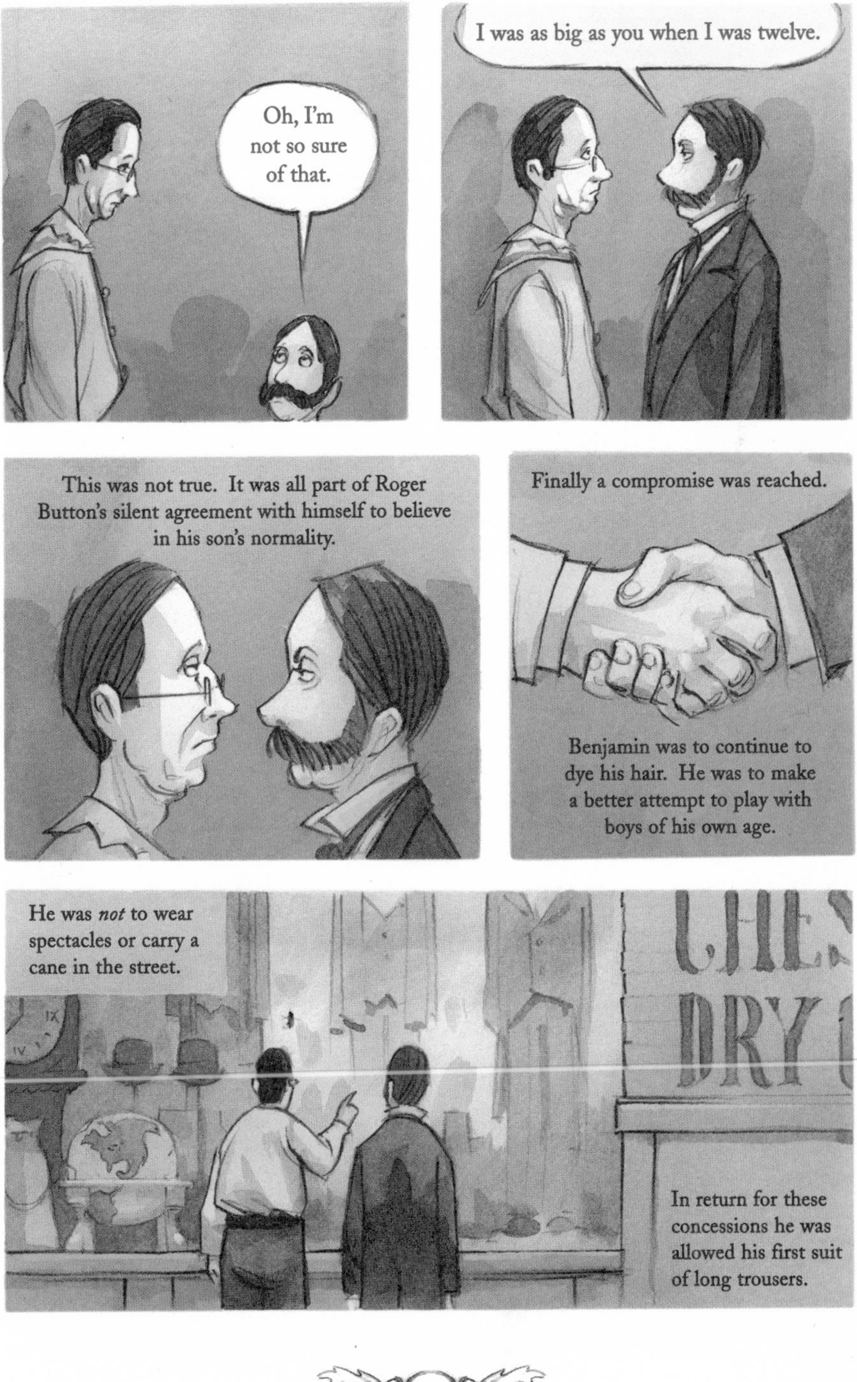
Oh, I'm not so sure of that.
I was as big as you when I was twelve.
This was not true. It was all part of Roger Button's silent agreement with himself to believe in his son's normality.
Finally a compromise was reached.
Benjamin was to continue to dye his hair. He was to make a better attempt to play with boys of his own age.
He was *not* to wear spectacles or carry a cane in the street.
DRY
In return for these concessions he was allowed his first suit of long trousers.

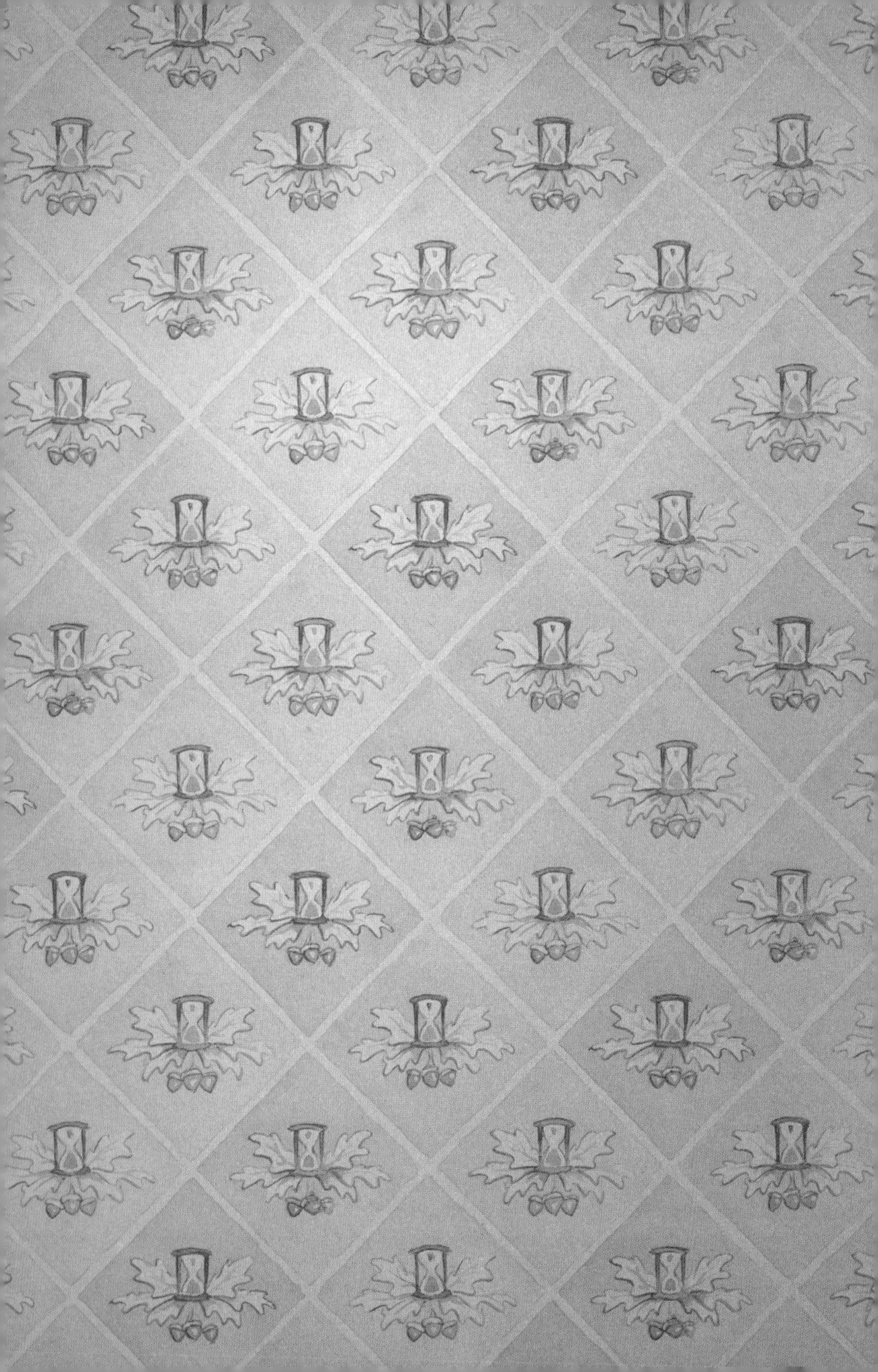

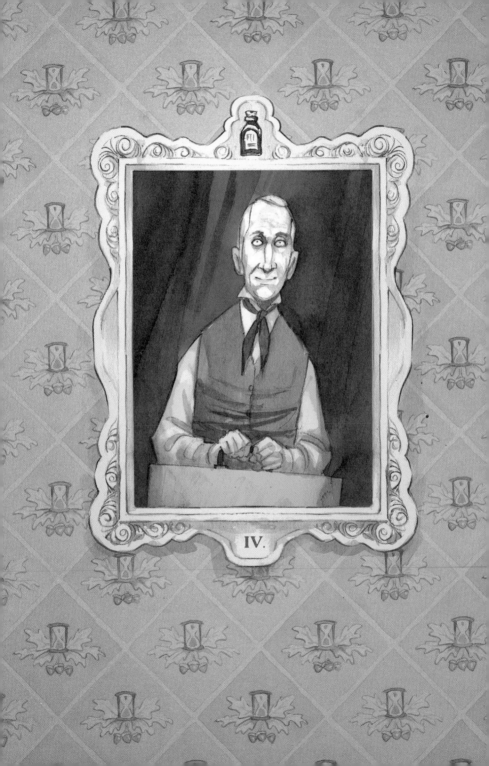

IV.

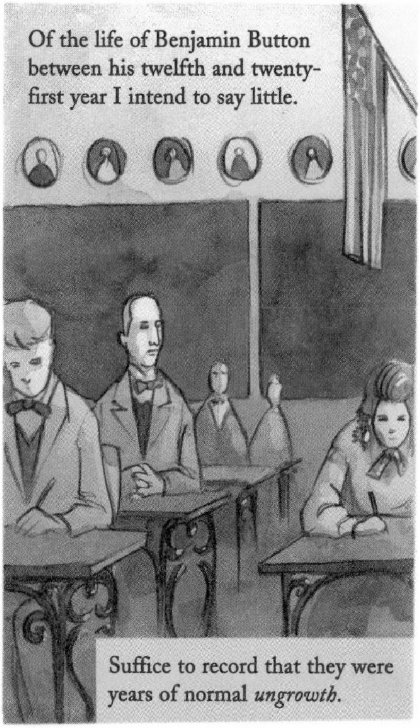
Of the life of Benjamin Button between his twelfth and twenty-first year I intend to say little.
Suffice to record that they were years of normal *ungrowth*.

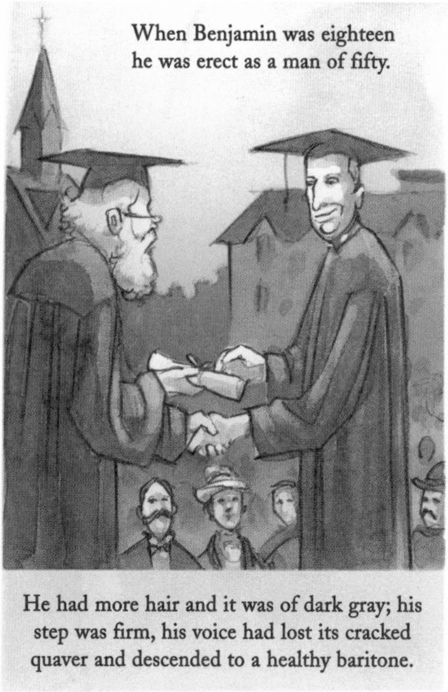
When Benjamin was eighteen he was erect as a man of fifty.
He had more hair and it was of dark gray; his step was firm, his voice had lost its cracked quaver and descended to a healthy baritone.

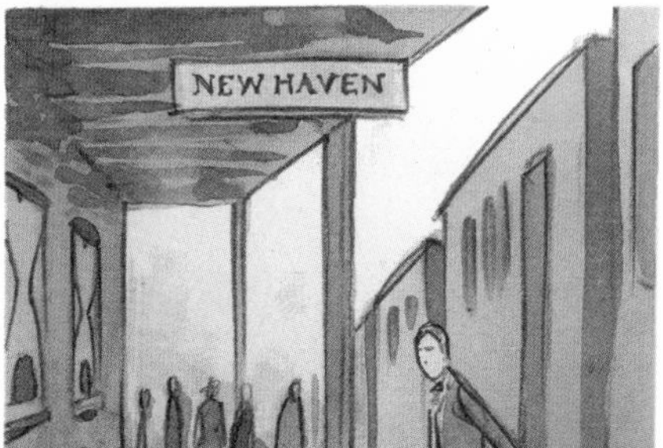
NEW HAVEN
So his father sent him up to Connecticut to take examinations for entrance to Yale College.

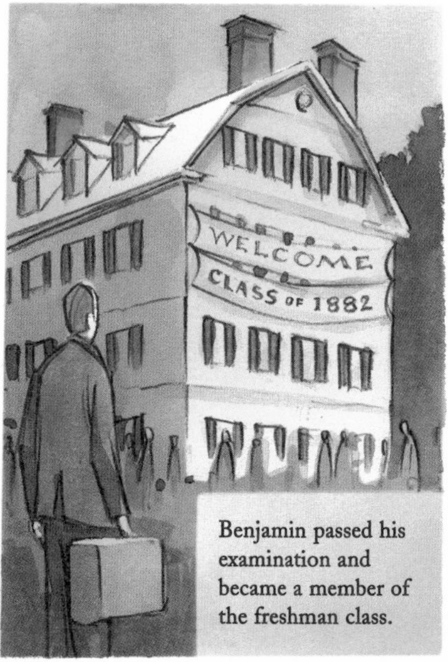
WELCOME
CLASS OF 1882
Benjamin passed his examination and became a member of the freshman class.

On the third day following his matriculation he received a notification from Mr. Hart, the college registrar, to call at his office and arrange his schedule.

Benjamin decided that his hair needed a new application of its brown dye.

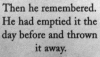

But an anxious inspection of his bureau drawer disclosed that the dye bottle was not there.

Then he remembered. He had emptied it the day before and thrown it away.

He was due at the registrar's in five minutes. There seemed to be no help for it—he must go as he was.

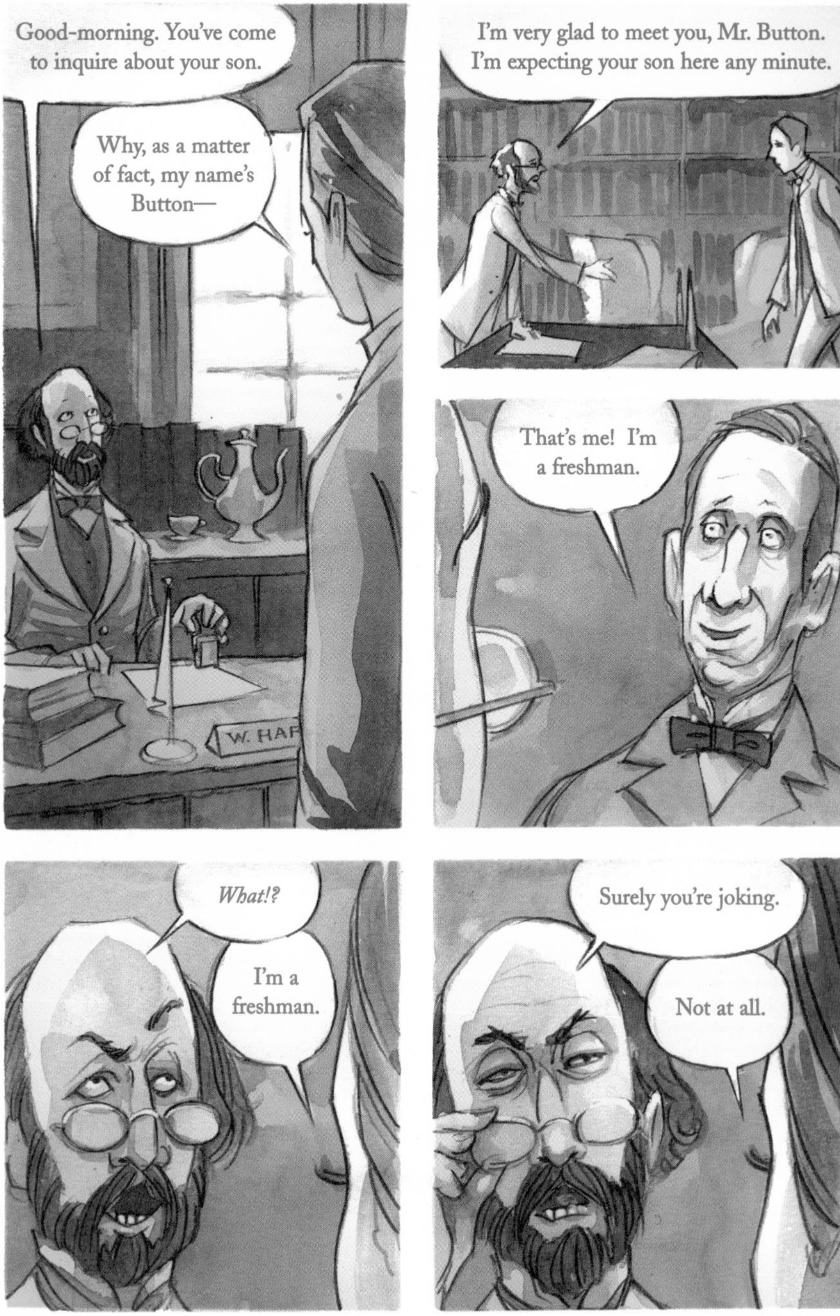
Good-morning. You've come to inquire about your son.
Why, as a matter of fact, my name's Button—
W. HAR
I'm very glad to meet you, Mr. Button. I'm expecting your son here any minute.
That's me! I'm a freshman.
What!?
I'm a freshman.
Surely you're joking.
Not at all.

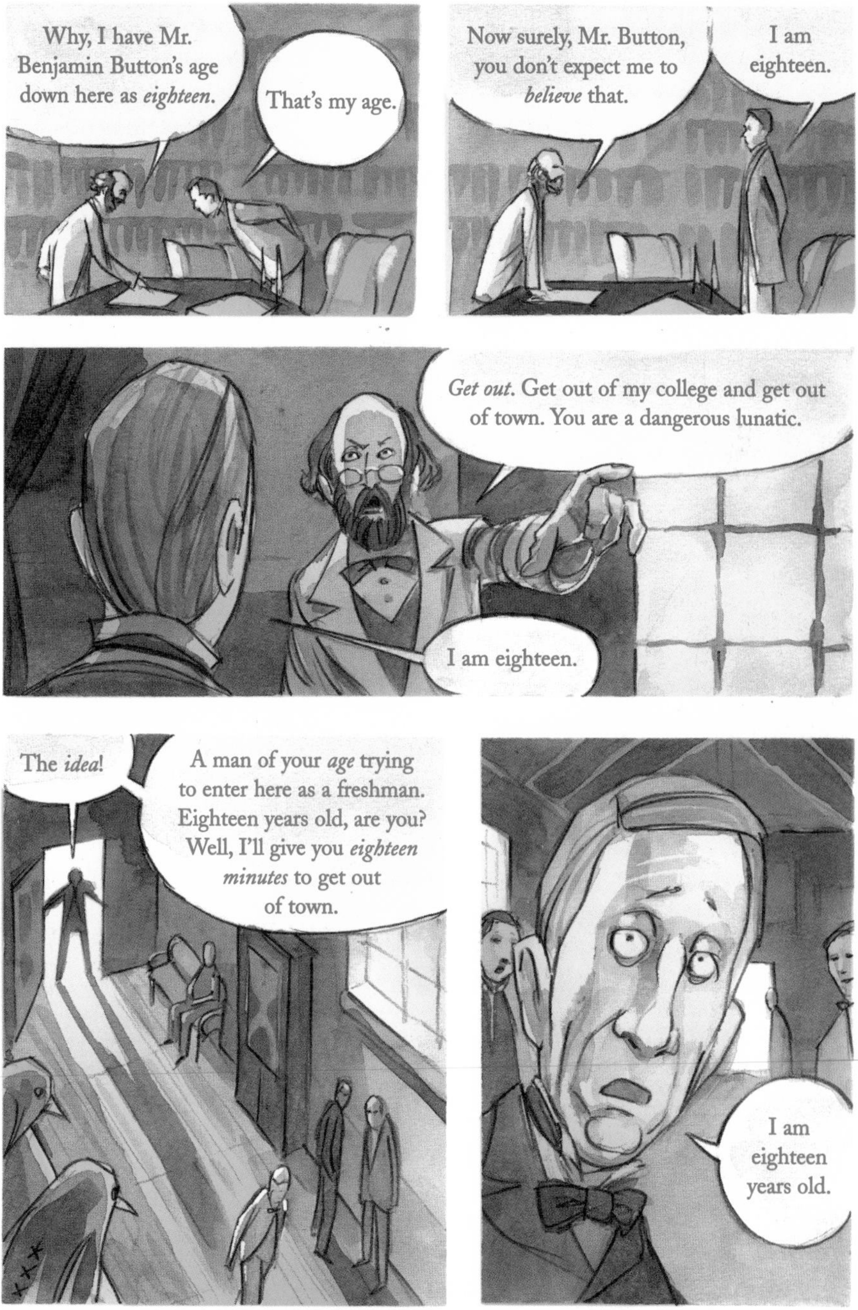
Why, I have Mr. Benjamin Button's age down here as *eighteen*.
That's my age.
Now surely, Mr. Button, you don't expect me to *believe* that.
I am eighteen.
Get out. Get out of my college and get out of town. You are a dangerous lunatic.
I am eighteen.
The *idea*!
A man of your *age* trying to enter here as a freshman. Eighteen years old, are you? Well, I'll give you *eighteen minutes* to get out of town.
I am eighteen years old.

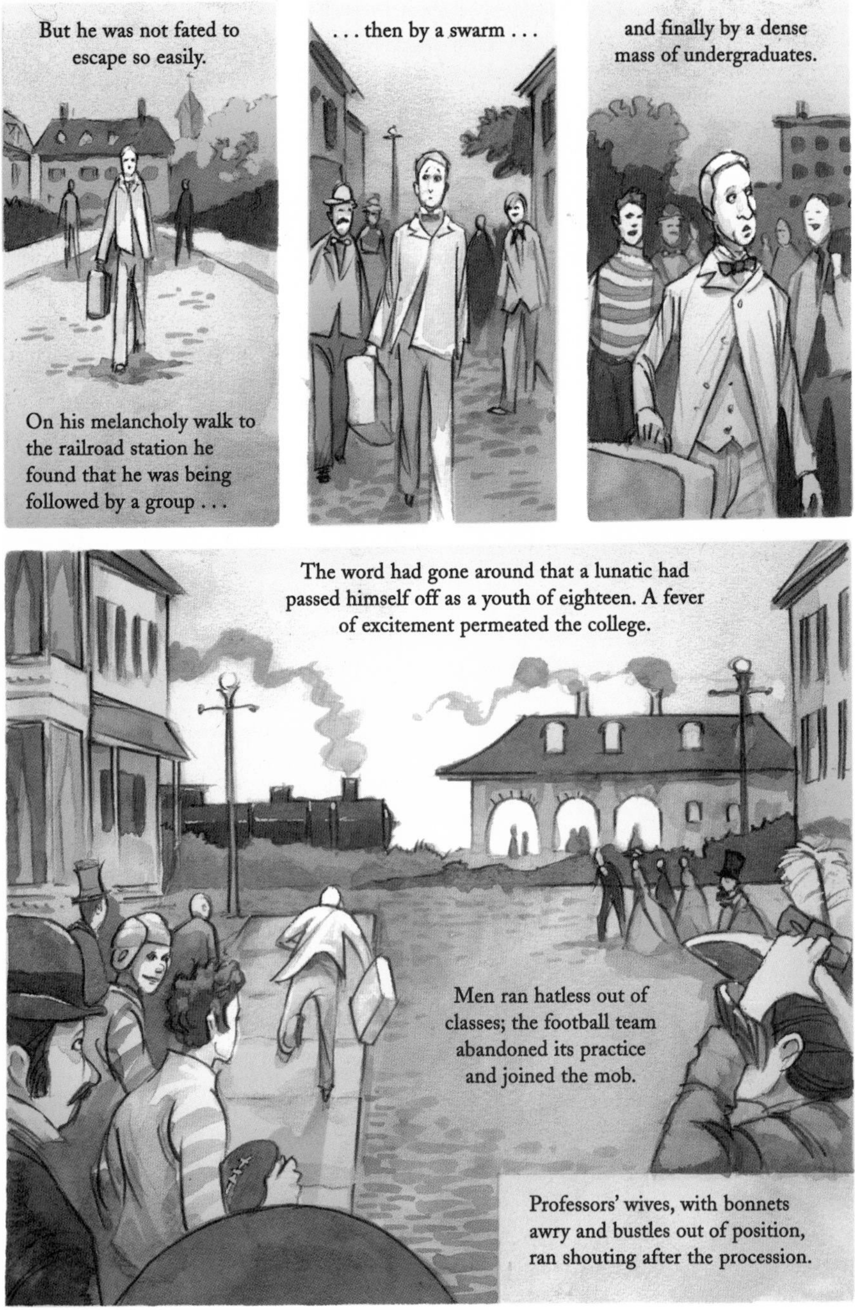
But he was not fated to escape so easily.
On his melancholy walk to the railroad station he found that he was being followed by a group . . .
. . . then by a swarm . . .
and finally by a dense mass of undergraduates.
The word had gone around that a lunatic had passed himself off as a youth of eighteen. A fever of excitement permeated the college.
Men ran hatless out of classes; the football team abandoned its practice and joined the mob.
Professors' wives, with bonnets awry and bustles out of position, ran shouting after the procession.

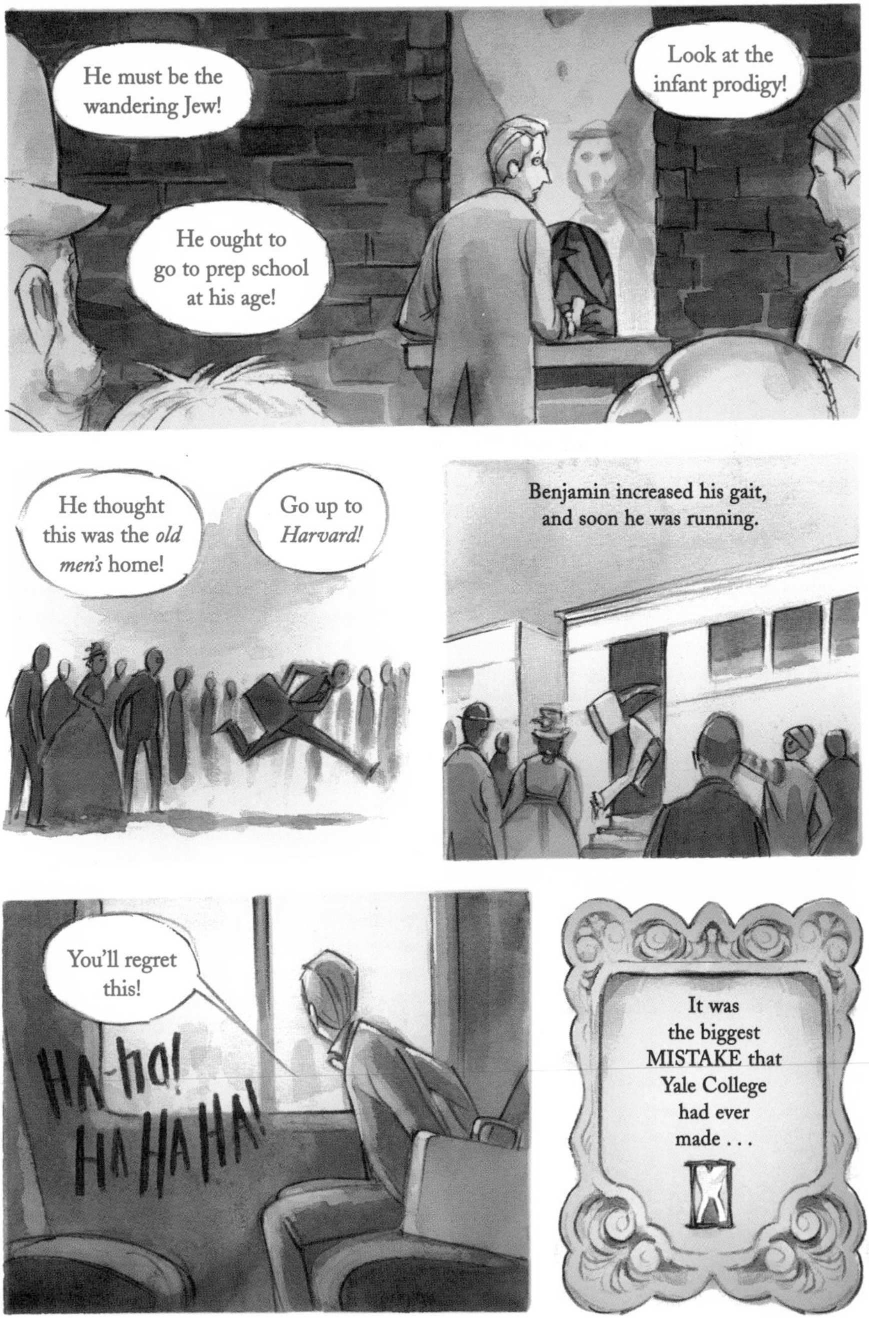
He must be the wandering Jew!
Look at the infant prodigy!
He ought to go to prep school at his age!
He thought this was the *old men's* home!
Go up to *Harvard!*
Benjamin increased his gait, and soon he was running.
You'll regret this!
HA-ha! HA HA HA!
It was the biggest MISTAKE that Yale College had ever made . . .

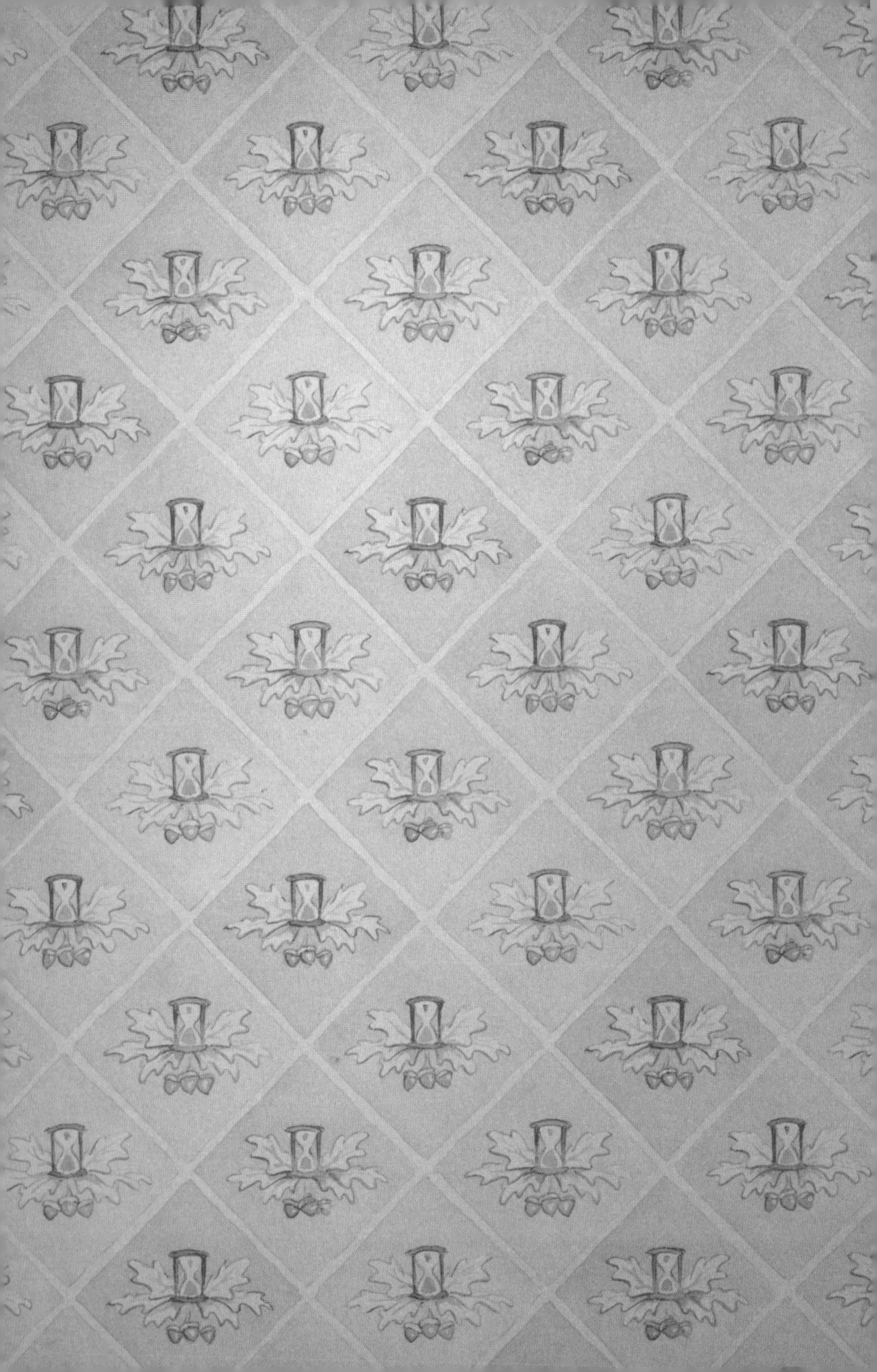

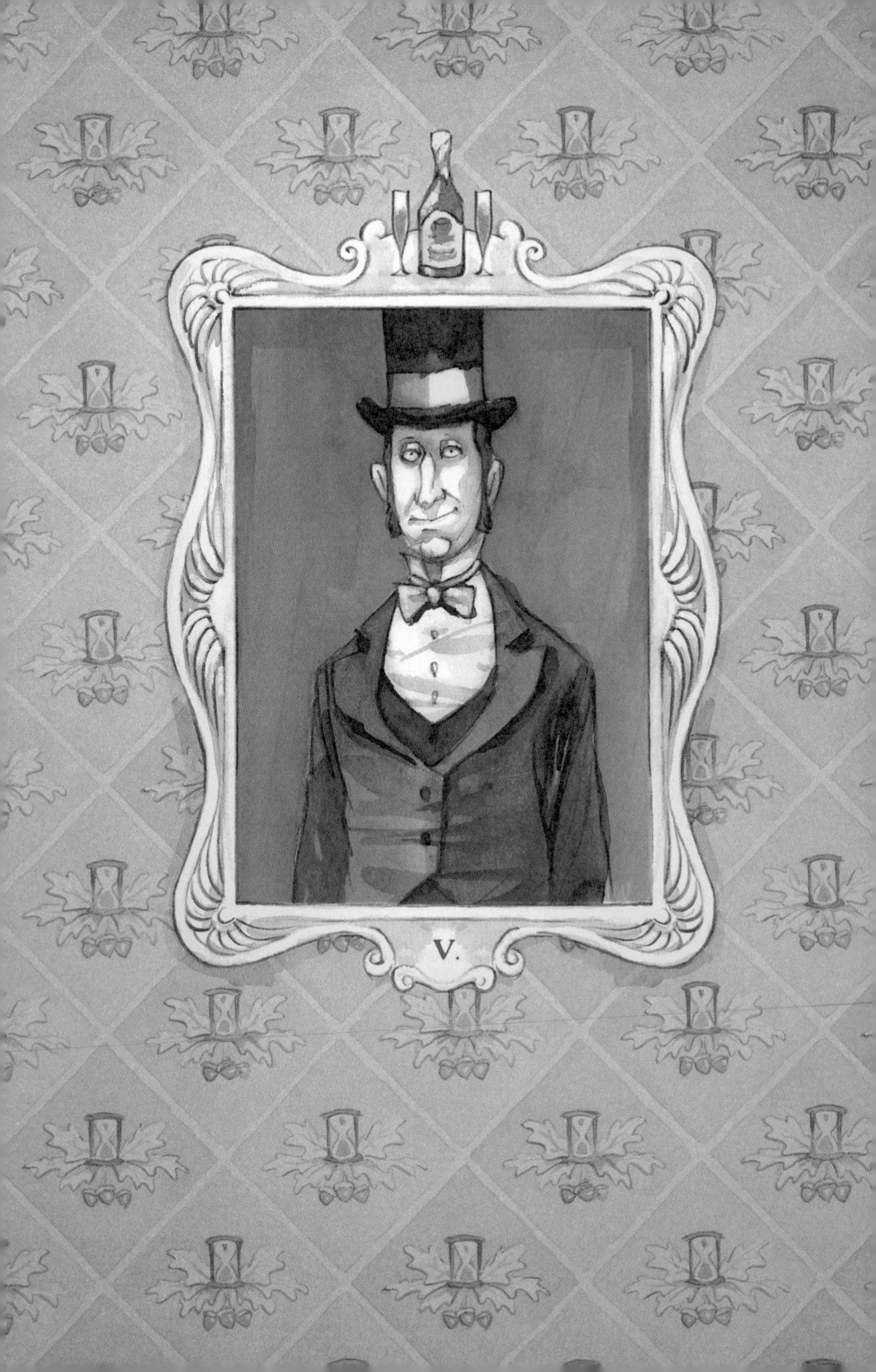
V.

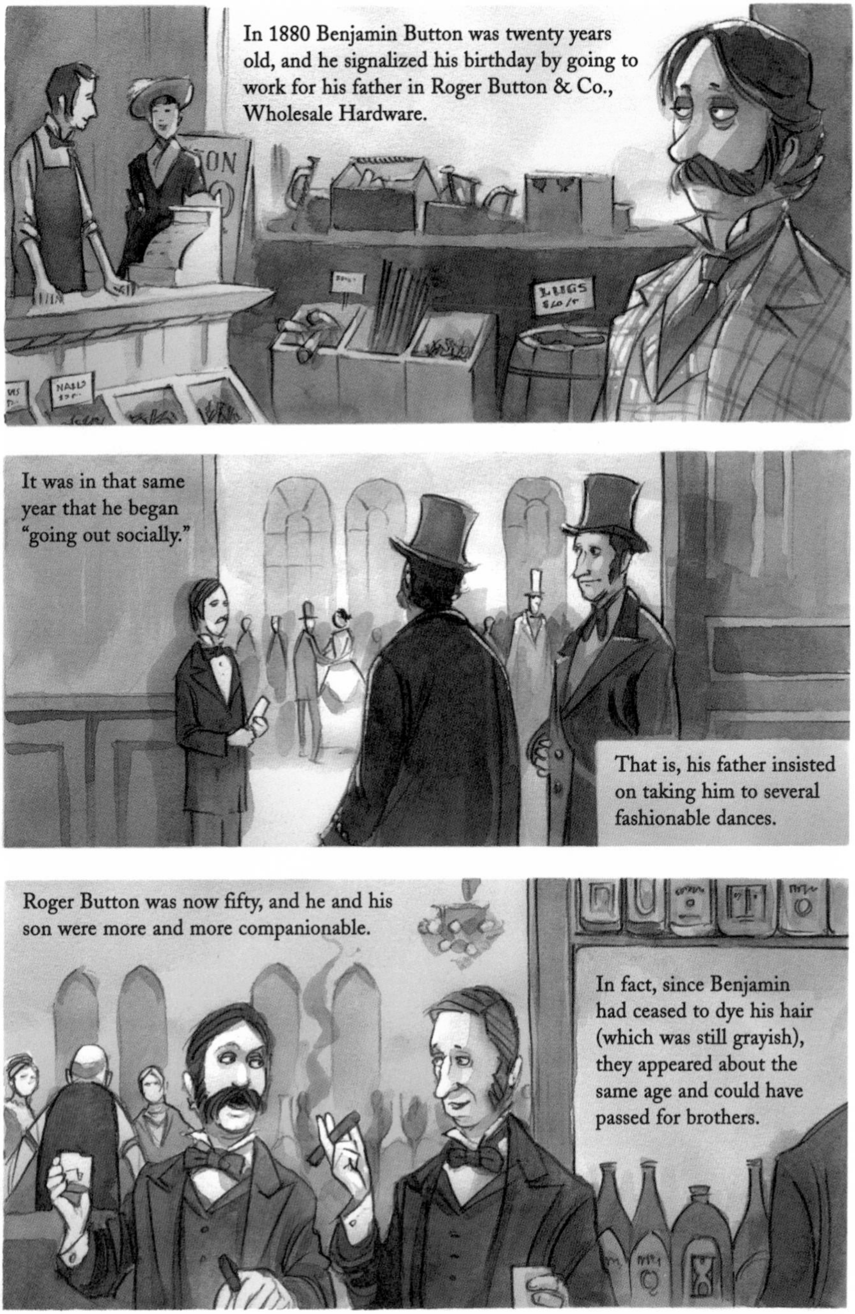
In 1880 Benjamin Button was twenty years old, and he signalized his birthday by going to work for his father in Roger Button & Co., Wholesale Hardware.
LUGS
NAILS
It was in that same year that he began "going out socially."
That is, his father insisted on taking him to several fashionable dances.
Roger Button was now fifty, and he and his son were more and more companionable.
In fact, since Benjamin had ceased to dye his hair (which was still grayish), they appeared about the same age and could have passed for brothers.

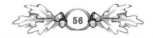

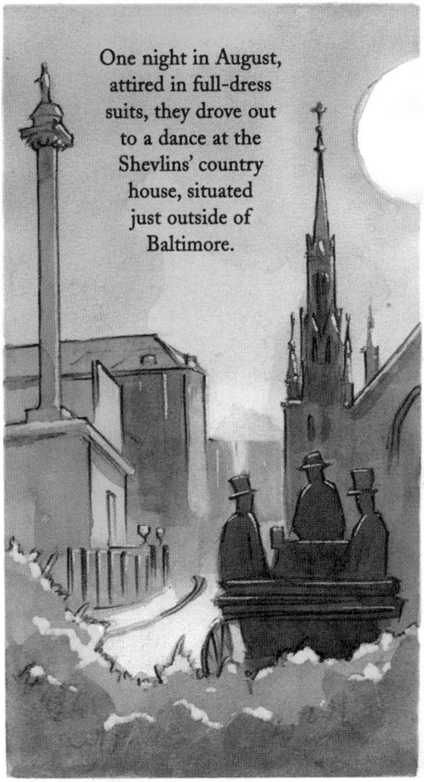
One night in August, attired in full-dress suits, they drove out to a dance at the Shevlins' country house, situated just outside of Baltimore.

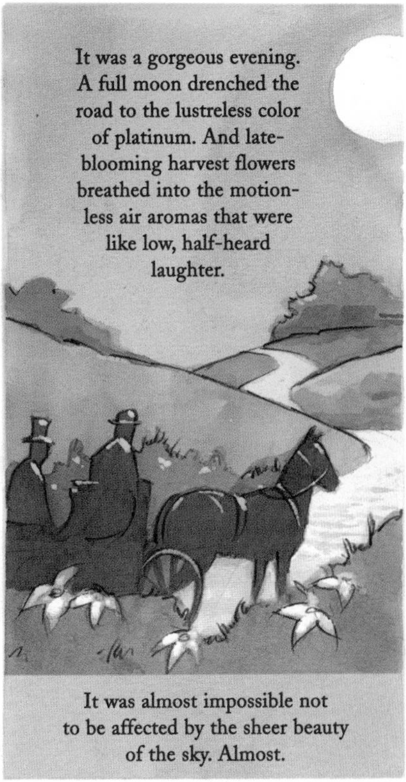
It was a gorgeous evening. A full moon drenched the road to the lustreless color of platinum. And late-blooming harvest flowers breathed into the motionless air aromas that were like low, half-heard laughter.
It was almost impossible not to be affected by the sheer beauty of the sky. Almost.

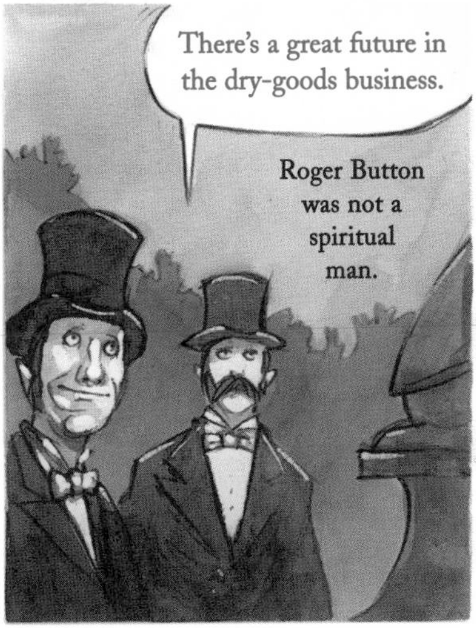
There's a great future in the dry-goods business.
Roger Button was not a spiritual man.

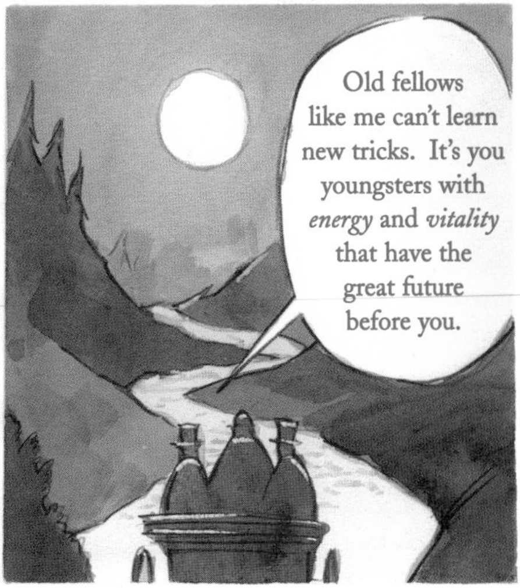
Old fellows like me can't learn new tricks. It's you youngsters with *energy* and *vitality* that have the great future before you.

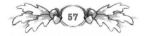

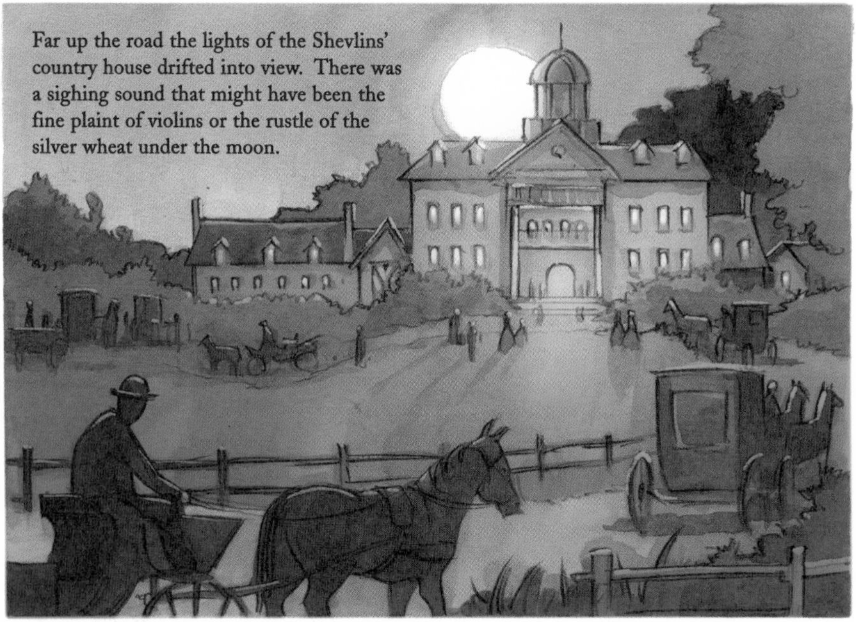
Far up the road the lights of the Shevlins' country house drifted into view. There was a sighing sound that might have been the fine plaint of violins or the rustle of the silver wheat under the moon.

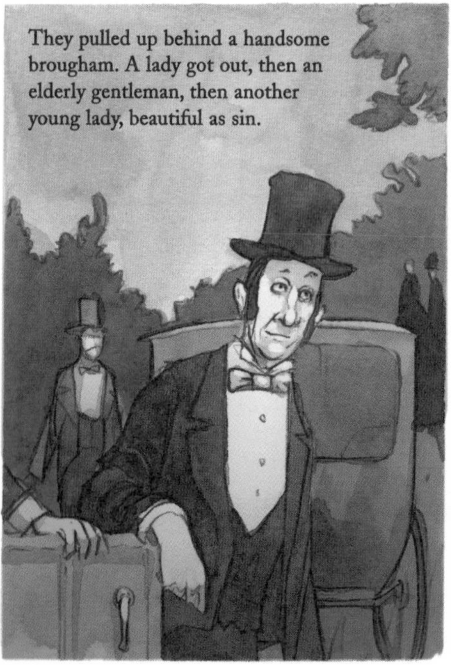
They pulled up behind a handsome brougham. A lady got out, then an elderly gentleman, then another young lady, beautiful as sin.

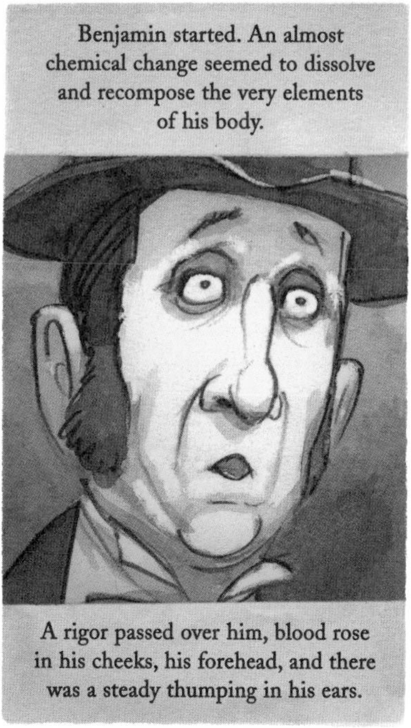
Benjamin started. An almost chemical change seemed to dissolve and recompose the very elements of his body.
A rigor passed over him, blood rose in his cheeks, his forehead, and there was a steady thumping in his ears.

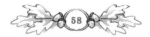

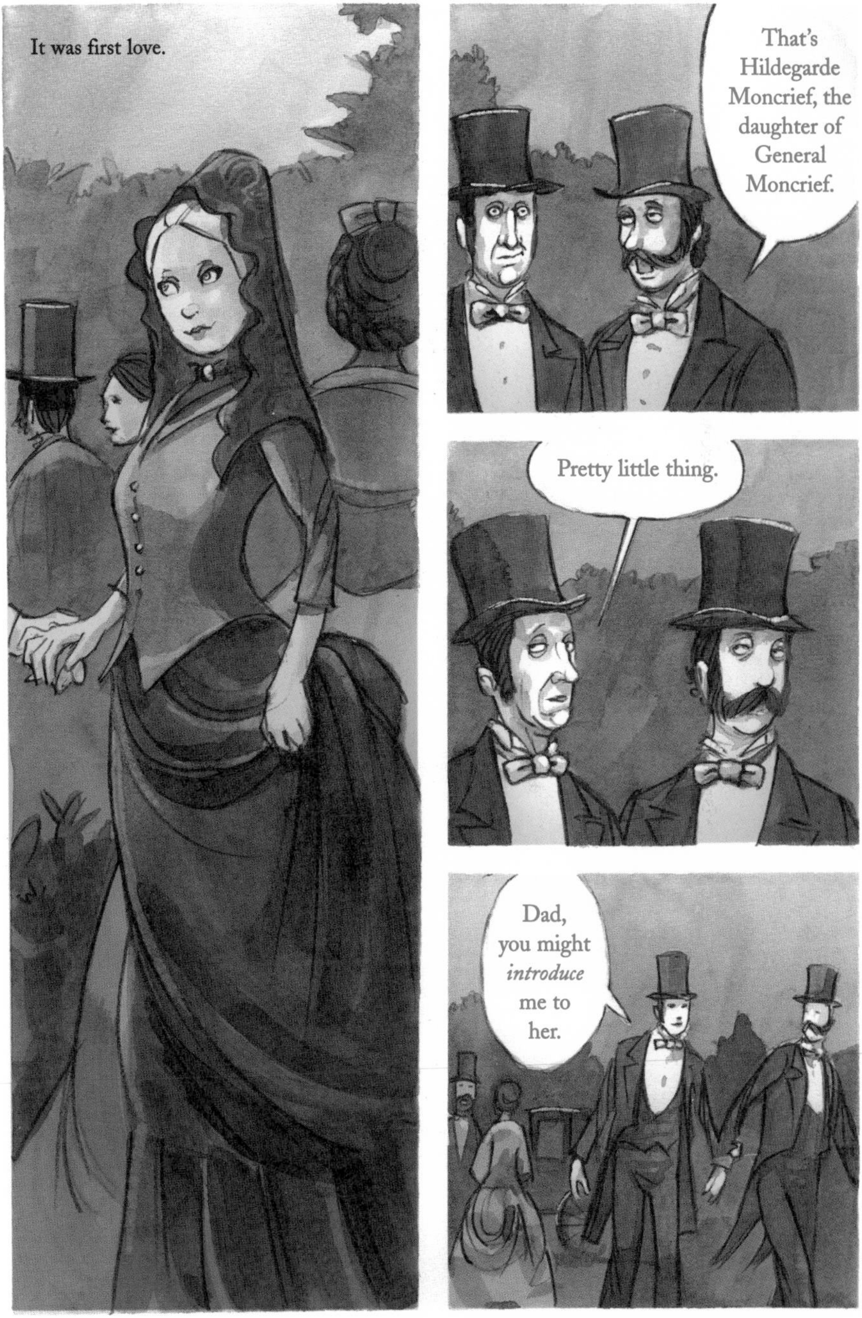
It was first love.
That's Hildegarde Moncrief, the daughter of General Moncrief.
Pretty little thing.
Dad, you might *introduce* me to her.

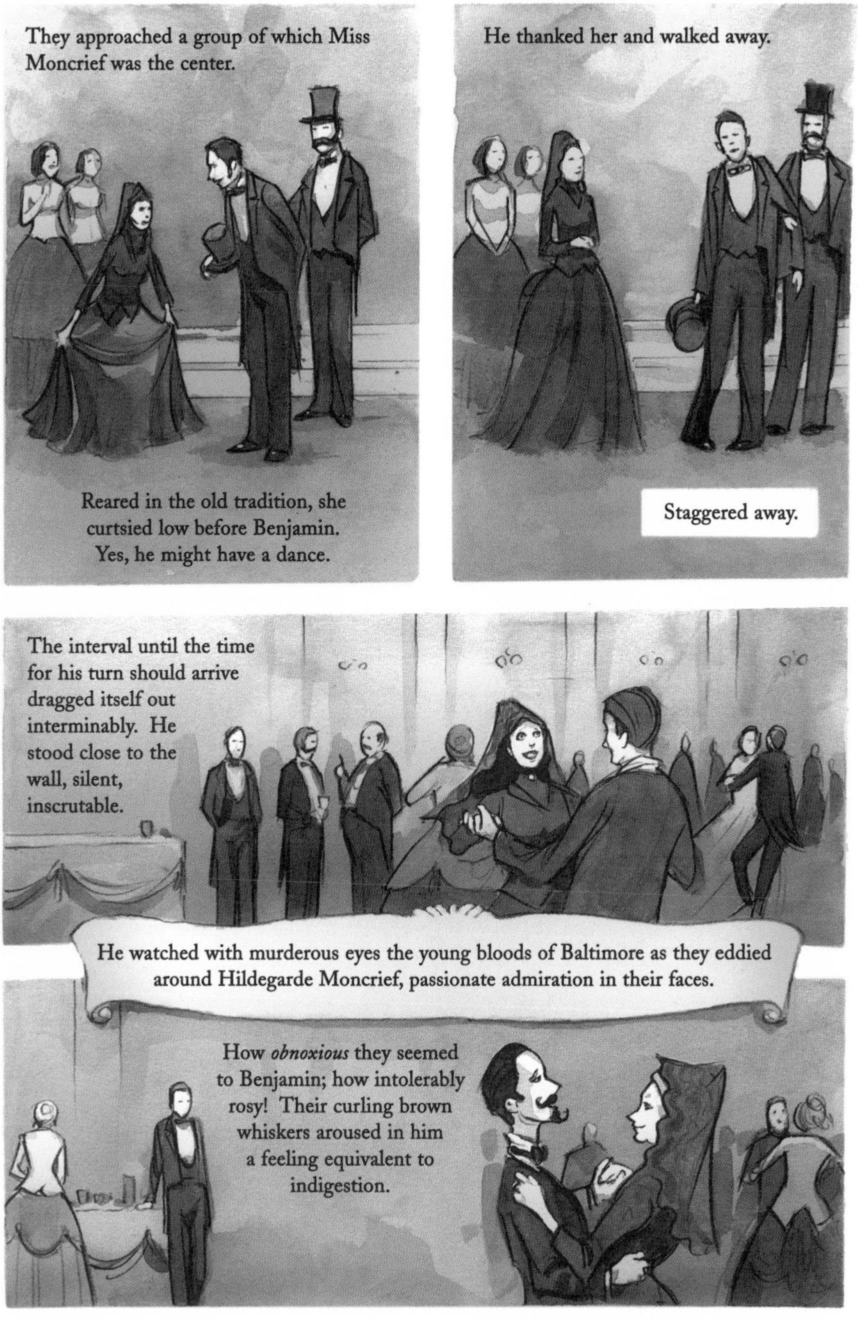
They approached a group of which Miss Moncrief was the center.
Reared in the old tradition, she curtsied low before Benjamin. Yes, he might have a dance.
He thanked her and walked away.
Staggered away.
The interval until the time for his turn should arrive dragged itself out interminably. He stood close to the wall, silent, inscrutable.
He watched with murderous eyes the young bloods of Baltimore as they eddied around Hildegarde Moncrief, passionate admiration in their faces.
How *obnoxious* they seemed to Benjamin; how intolerably rosy! Their curling brown whiskers aroused in him a feeling equivalent to indigestion.

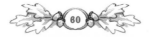

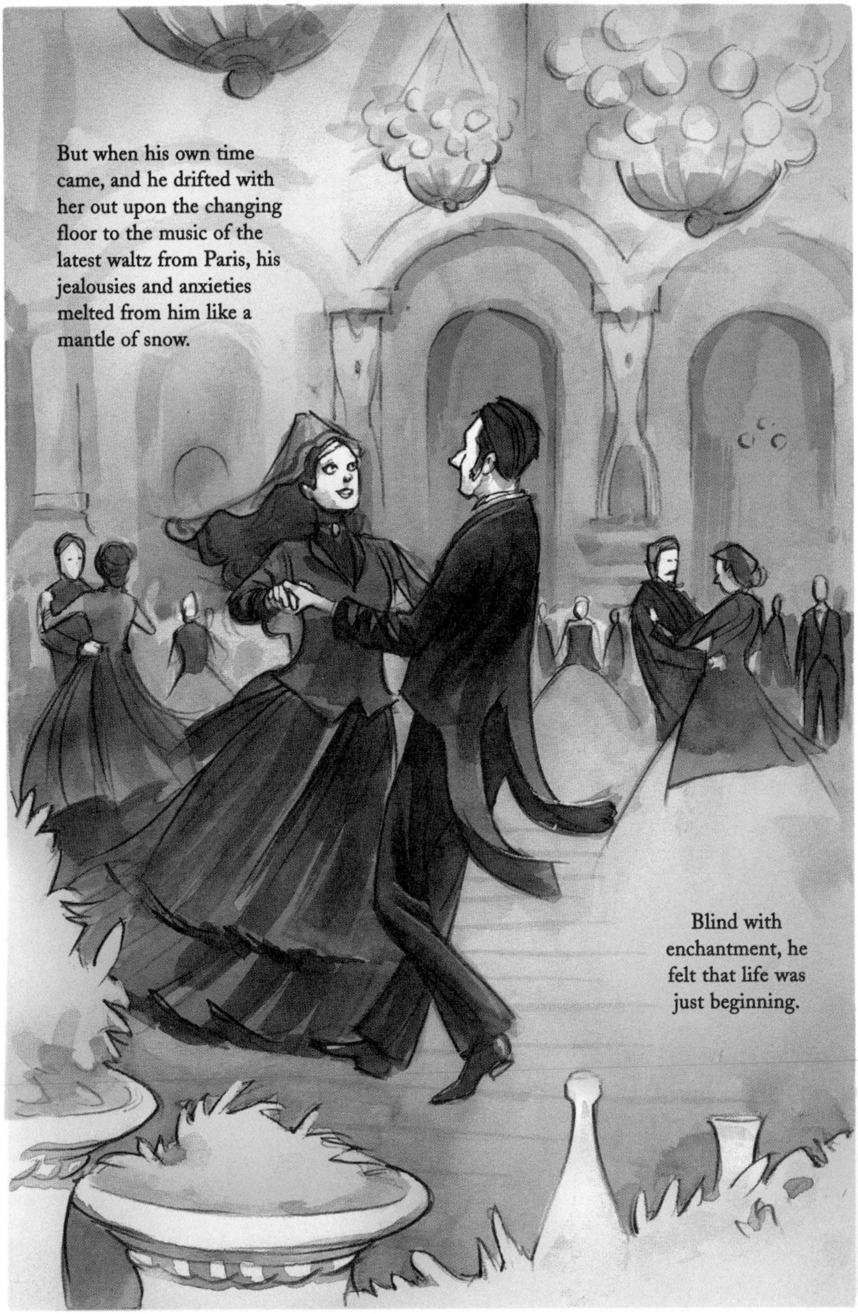
But when his own time came, and he drifted with her out upon the changing floor to the music of the latest waltz from Paris, his jealousies and anxieties melted from him like a mantle of snow.
Blind with enchantment, he felt that life was just beginning.

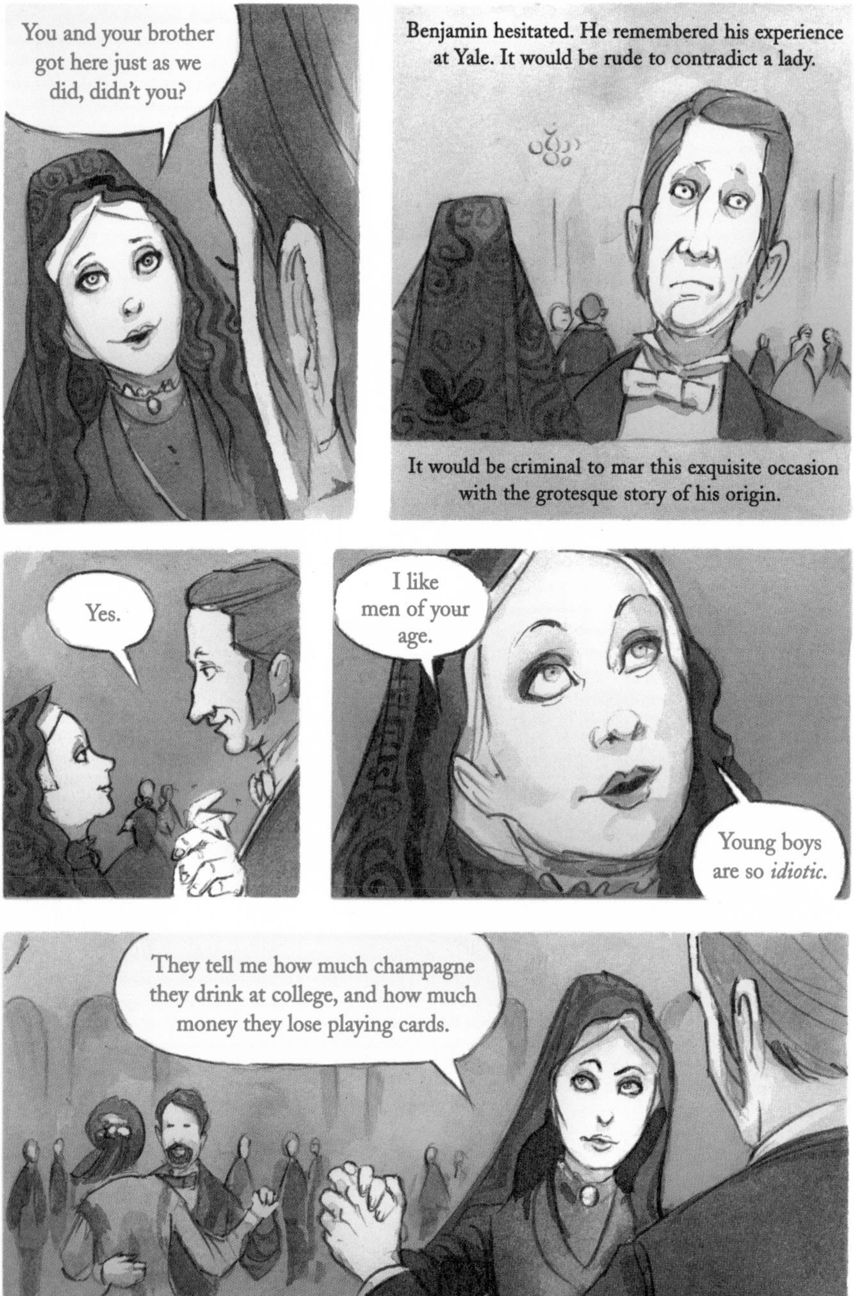
You and your brother got here just as we did, didn't you?
Benjamin hesitated. He remembered his experience at Yale. It would be rude to contradict a lady.
It would be criminal to mar this exquisite occasion with the grotesque story of his origin.
Yes.
I like men of your age.
Young boys are so *idiotic*.
They tell me how much champagne they drink at college, and how much money they lose playing cards.

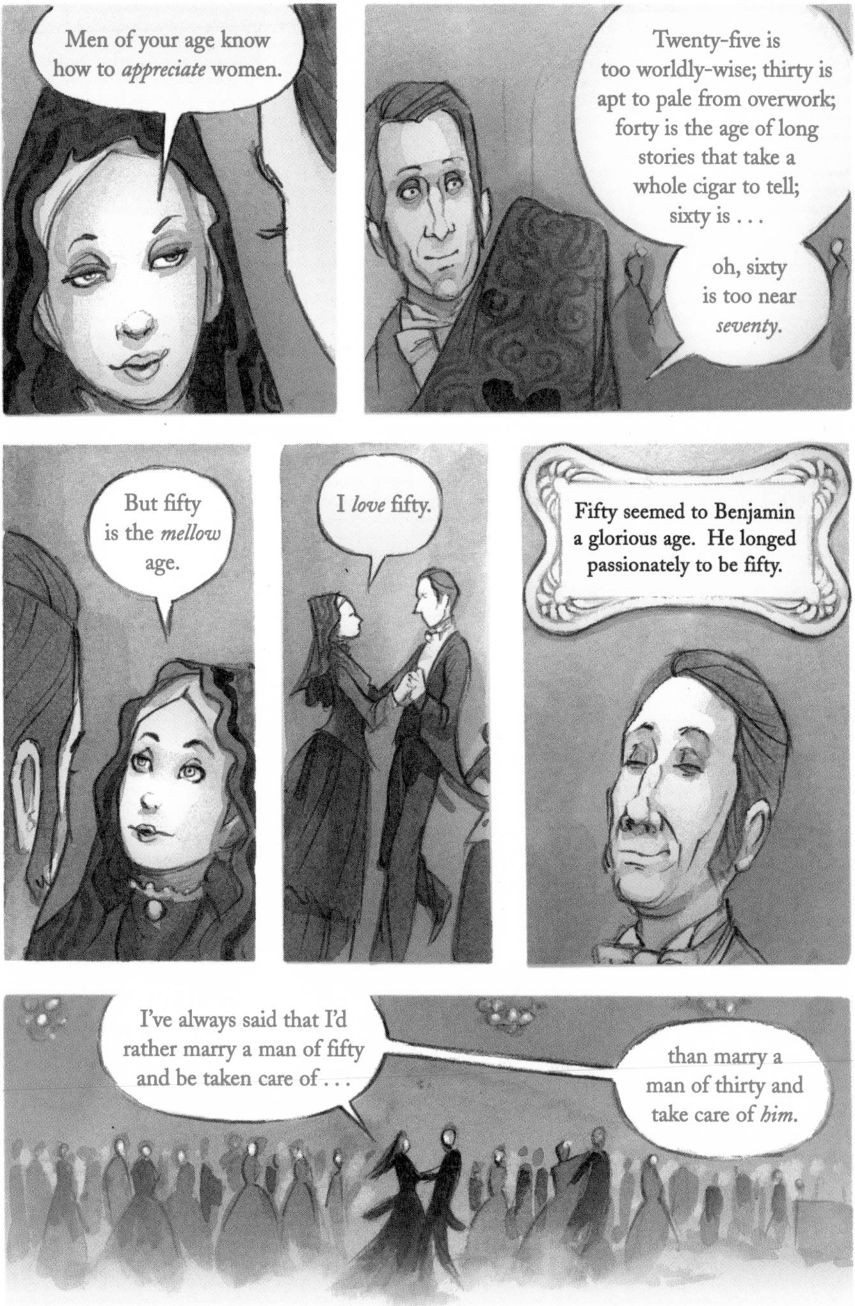
Men of your age know how to *appreciate* women.
Twenty-five is too worldly-wise; thirty is apt to pale from overwork; forty is the age of long stories that take a whole cigar to tell; sixty is . . .
oh, sixty is too near *seventy*.
But fifty is the *mellow* age.
I *love* fifty.
Fifty seemed to Benjamin a glorious age. He longed passionately to be fifty.
I've always said that I'd rather marry a man of fifty and be taken care of . . .
than marry a man of thirty and take care of *him*.

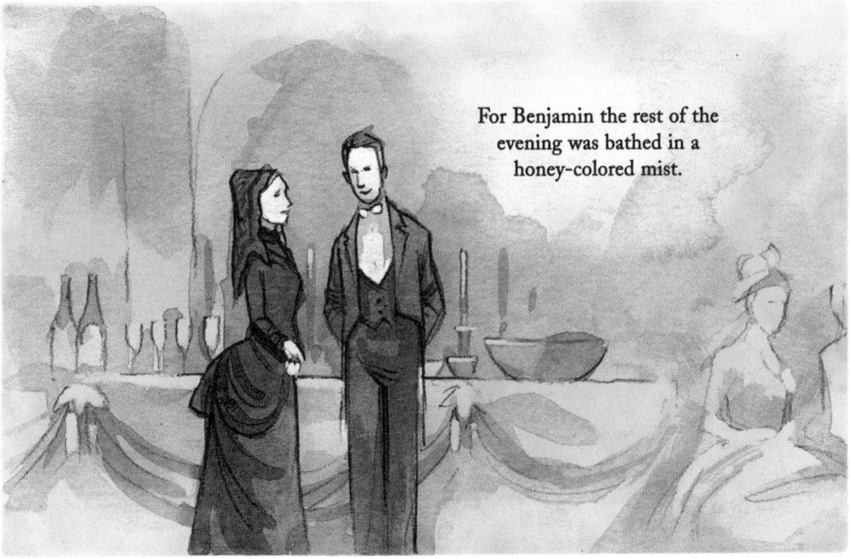
For Benjamin the rest of the evening was bathed in a honey-colored mist.

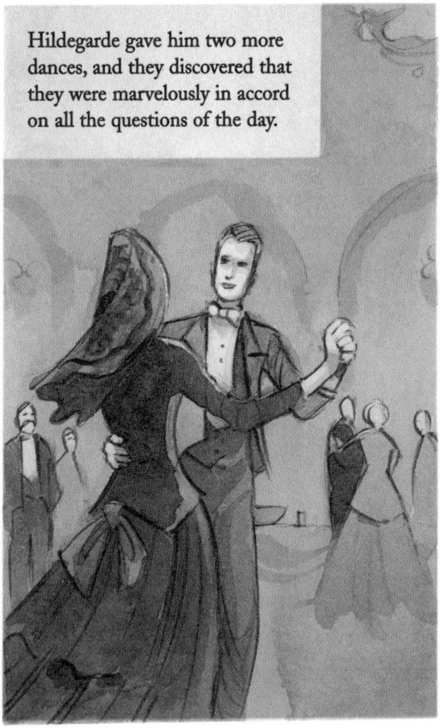
Hildegarde gave him two more dances, and they discovered that they were marvelously in accord on all the questions of the day.

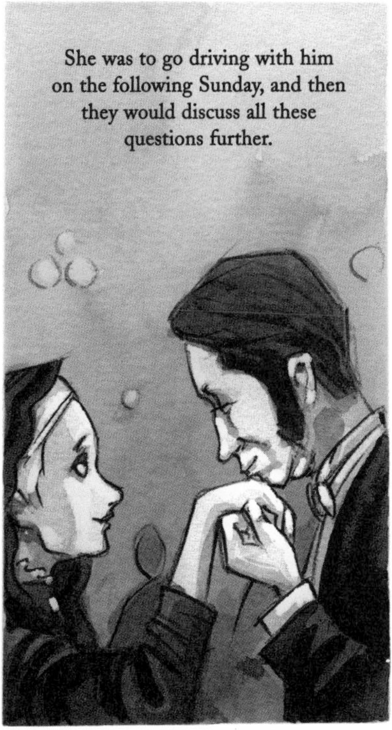
She was to go driving with him on the following Sunday, and then they would discuss all these questions further.

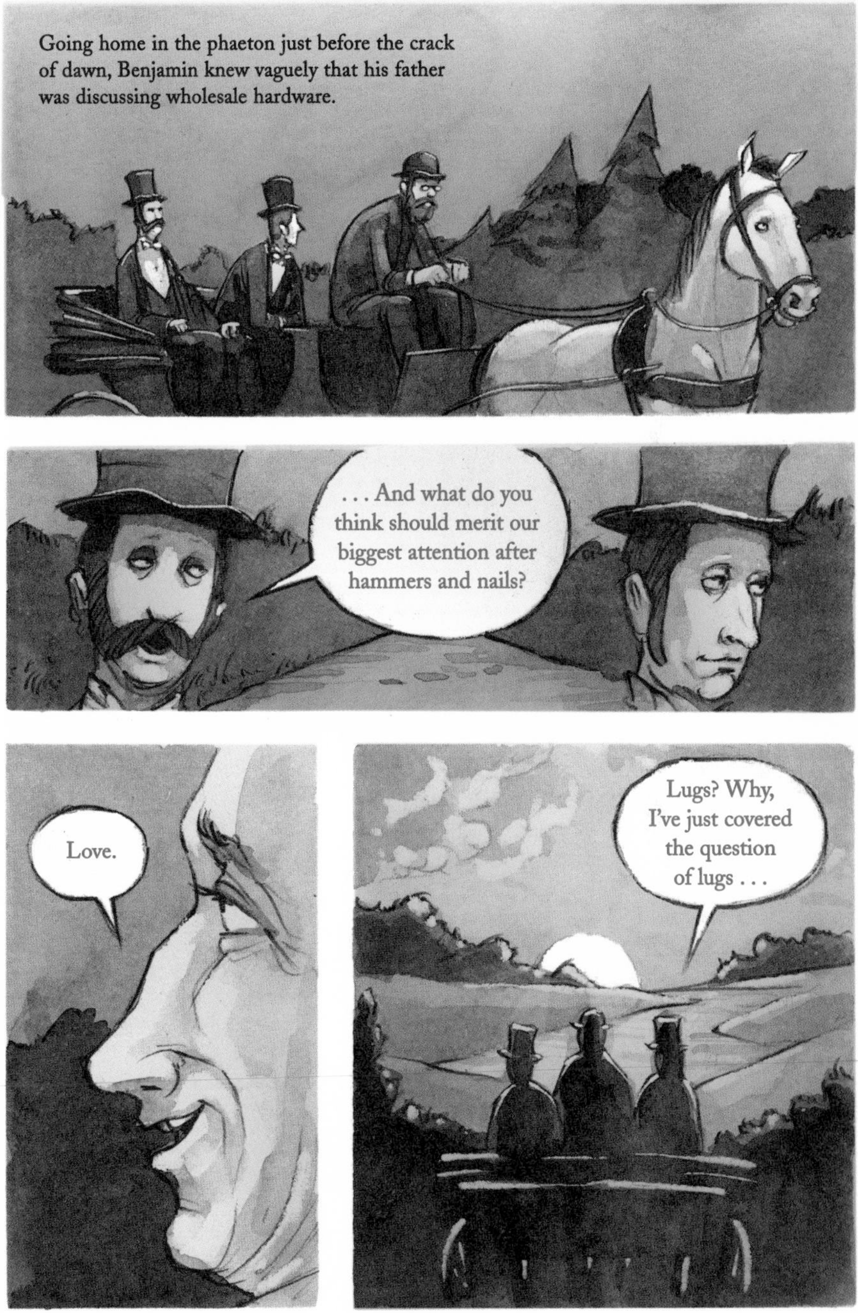
Going home in the phaeton just before the crack of dawn, Benjamin knew vaguely that his father was discussing wholesale hardware.
. . . And what do you think should merit our biggest attention after hammers and nails?
Love.
Lugs? Why, I've just covered the question of lugs . . .

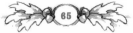

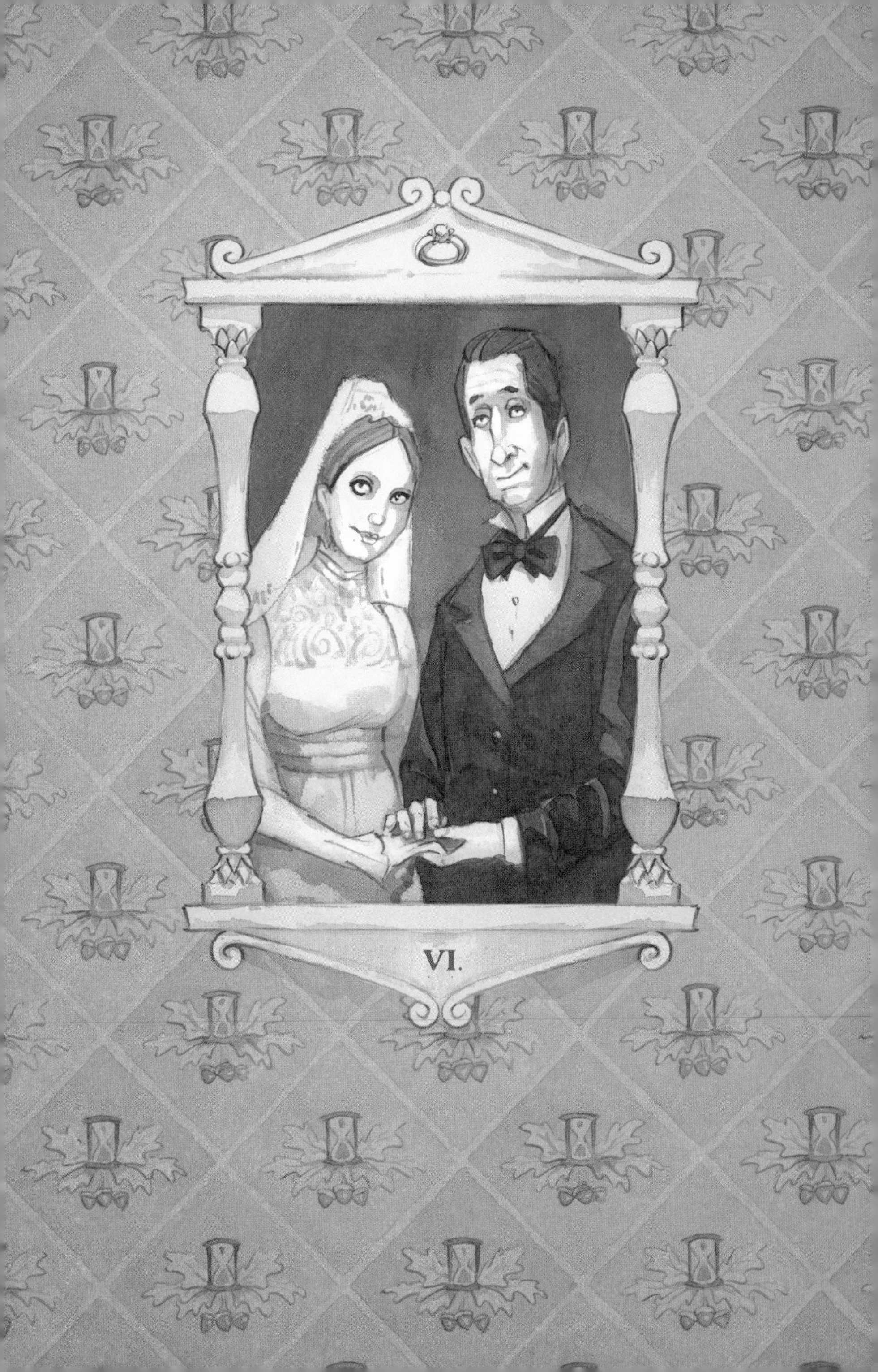
VI.

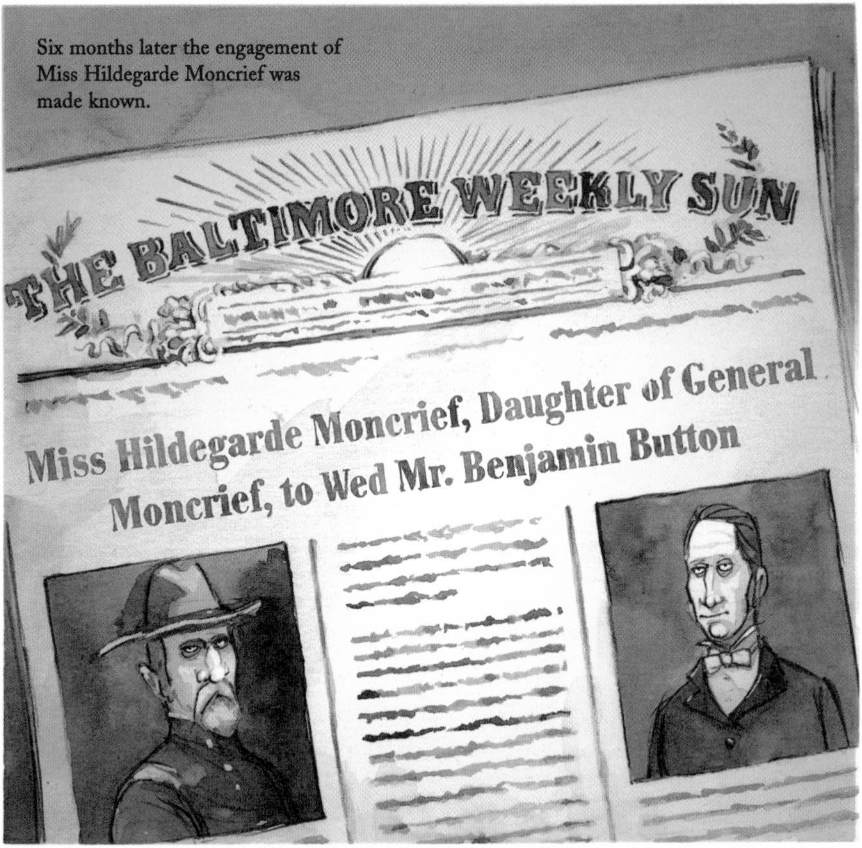
Six months later the engagement of Miss Hildegarde Moncrief was made known.
THE BALTIMORE WEEKLY SUN
Miss Hildegarde Moncrief, Daughter of General Moncrief, to Wed Mr. Benjamin Button

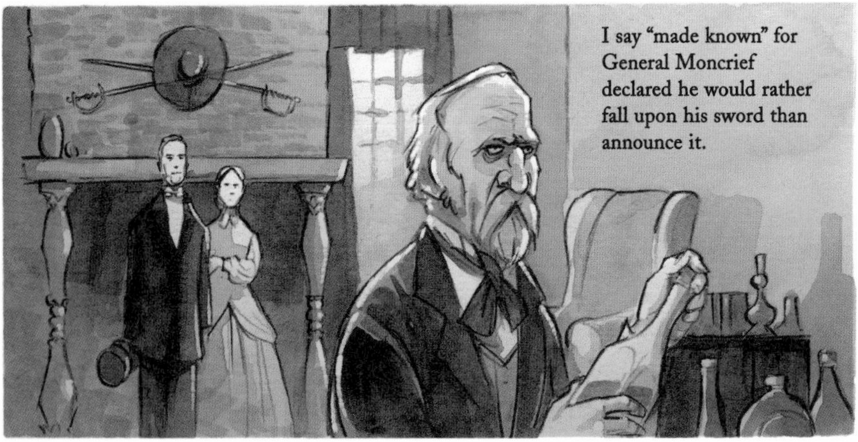
I say "made known" for General Moncrief declared he would rather fall upon his sword than announce it.

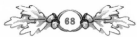

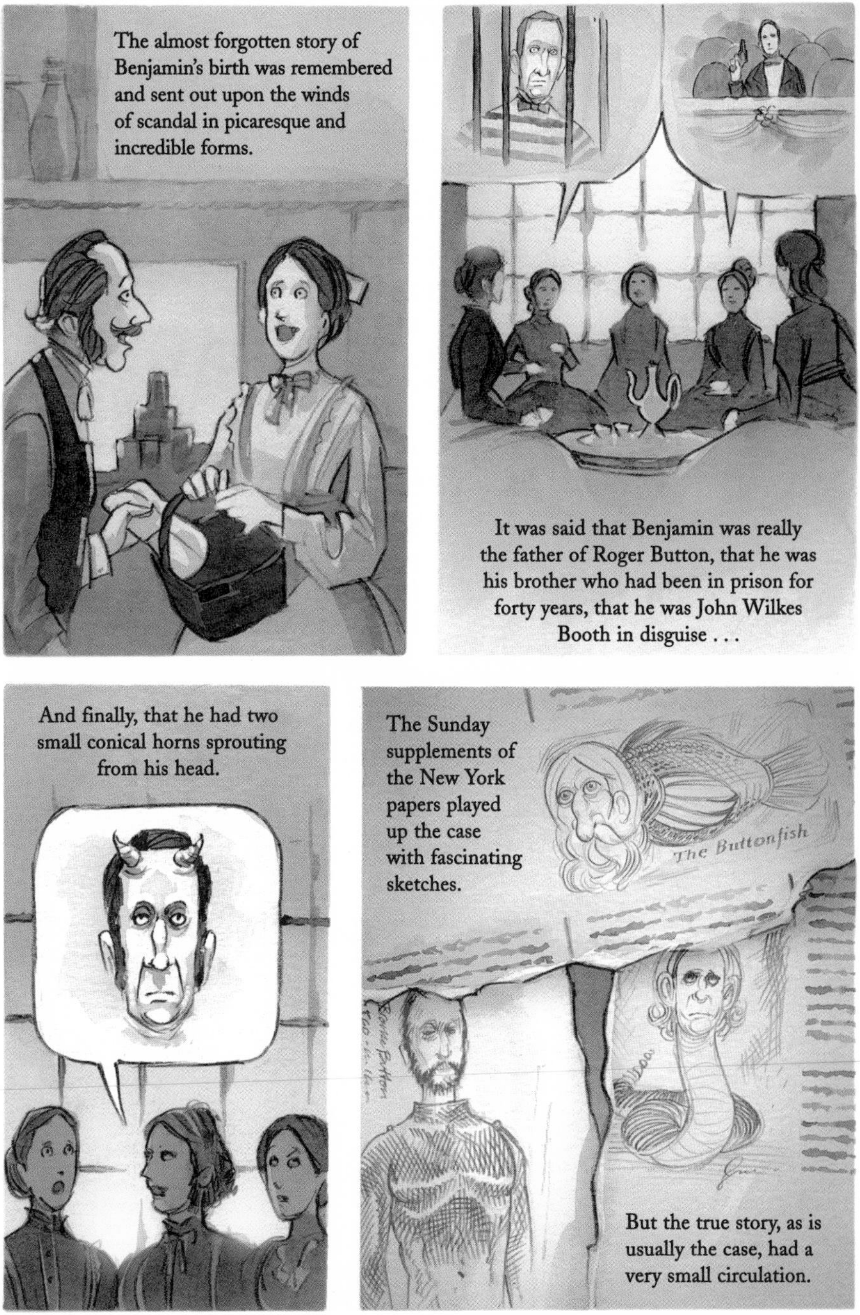
The almost forgotten story of Benjamin's birth was remembered and sent out upon the winds of scandal in picaresque and incredible forms.
It was said that Benjamin was really the father of Roger Button, that he was his brother who had been in prison for forty years, that he was John Wilkes Booth in disguise . . .
And finally, that he had two small conical horns sprouting from his head.
The Sunday supplements of the New York papers played up the case with fascinating sketches.
The Buttonfish
But the true story, as is usually the case, had a very small circulation.

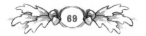

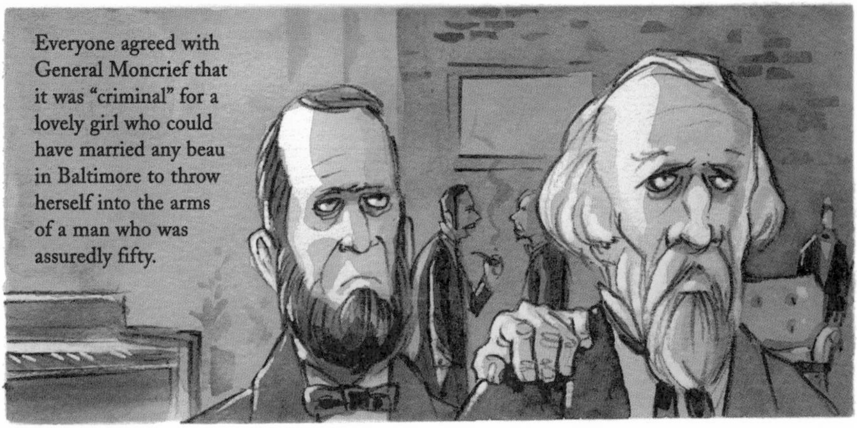
Everyone agreed with General Moncrief that it was "criminal" for a lovely girl who could have married any beau in Baltimore to throw herself into the arms of a man who was assuredly fifty.

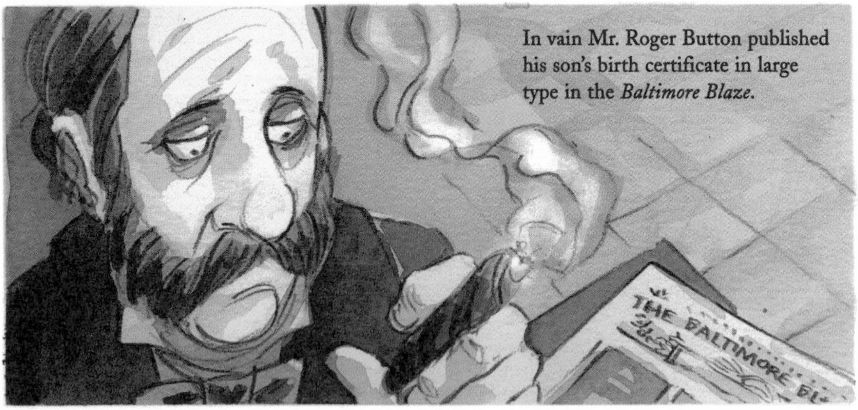
In vain Mr. Roger Button published his son's birth certificate in large type in the *Baltimore Blaze*.
THE BALTIMORE

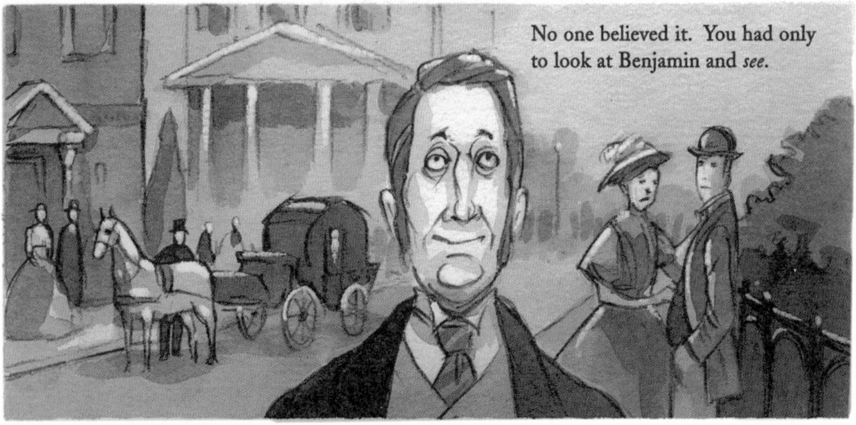
No one believed it. You had only to look at Benjamin and *see*.

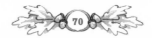

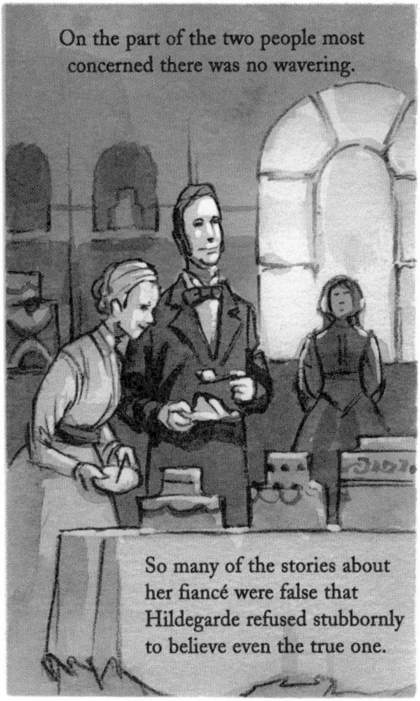
On the part of the two people most concerned there was no wavering.
So many of the stories about her fiancé were false that Hildegarde refused stubbornly to believe even the true one.

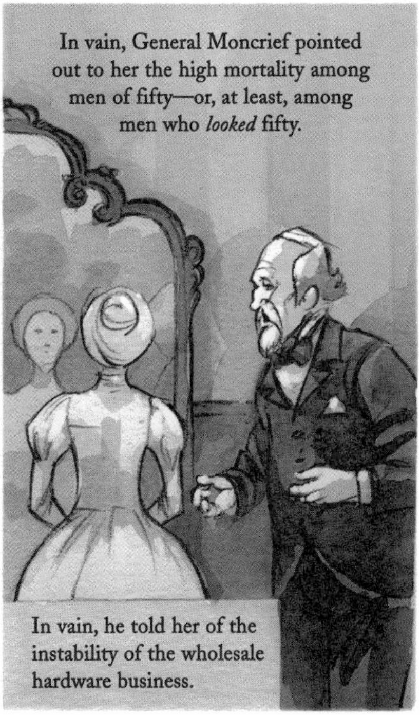
In vain, General Moncrief pointed out to her the high mortality among men of fifty—or, at least, among men who *looked* fifty.
In vain, he told her of the instability of the wholesale hardware business.

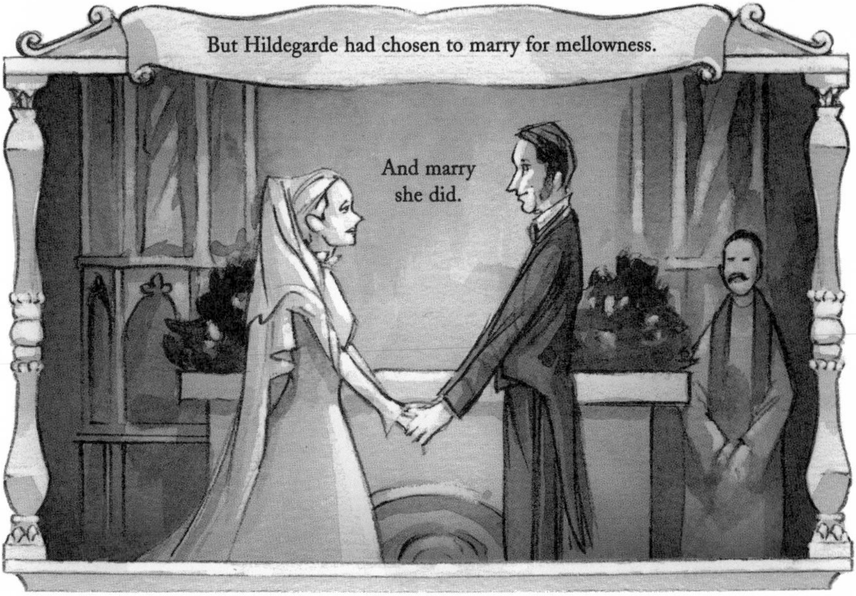
But Hildegarde had chosen to marry for mellowness.
And marry she did.

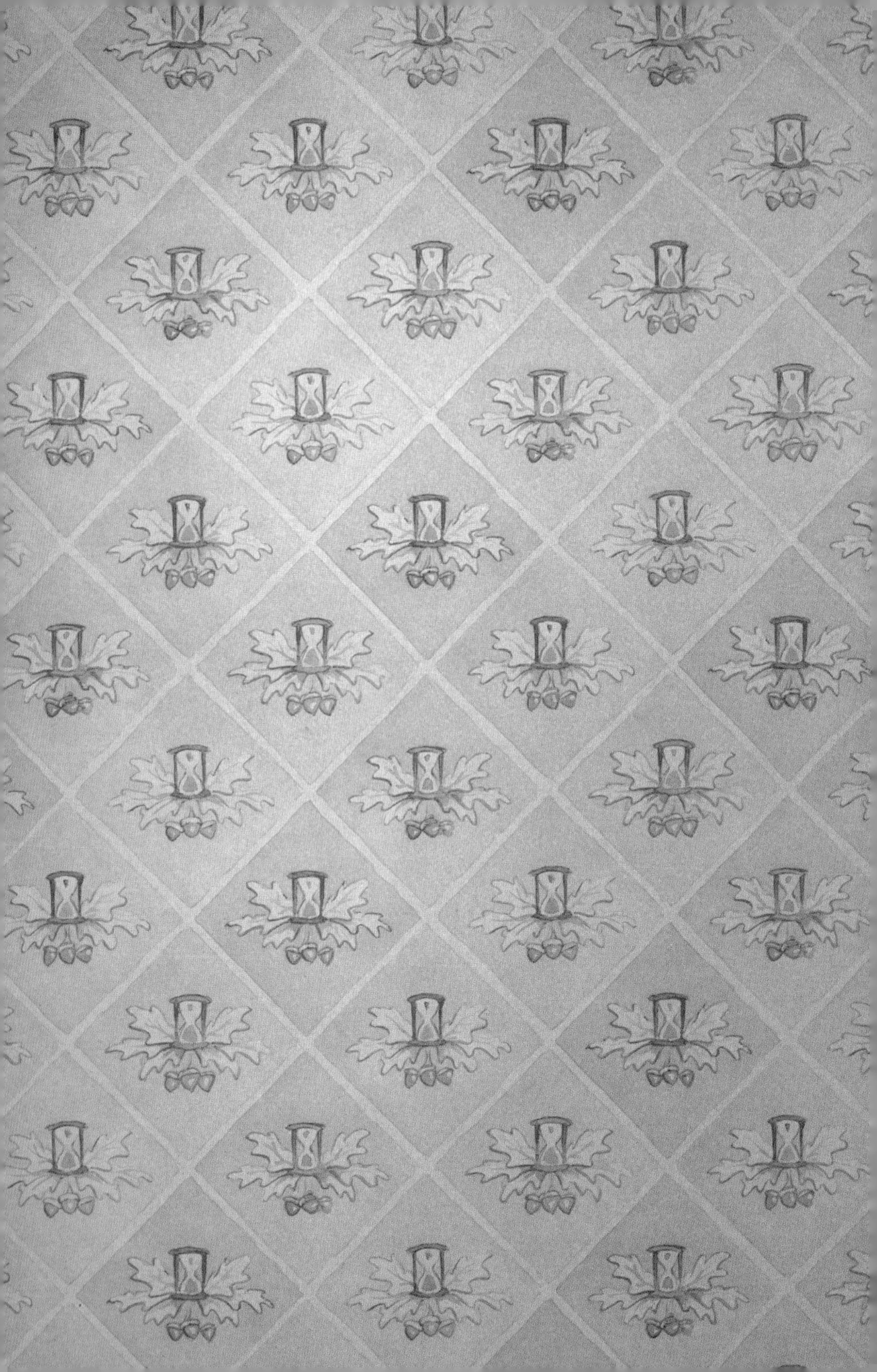

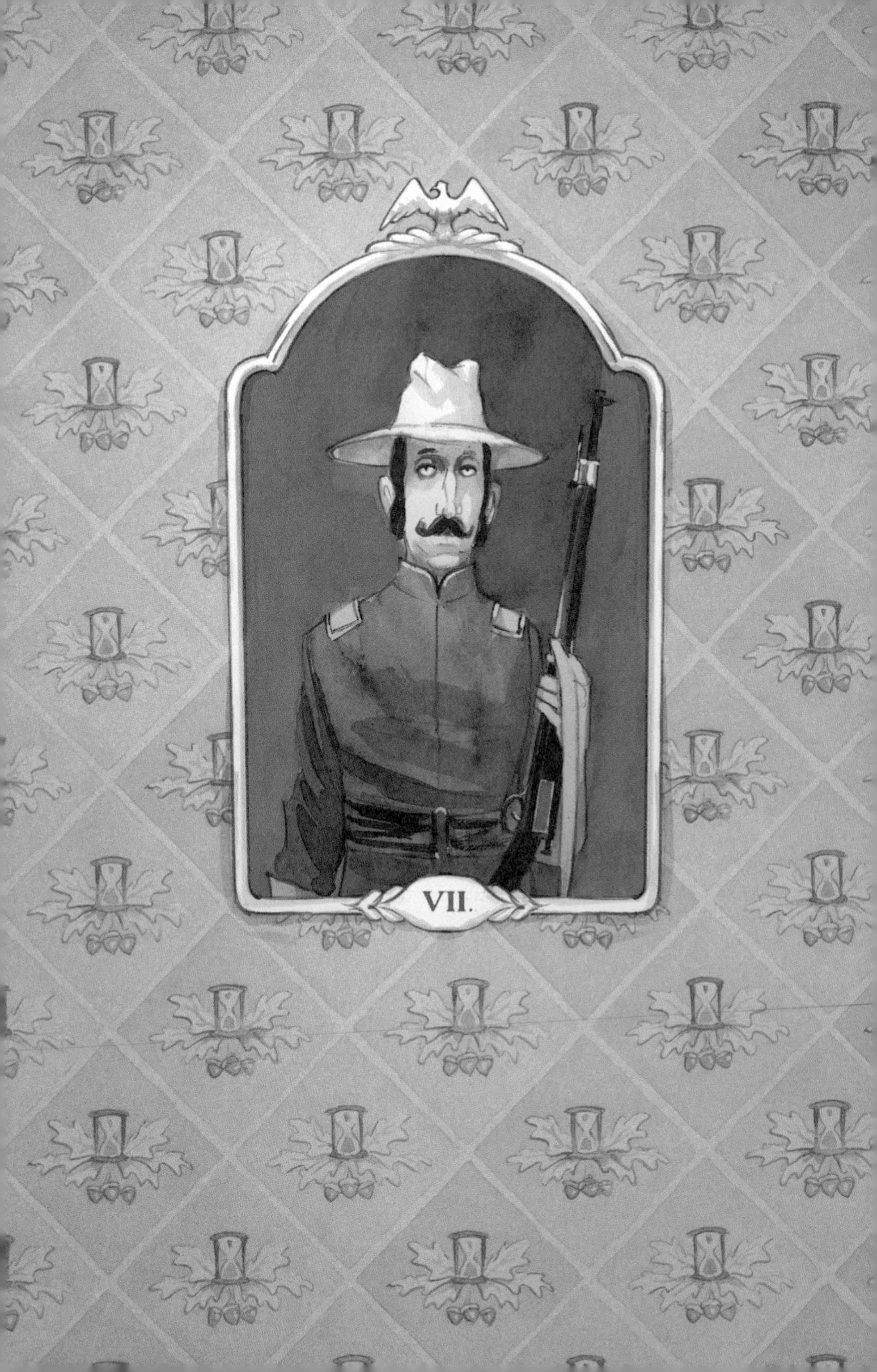
VII.

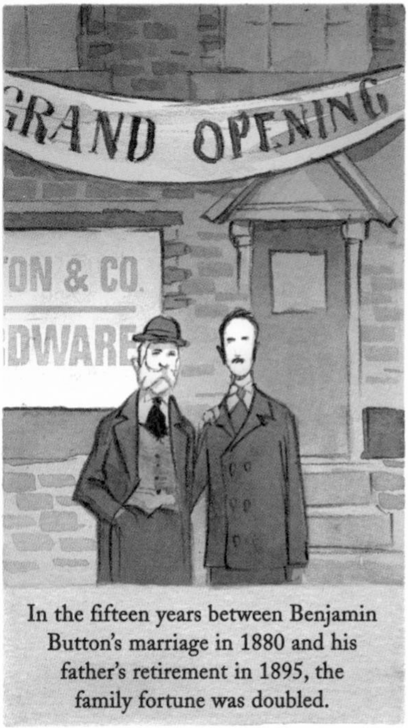
GRAND OPENING
In the fifteen years between Benjamin Button's marriage in 1880 and his father's retirement in 1895, the family fortune was doubled.

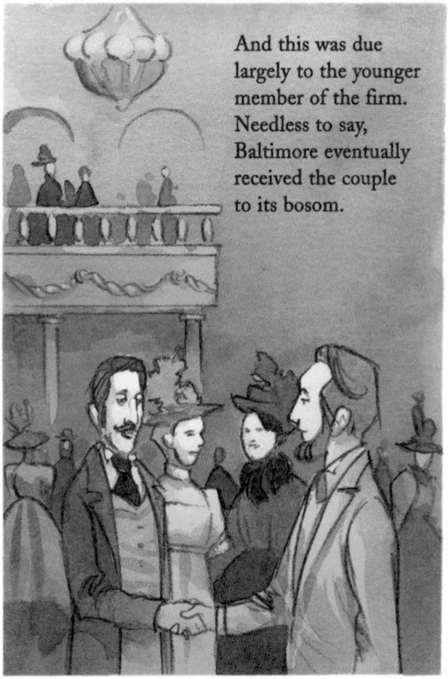
And this was due largely to the younger member of the firm. Needless to say, Baltimore eventually received the couple to its bosom.

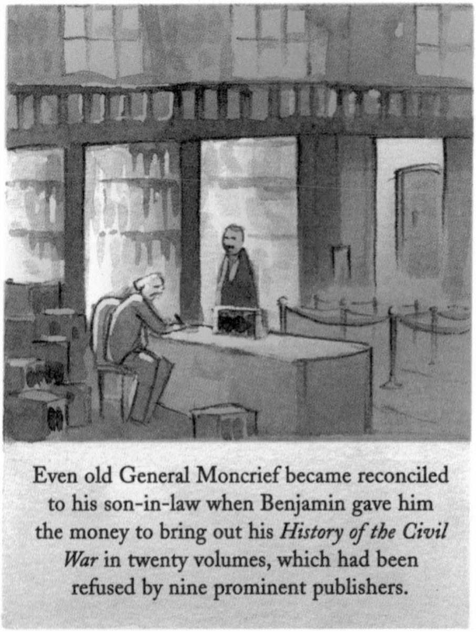
Even old General Moncrief became reconciled to his son-in-law when Benjamin gave him the money to bring out his *History of the Civil War* in twenty volumes, which had been refused by nine prominent publishers.

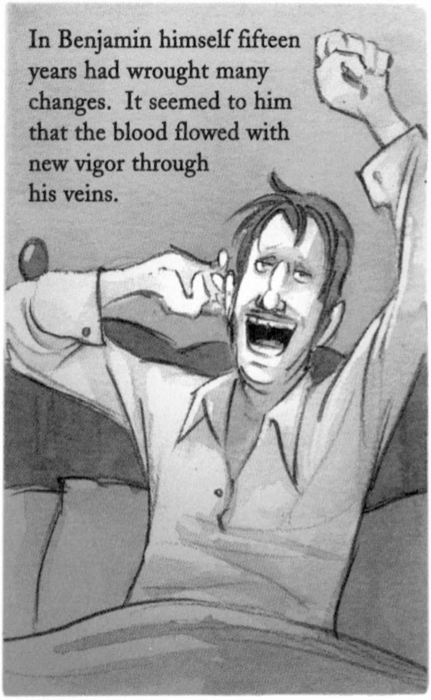
In Benjamin himself fifteen years had wrought many changes. It seemed to him that the blood flowed with new vigor through his veins.

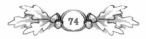

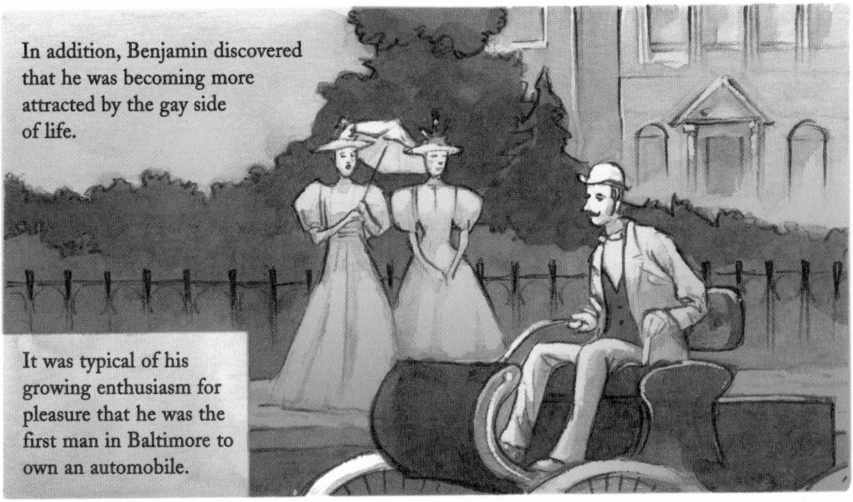
In addition, Benjamin discovered that he was becoming more attracted by the gay side of life.
It was typical of his growing enthusiasm for pleasure that he was the first man in Baltimore to own an automobile.

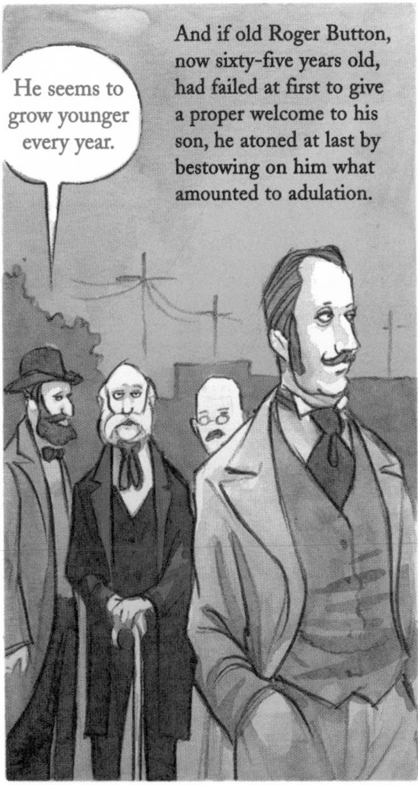
And if old Roger Button, now sixty-five years old, had failed at first to give a proper welcome to his son, he atoned at last by bestowing on him what amounted to adulation.
He seems to grow younger every year.

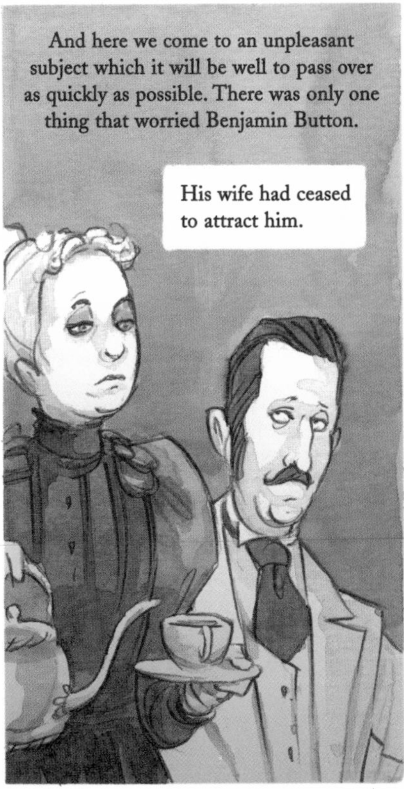
And here we come to an unpleasant subject which it will be well to pass over as quickly as possible. There was only one thing that worried Benjamin Button.
His wife had ceased to attract him.

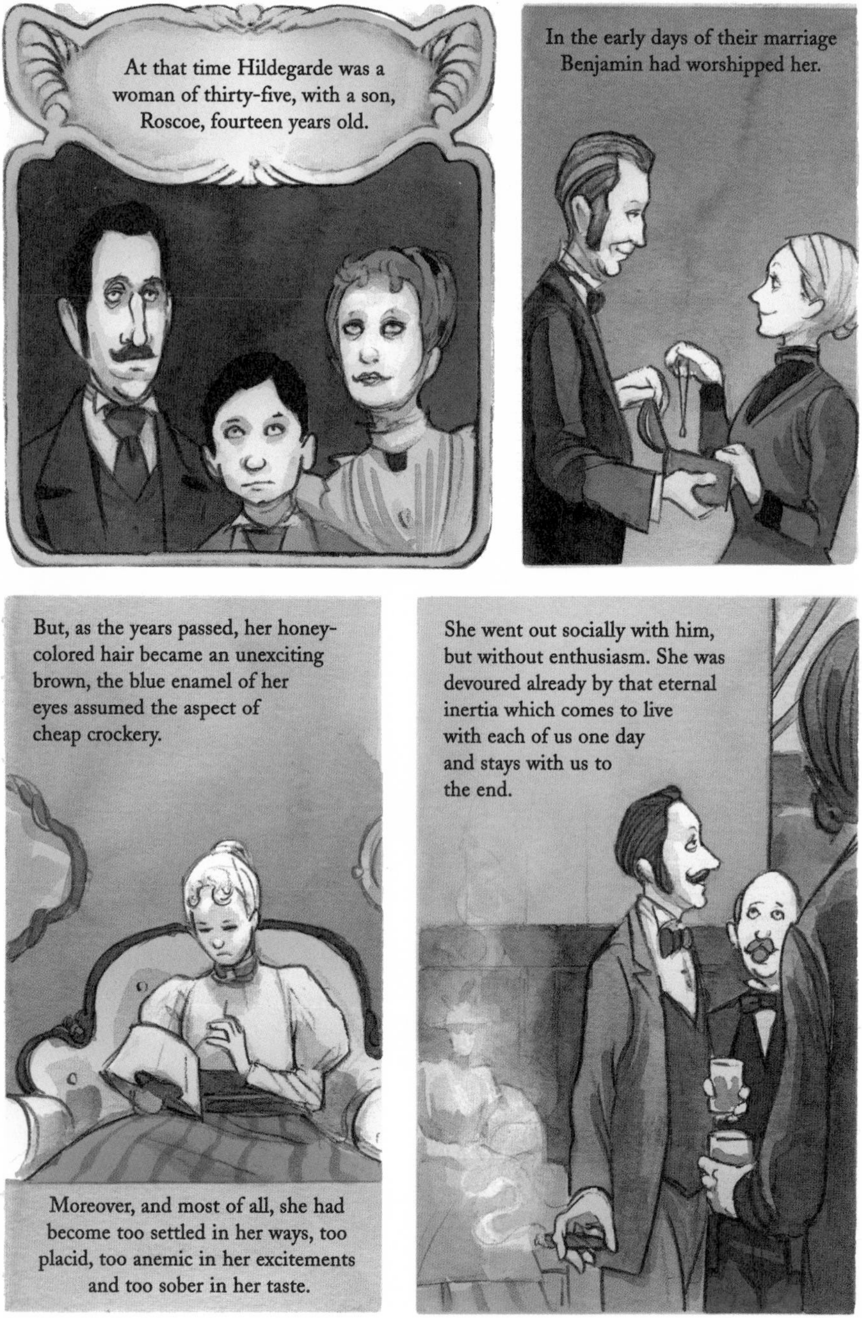
At that time Hildegarde was a woman of thirty-five, with a son, Roscoe, fourteen years old.
In the early days of their marriage Benjamin had worshipped her.
But, as the years passed, her honey-colored hair became an unexciting brown, the blue enamel of her eyes assumed the aspect of cheap crockery.
Moreover, and most of all, she had become too settled in her ways, too placid, too anemic in her excitements and too sober in her taste.
She went out socially with him, but without enthusiasm. She was devoured already by that eternal inertia which comes to live with each of us one day and stays with us to the end.

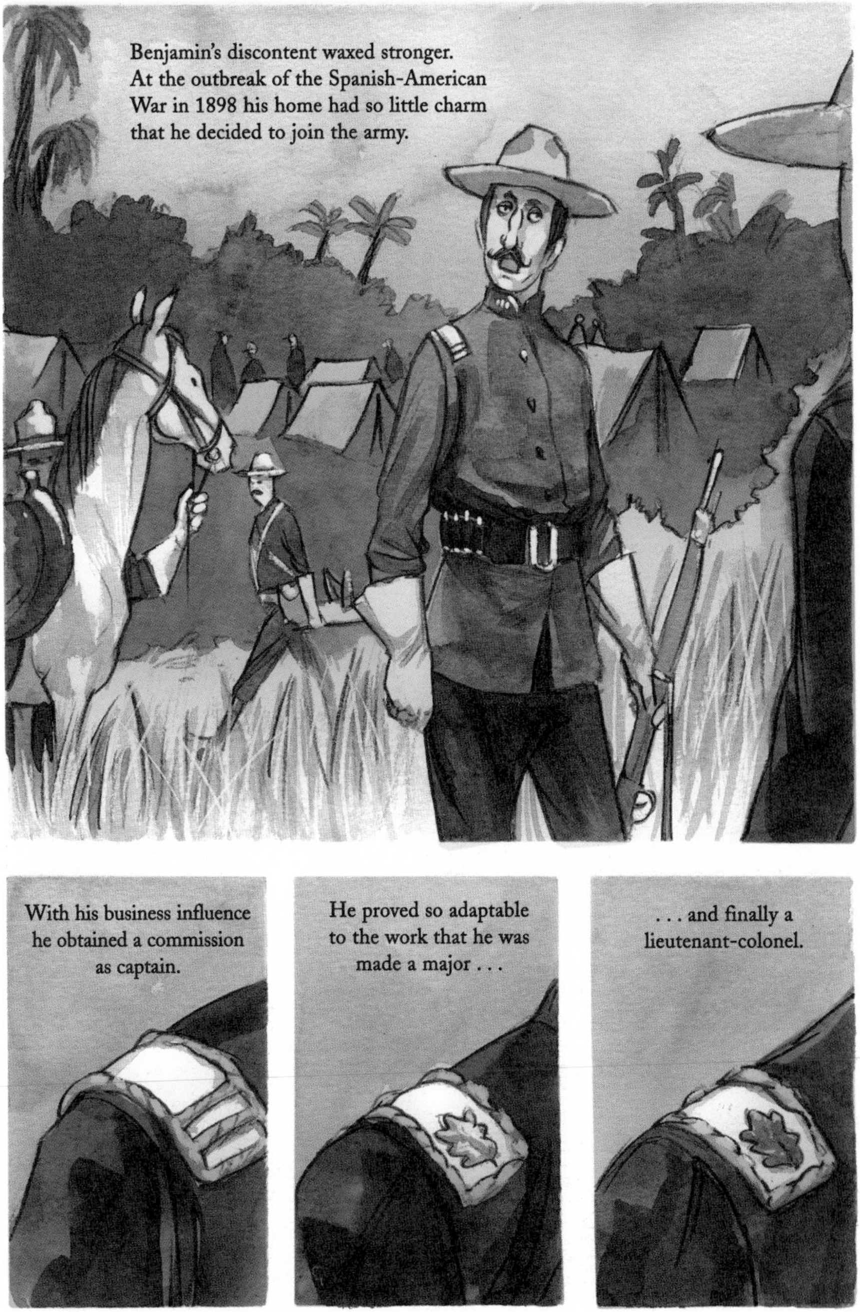
Benjamin's discontent waxed stronger. At the outbreak of the Spanish-American War in 1898 his home had so little charm that he decided to join the army.
With his business influence he obtained a commission as captain.
He proved so adaptable to the work that he was made a major . . .
. . . and finally a lieutenant-colonel.

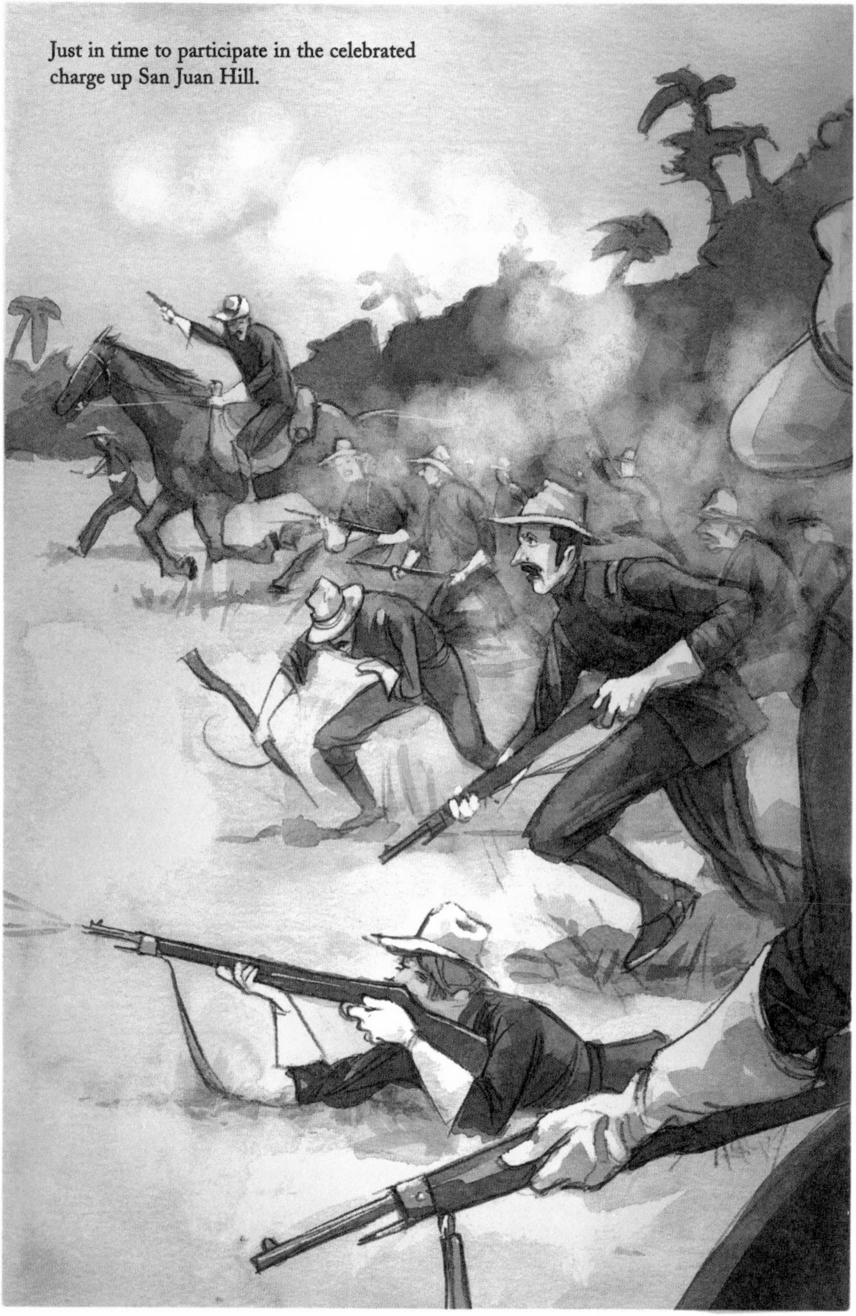

Just in time to participate in the celebrated charge up San Juan Hill.

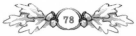

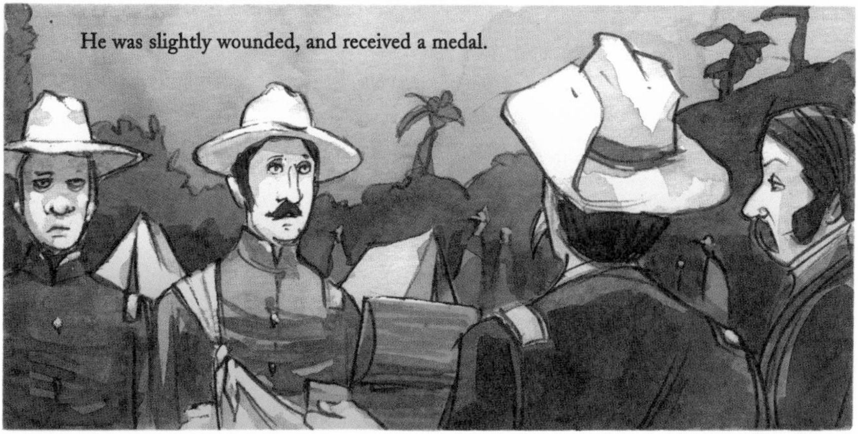
He was slightly wounded, and received a medal.

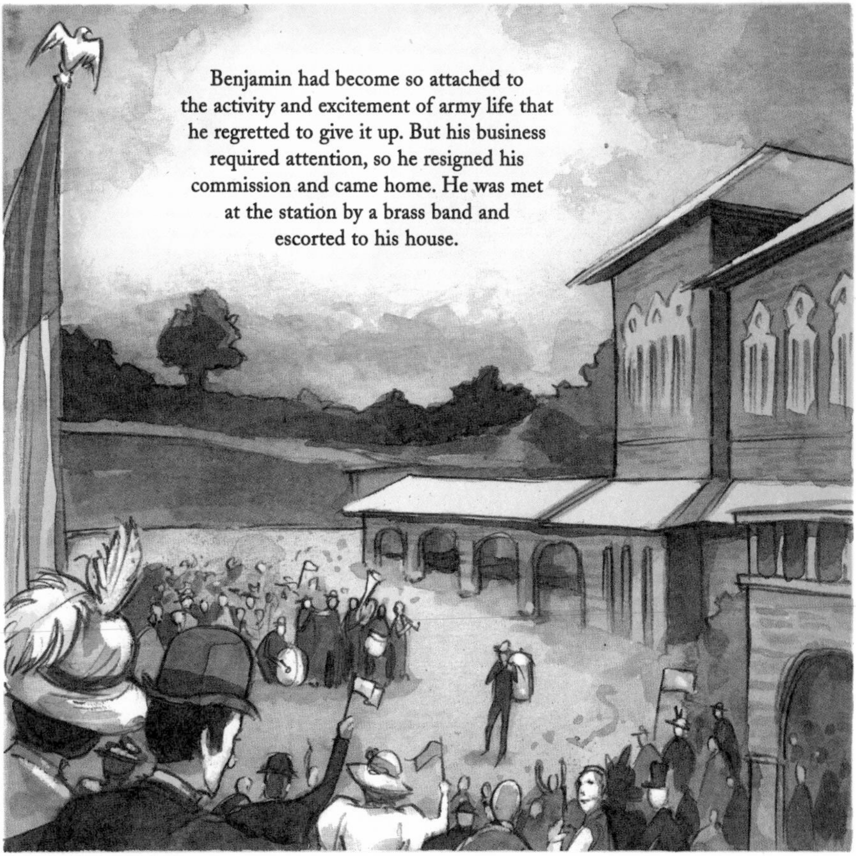
Benjamin had become so attached to the activity and excitement of army life that he regretted to give it up. But his business required attention, so he resigned his commission and came home. He was met at the station by a brass band and escorted to his house.

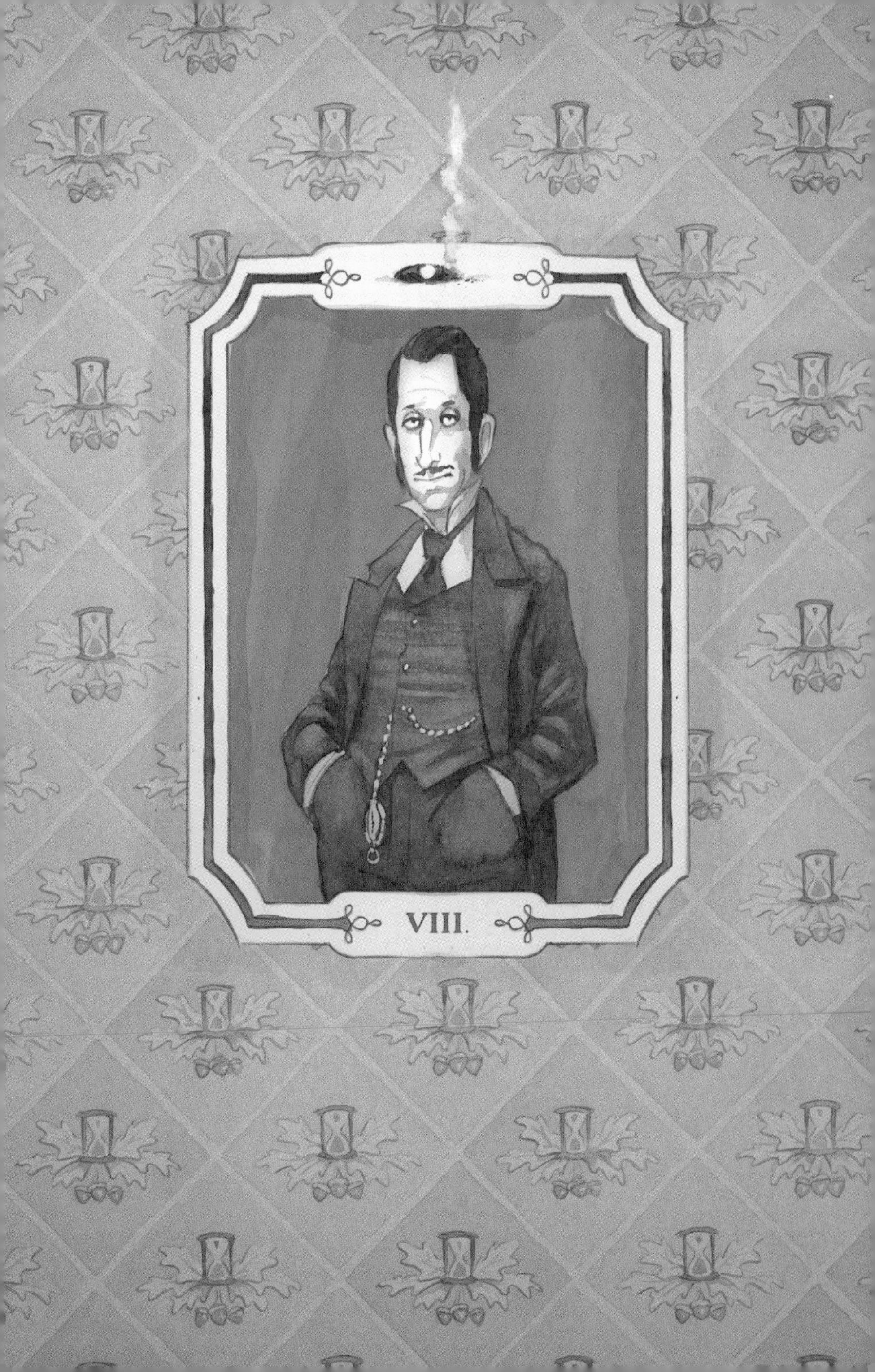
VIII.

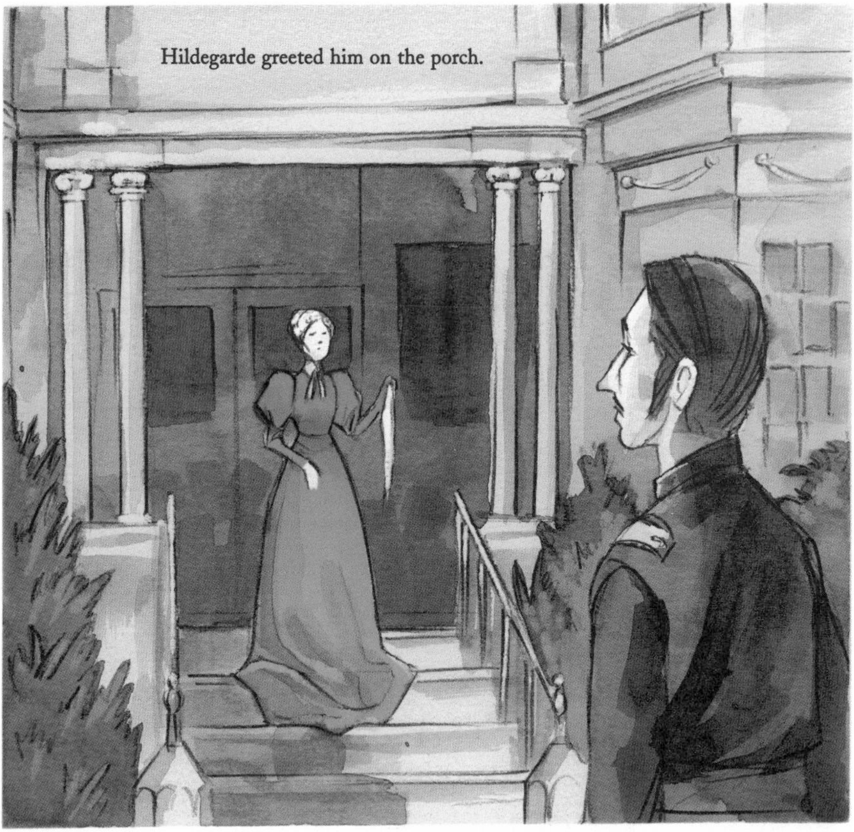
Hildegarde greeted him on the porch.

But even as Benjamin kissed her, he felt with a sinking heart that these years had taken their toll.

She was a woman of forty now, with a faint skirmish line of gray hairs in her head.

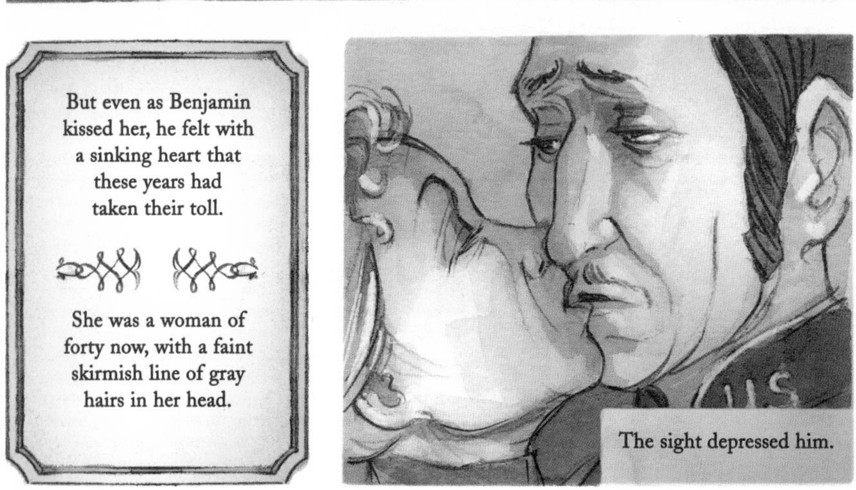
The sight depressed him.

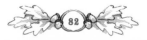

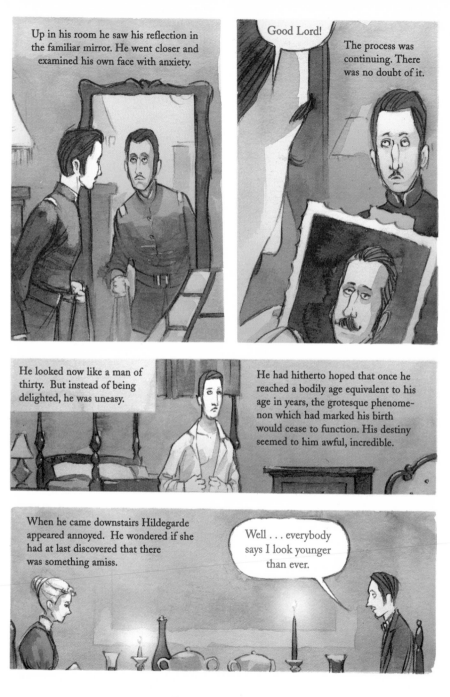

Up in his room he saw his reflection in the familiar mirror. He went closer and examined his own face with anxiety.

Good Lord!

The process was continuing. There was no doubt of it.

He looked now like a man of thirty. But instead of being delighted, he was uneasy.

He had hitherto hoped that once he reached a bodily age equivalent to his age in years, the grotesque phenomenon which had marked his birth would cease to function. His destiny seemed to him awful, incredible.

When he came downstairs Hildegarde appeared annoyed. He wondered if she had at last discovered that there was something amiss.

Well . . . everybody says I look younger than ever.

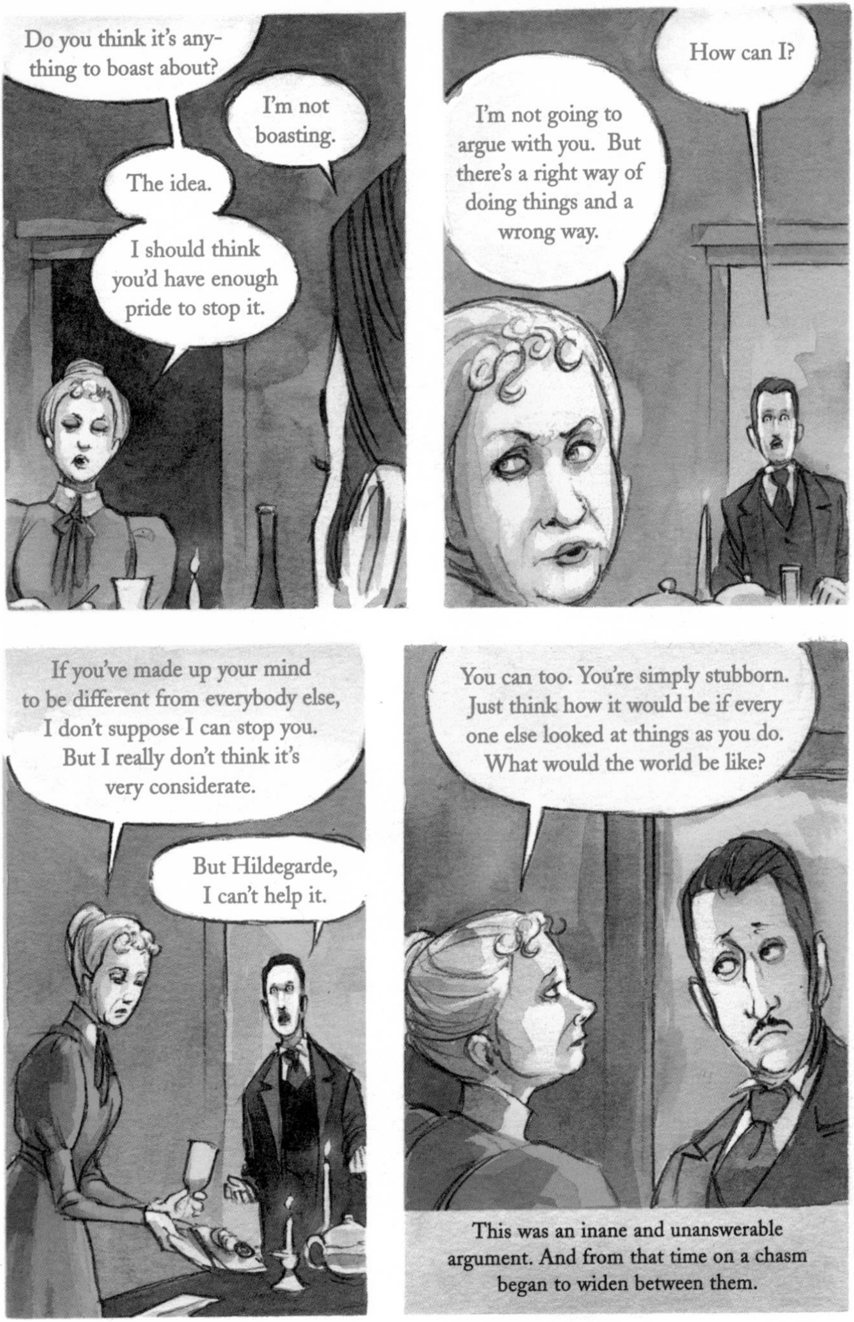
Do you think it's anything to boast about?
I'm not boasting.
The idea.
I should think you'd have enough pride to stop it.
How can I?
I'm not going to argue with you. But there's a right way of doing things and a wrong way.
If you've made up your mind to be different from everybody else, I don't suppose I can stop you. But I really don't think it's very considerate.
But Hildegarde, I can't help it.
You can too. You're simply stubborn. Just think how it would be if every one else looked at things as you do. What would the world be like?
This was an inane and unanswerable argument. And from that time on a chasm began to widen between them.

To add to the breach, he found, as the new century gathered headway, that his thirst for gayety grew stronger. Never a party of any kind in the city of Baltimore but he was there.

Dancing with the prettiest of the young married women, chatting with the most popular of debutantes . . .

. . . while his wife, a dowager of evil omen, sat among the chaperones, now in haughty disapproval, and now following him with solemn, puzzled and reproachful eyes.

Look! What a pity! A young fellow that age tied to a woman of forty-five.

He must be twenty years younger than his wife.

They had forgotten—as people inevitably forget— that back in 1880 their mammas and papas had also remarked about this same ill-matched pair.

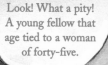

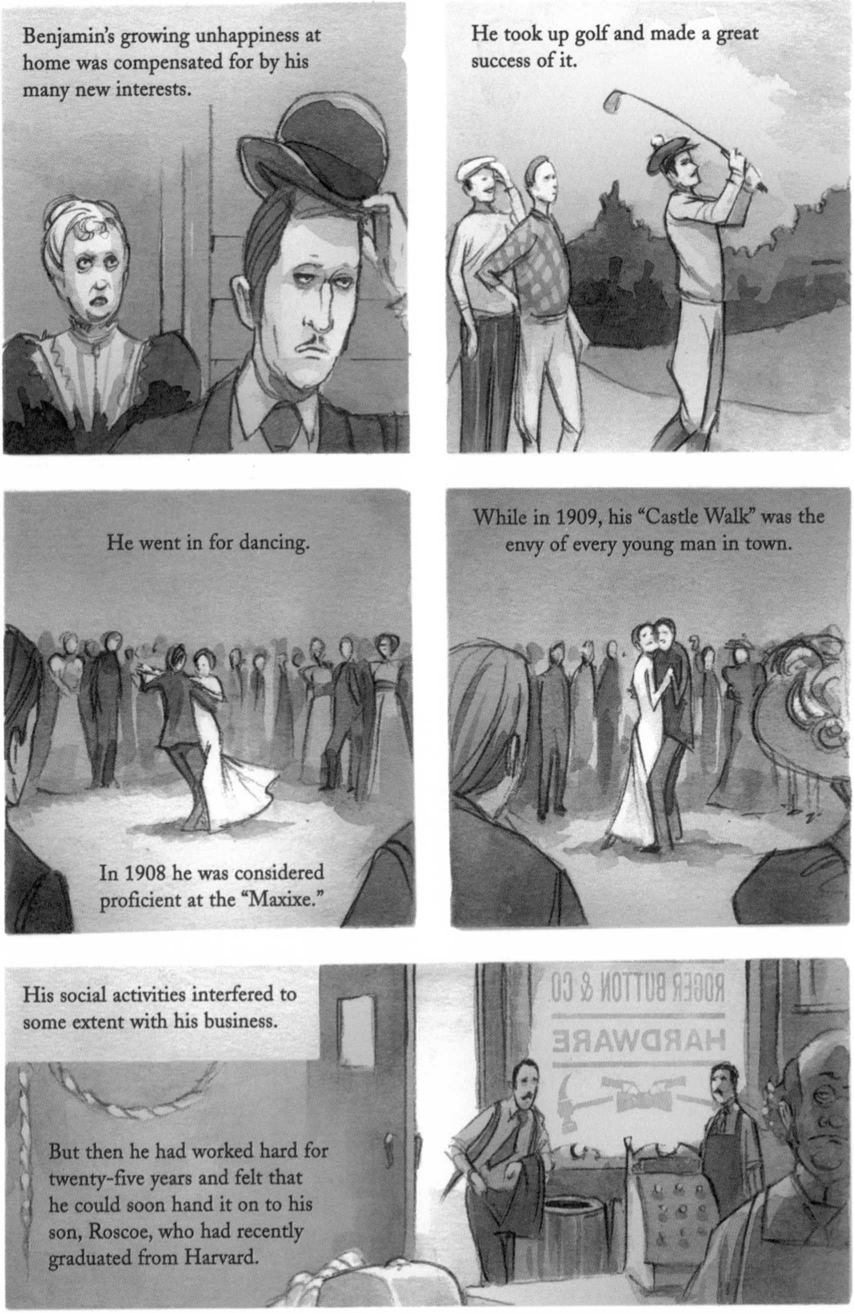
Benjamin's growing unhappiness at home was compensated for by his many new interests.
He took up golf and made a great success of it.
He went in for dancing.
In 1908 he was considered proficient at the "Maxixe."
While in 1909, his "Castle Walk" was the envy of every young man in town.
His social activities interfered to some extent with his business.
But then he had worked hard for twenty-five years and felt that he could soon hand it on to his son, Roscoe, who had recently graduated from Harvard.
ROGER BUTTON & CO.
HARDWARE

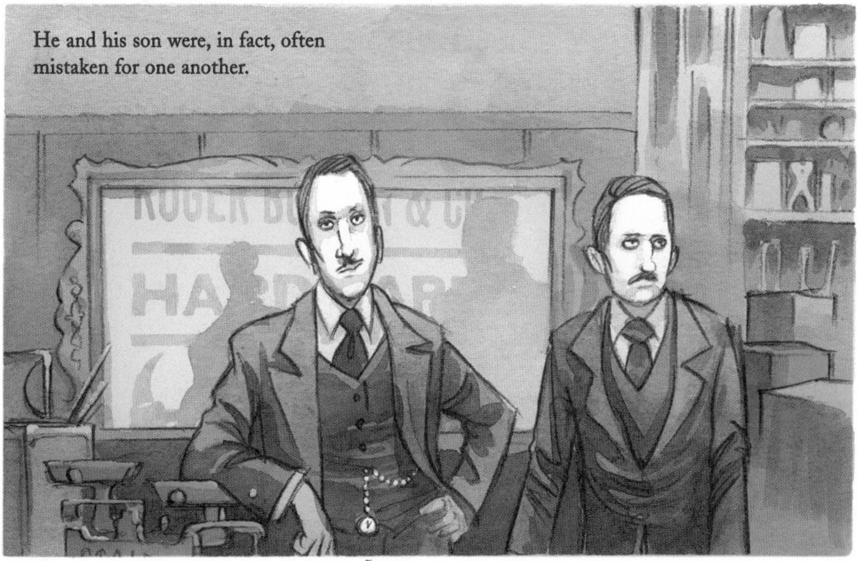
He and his son were, in fact, often mistaken for one another.

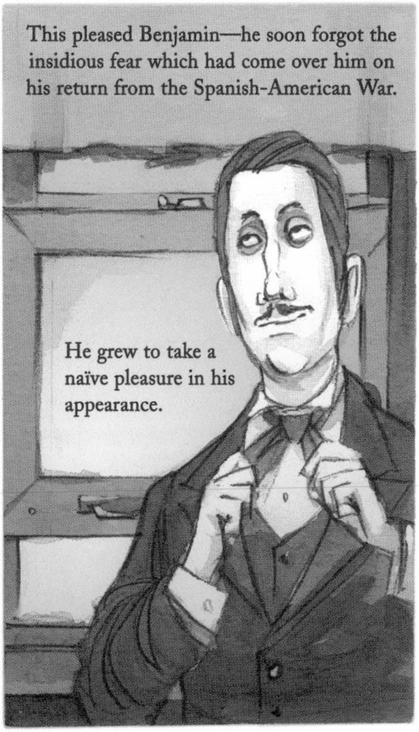
This pleased Benjamin—he soon forgot the insidious fear which had come over him on his return from the Spanish-American War.
He grew to take a naïve pleasure in his appearance.

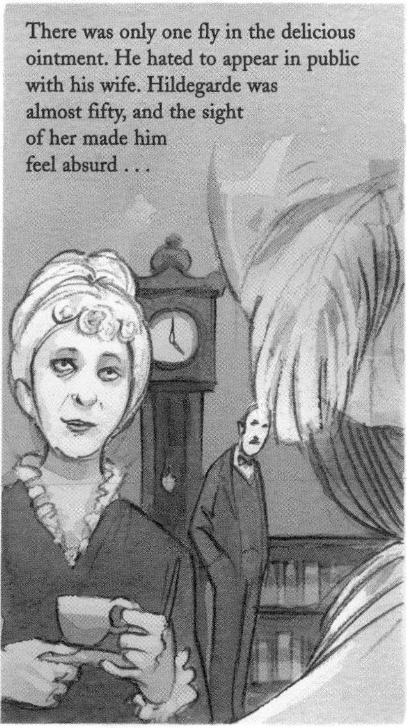
There was only one fly in the delicious ointment. He hated to appear in public with his wife. Hildegarde was almost fifty, and the sight of her made him feel absurd . . .

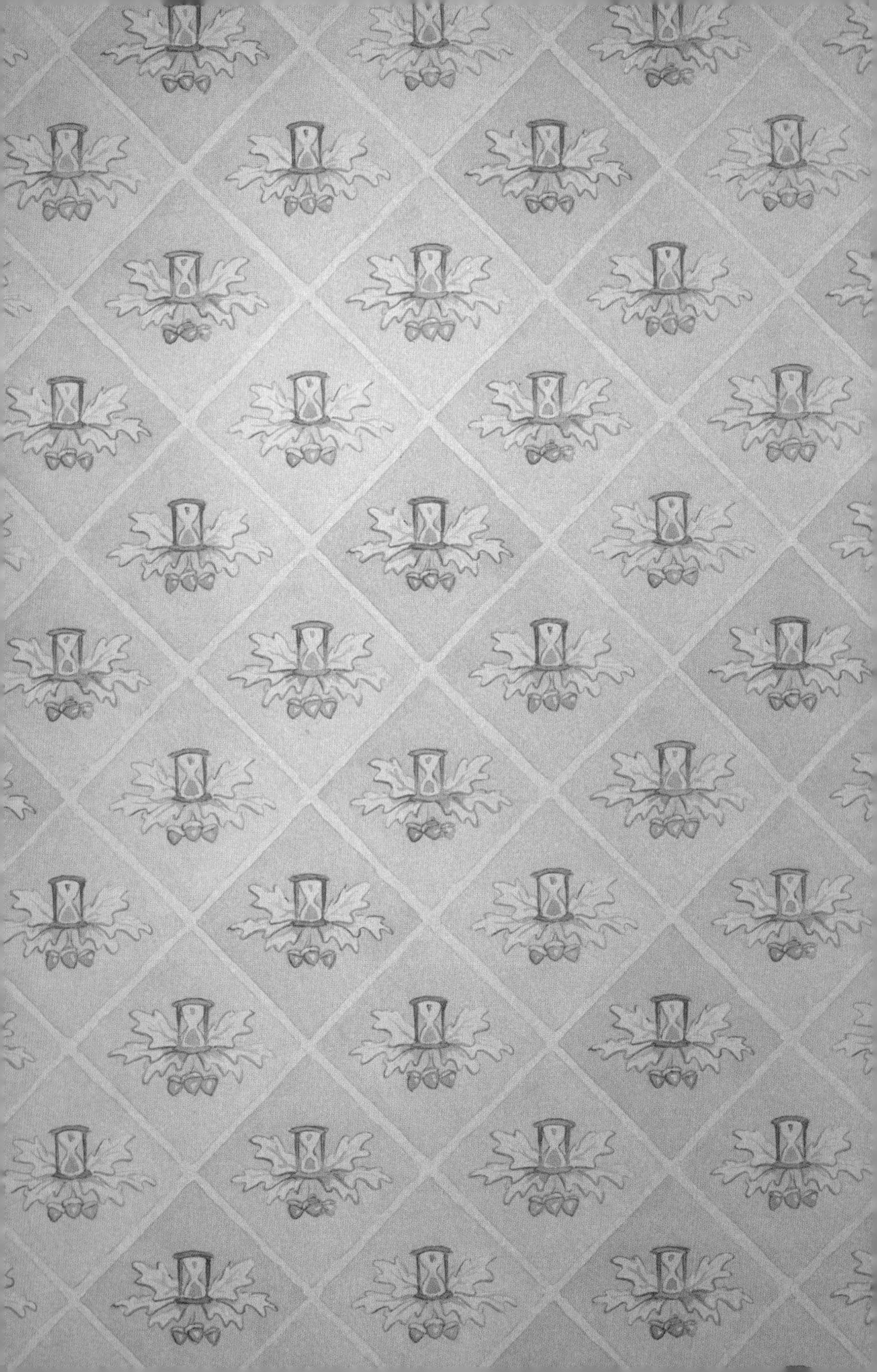

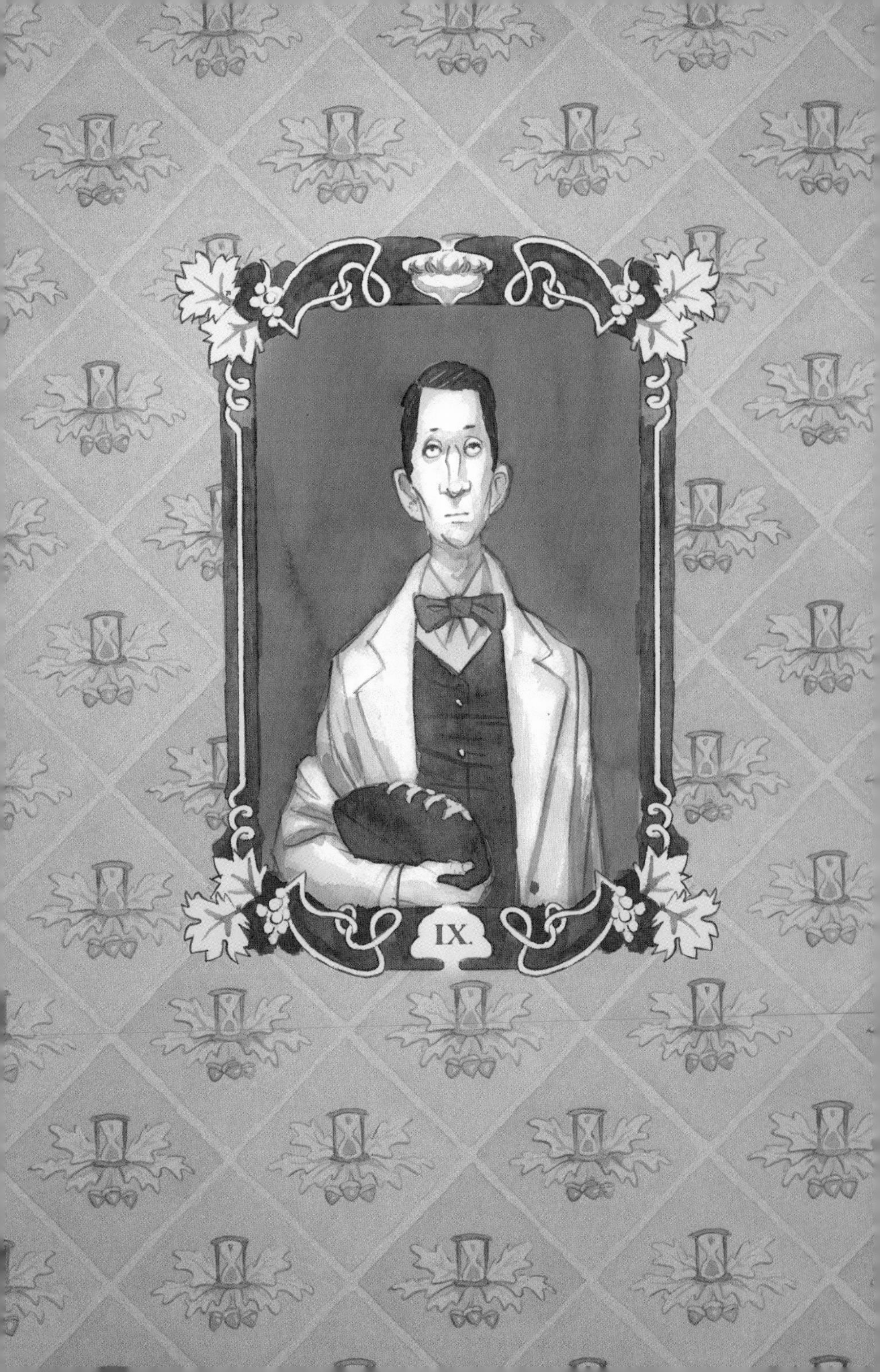
IX.

One September day in 1910—a few years after Roger Button & Co., Wholesale Hardware had been handed over to young Roscoe Button . . .

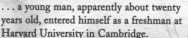

. . . a young man, apparently about twenty years old, entered himself as a freshman at Harvard University in Cambridge.

He did not make the mistake of announcing that he would never see fifty again, nor did he mention the fact that his son had been graduated from the same institution ten years before.

He was admitted, and almost immediately attained a prominent position in the class, partly because he seemed a little older than the other freshmen, whose average age was about eighteen.

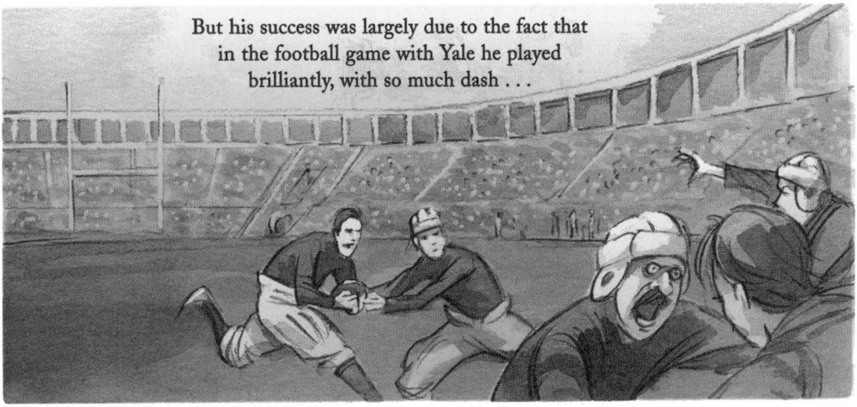
But his success was largely due to the fact that in the football game with Yale he played brilliantly, with so much dash . . .

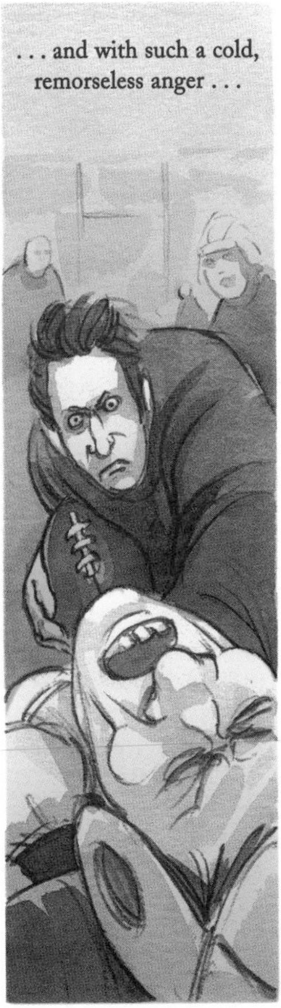
. . . and with such a cold, remorseless anger . . .

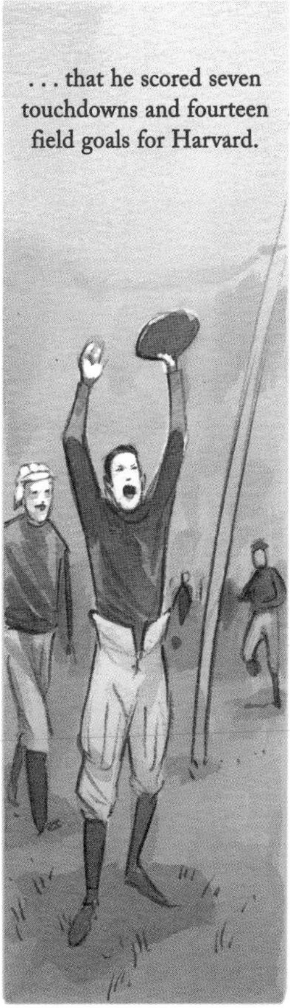
. . . that he scored seven touchdowns and fourteen field goals for Harvard.

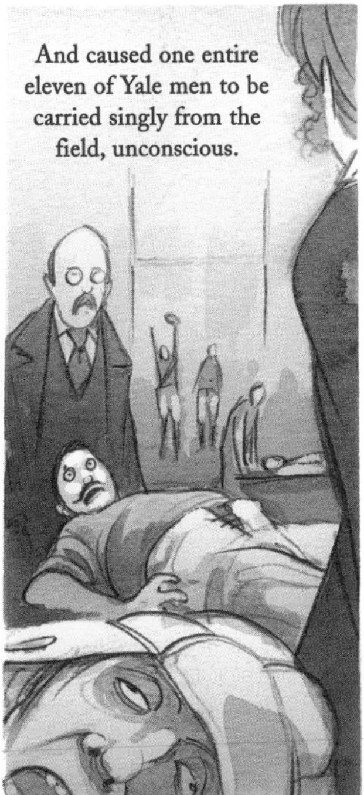
And caused one entire eleven of Yale men to be carried singly from the field, unconscious.

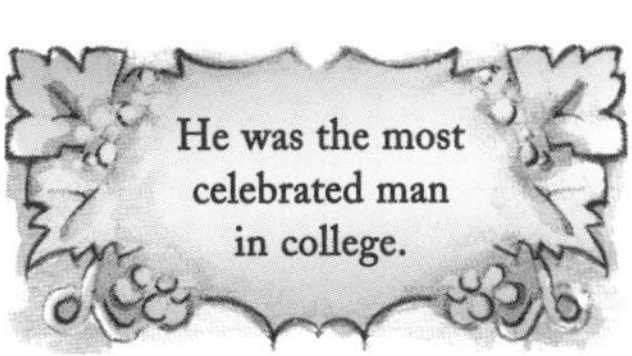
He was the most celebrated man in college.

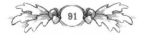

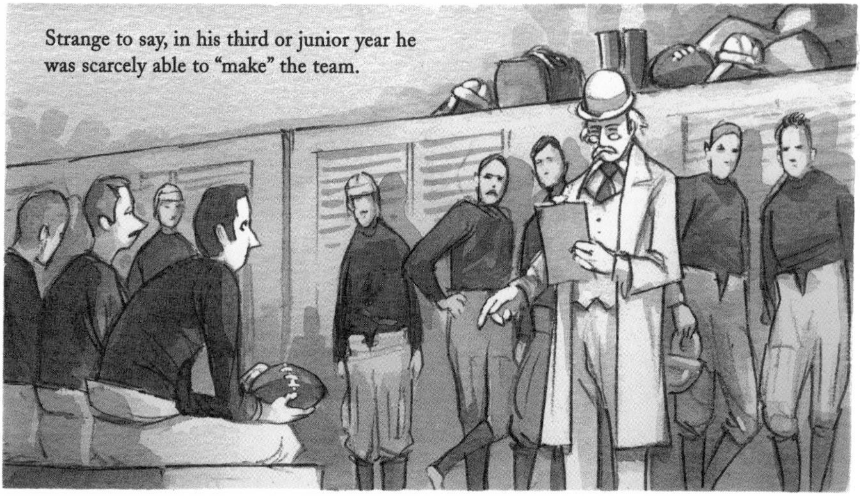
Strange to say, in his third or junior year he was scarcely able to "make" the team.

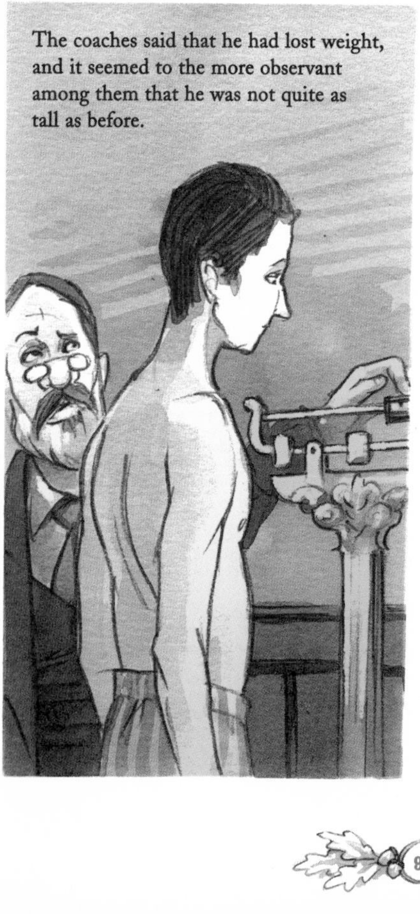
The coaches said that he had lost weight, and it seemed to the more observant among them that he was not quite as tall as before.

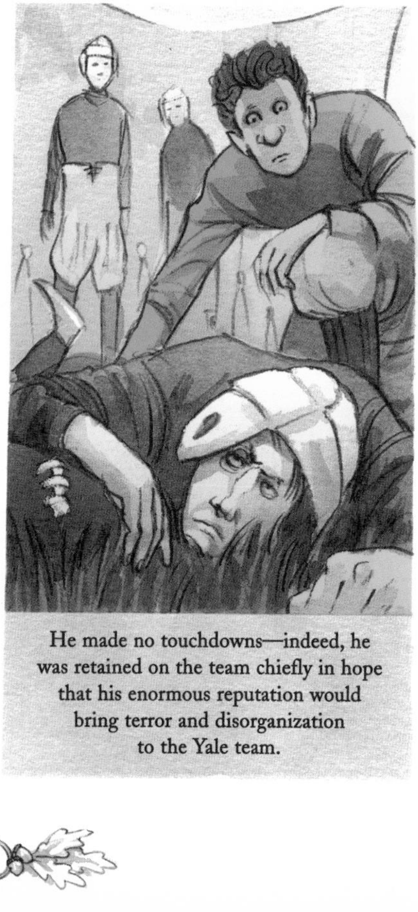
He made no touchdowns—indeed, he was retained on the team chiefly in hope that his enormous reputation would bring terror and disorganization to the Yale team.

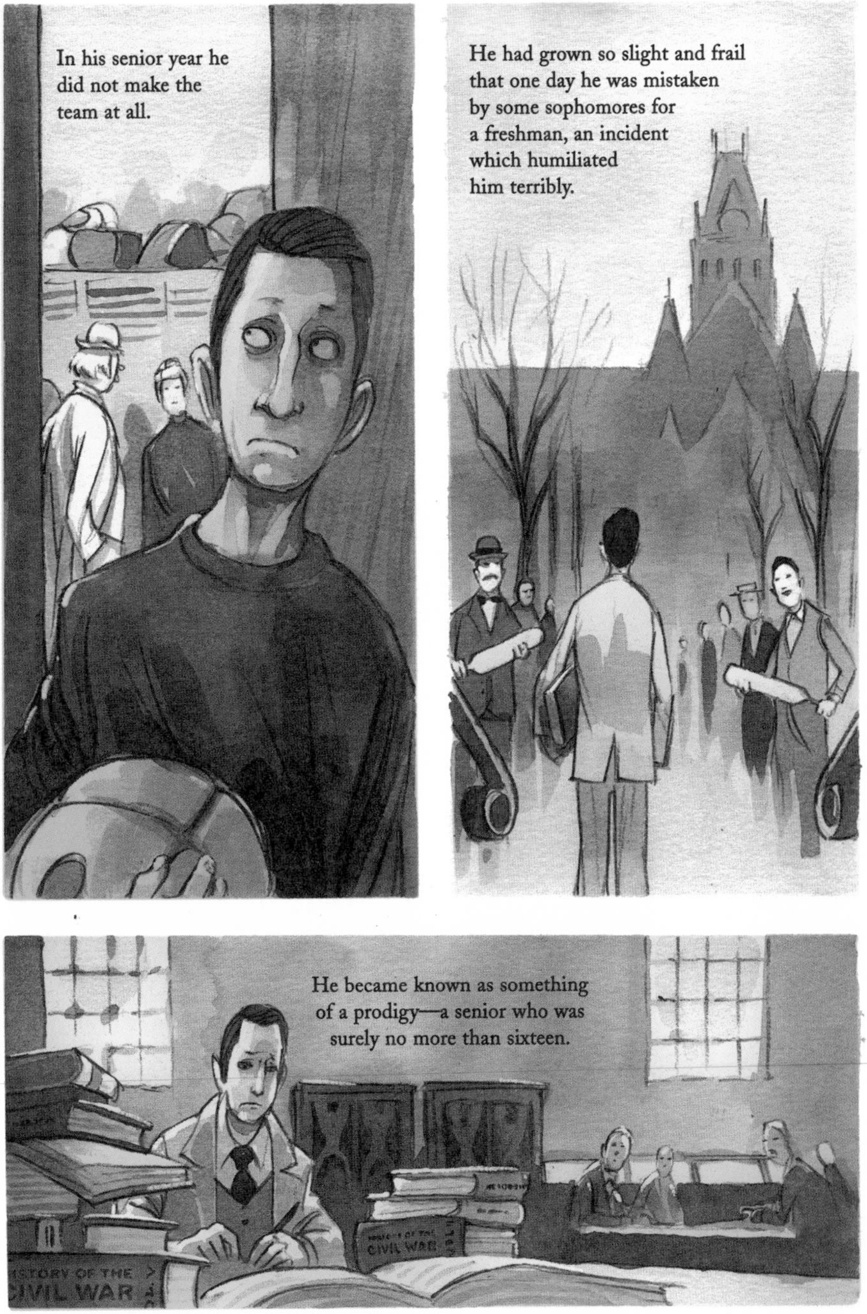
In his senior year he did not make the team at all.
He had grown so slight and frail that one day he was mistaken by some sophomores for a freshman, an incident which humiliated him terribly.
He became known as something of a prodigy—a senior who was surely no more than sixteen.

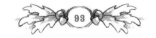

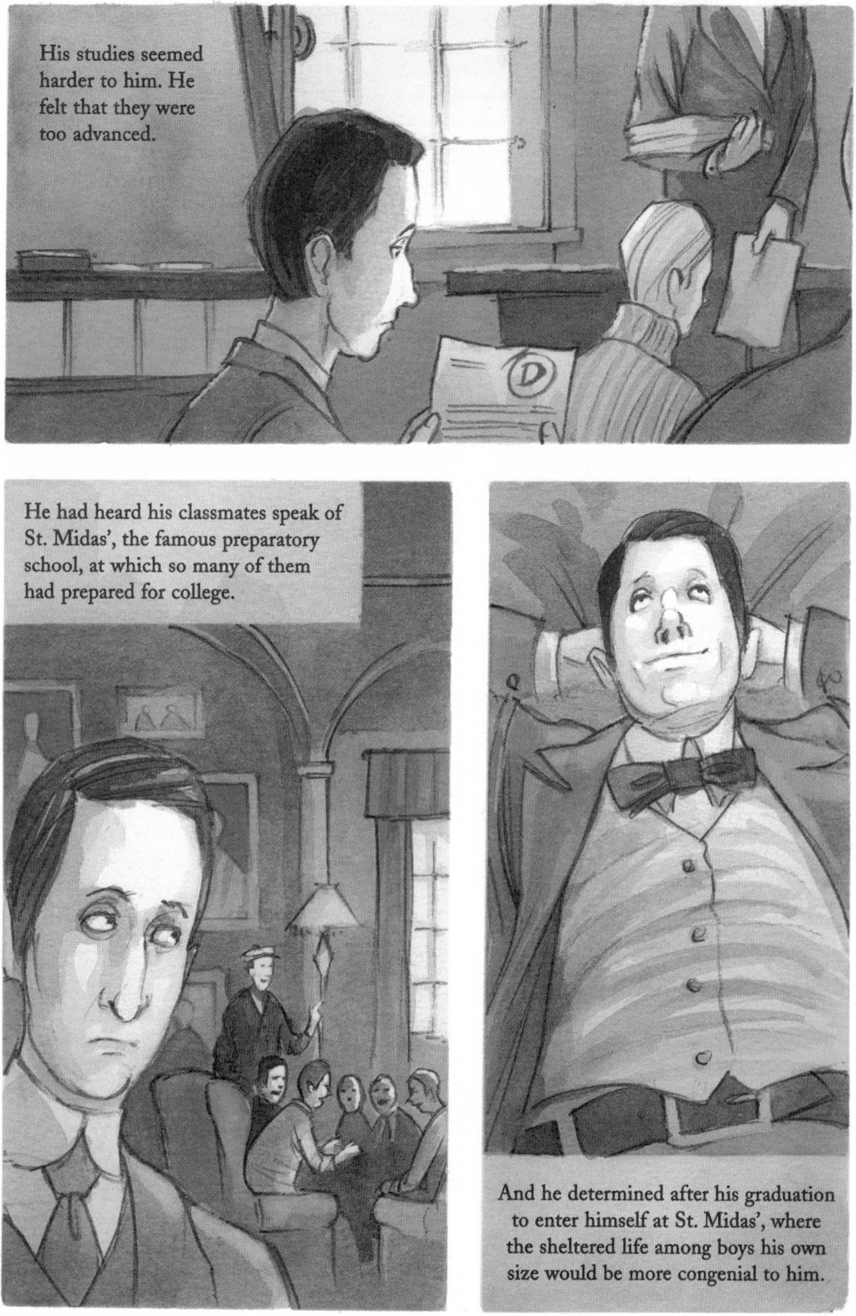
His studies seemed harder to him. He felt that they were too advanced.
D
He had heard his classmates speak of St. Midas', the famous preparatory school, at which so many of them had prepared for college.
And he determined after his graduation to enter himself at St. Midas', where the sheltered life among boys his own size would be more congenial to him.

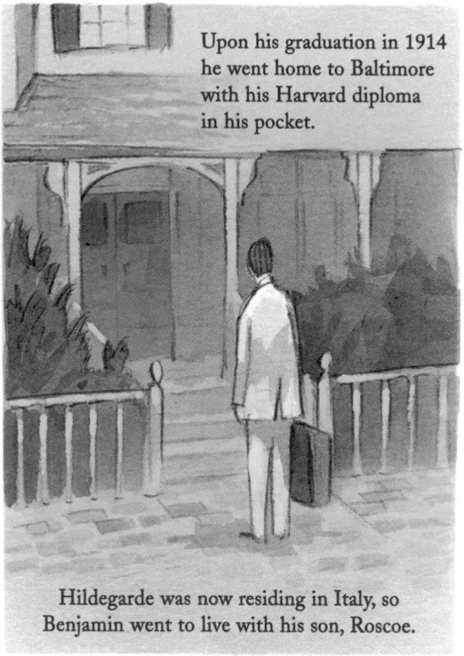
Upon his graduation in 1914 he went home to Baltimore with his Harvard diploma in his pocket.
Hildegarde was now residing in Italy, so Benjamin went to live with his son, Roscoe.

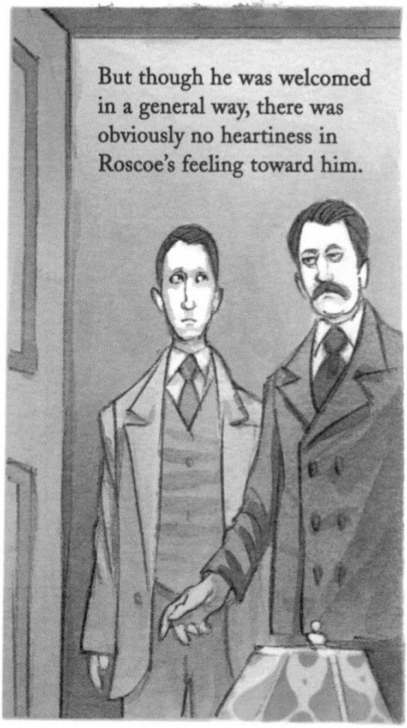
But though he was welcomed in a general way, there was obviously no heartiness in Roscoe's feeling toward him.

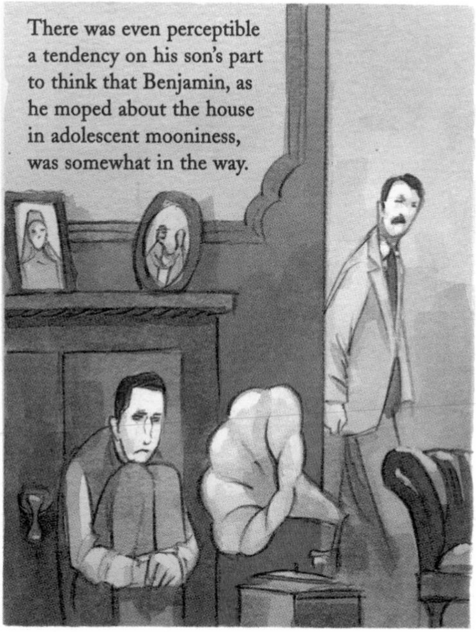
There was even perceptible a tendency on his son's part to think that Benjamin, as he moped about the house in adolescent mooniness, was somewhat in the way.

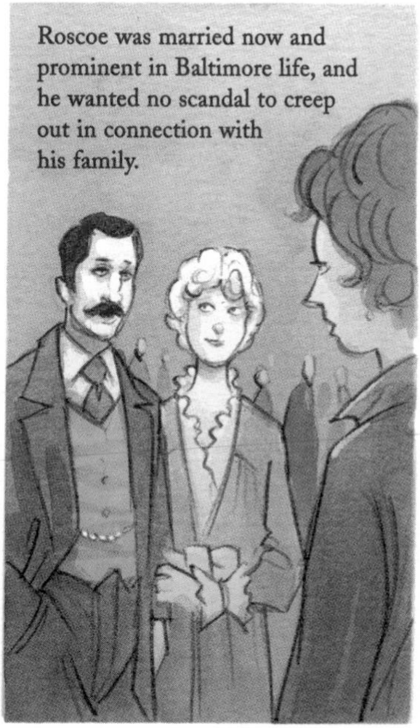
Roscoe was married now and prominent in Baltimore life, and he wanted no scandal to creep out in connection with his family.

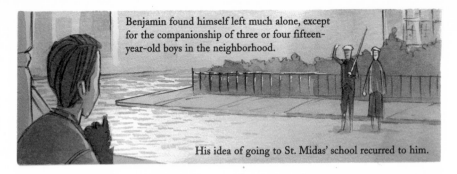

Benjamin found himself left much alone, except for the companionship of three or four fifteen-year-old boys in the neighborhood.

His idea of going to St. Midas' school recurred to him.

Say, I've told you over and over that I want to go to prep school.

Well, go then.

I can't go alone. You'll have to enter me and take me up there.

I haven't got time.

As a matter of fact, you'd better not go on with this business much longer. You better pull up short.

You better turn right around and start back the other way. This has gone too far to be a joke. It isn't funny anymore.

You . . . you behave yourself!

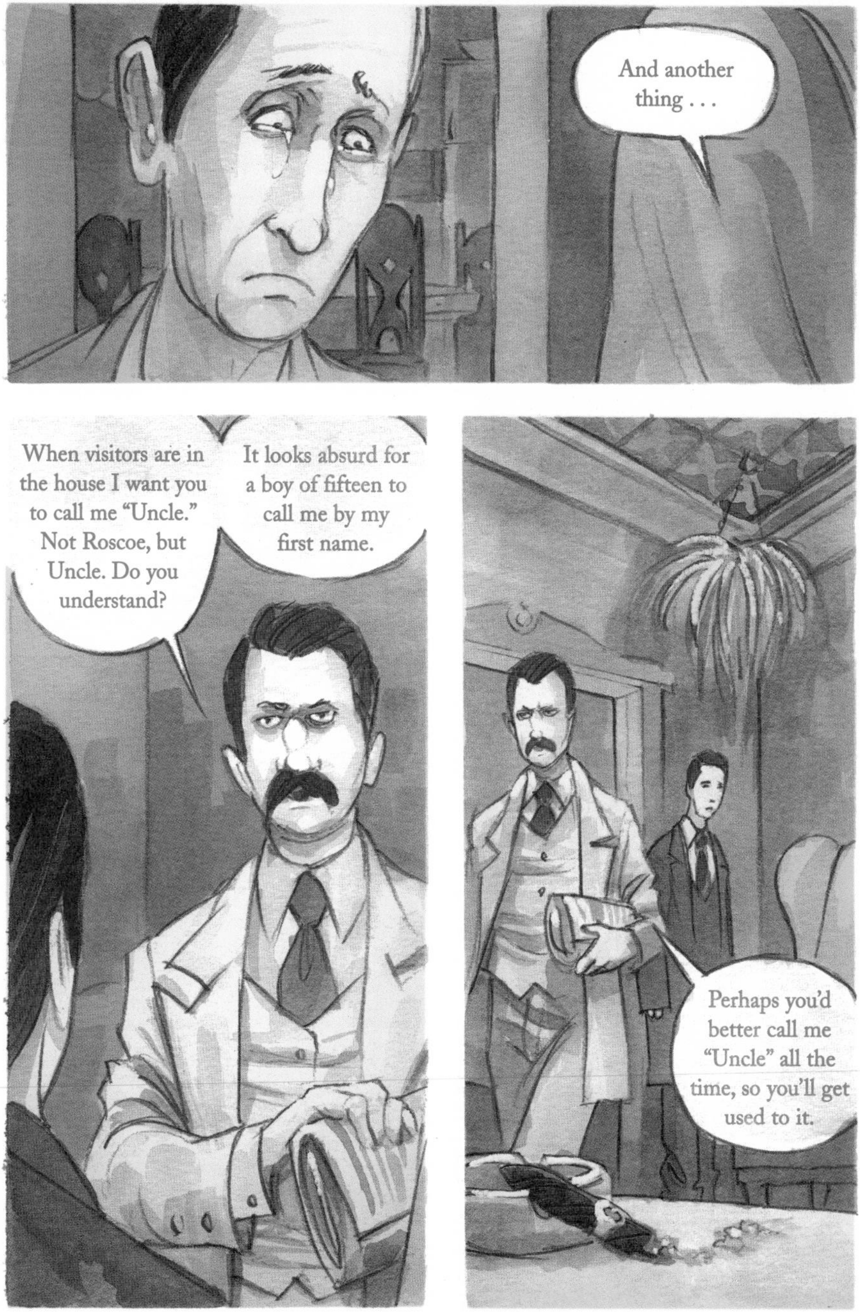

And another thing . . .
When visitors are in the house I want you to call me "Uncle." Not Roscoe, but Uncle. Do you understand?
It looks absurd for a boy of fifteen to call me by my first name.
Perhaps you'd better call me "Uncle" all the time, so you'll get used to it.

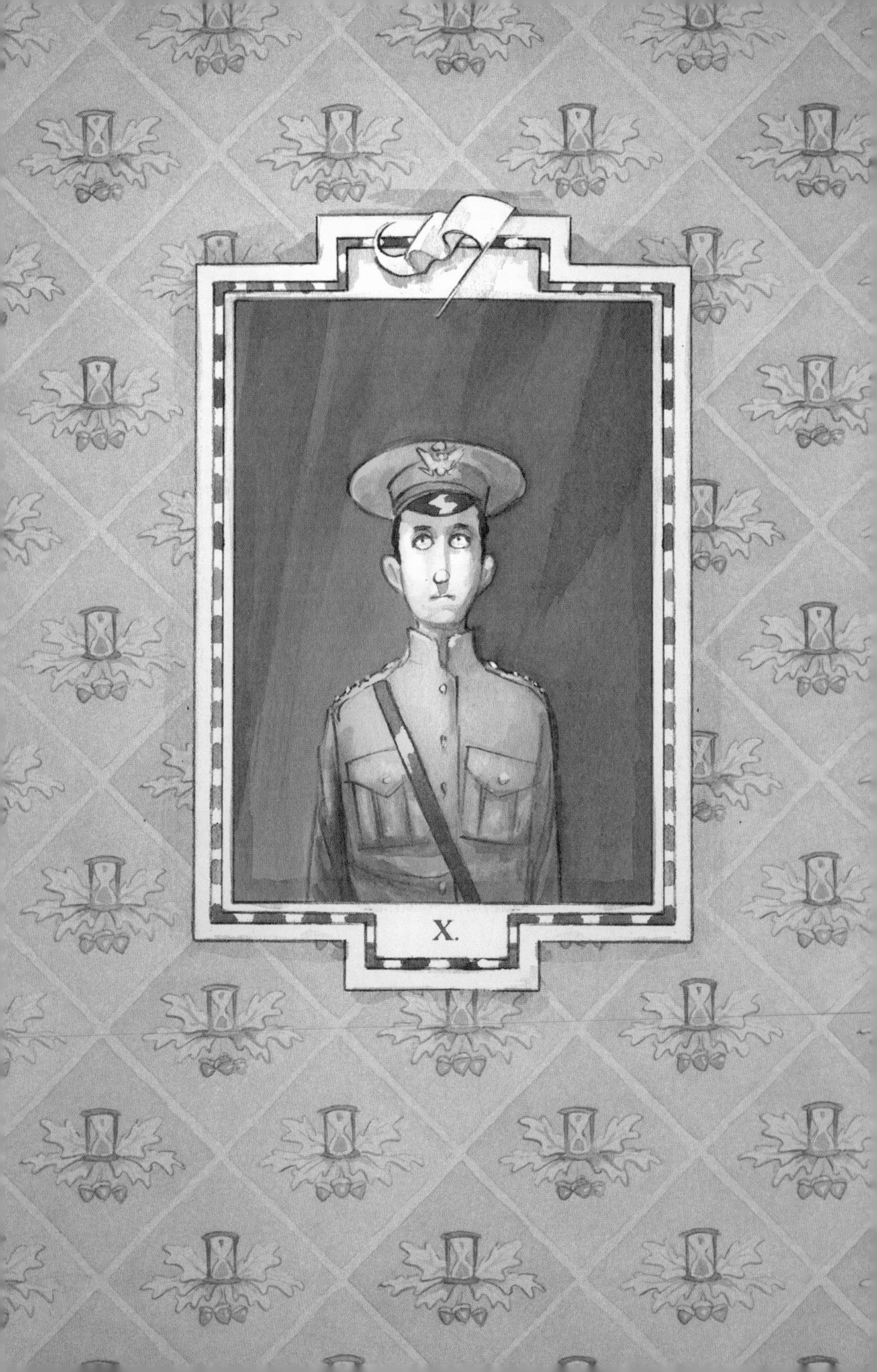
X.

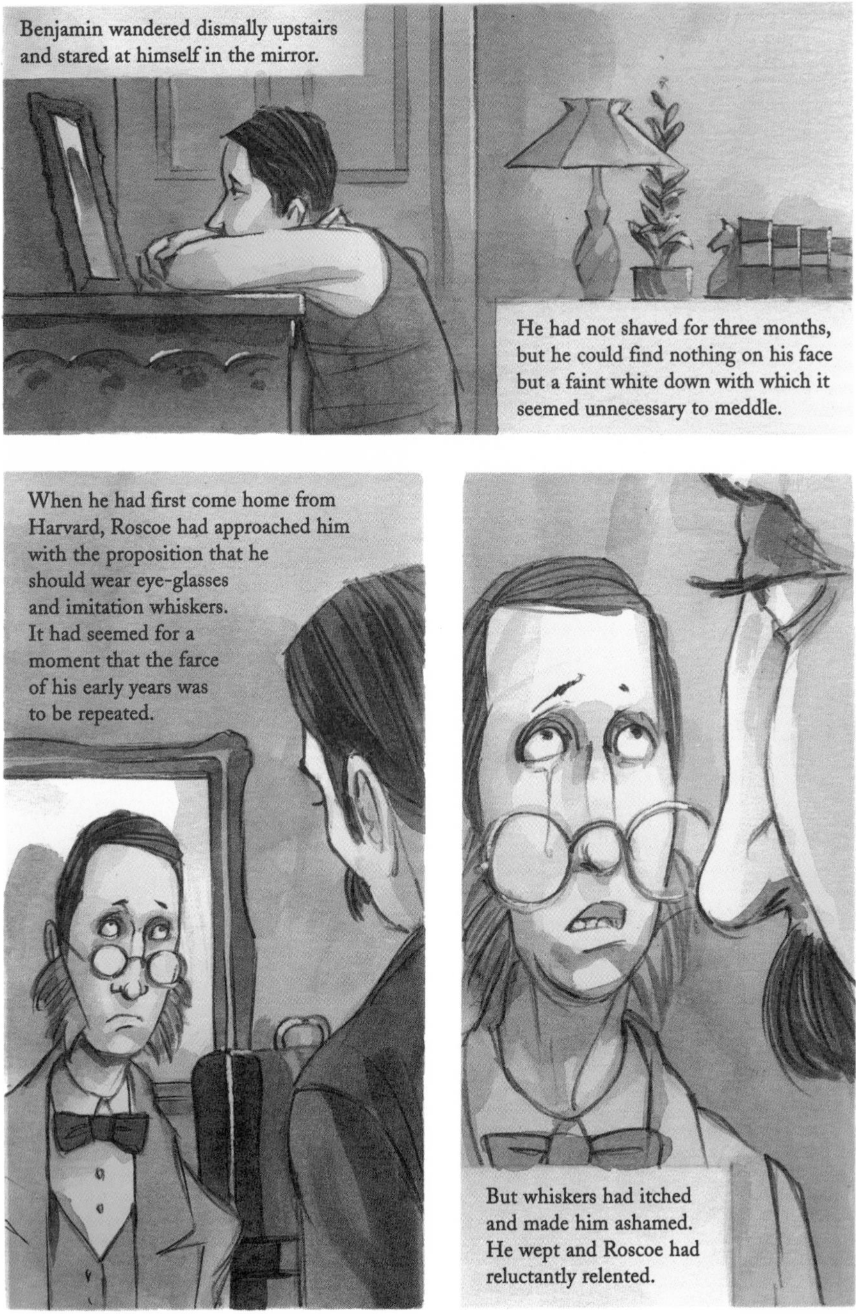
Benjamin wandered dismally upstairs and stared at himself in the mirror.
He had not shaved for three months, but he could find nothing on his face but a faint white down with which it seemed unnecessary to meddle.
When he had first come home from Harvard, Roscoe had approached him with the proposition that he should wear eye-glasses and imitation whiskers. It had seemed for a moment that the farce of his early years was to be repeated.
But whiskers had itched and made him ashamed. He wept and Roscoe had reluctantly relented.

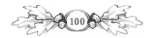

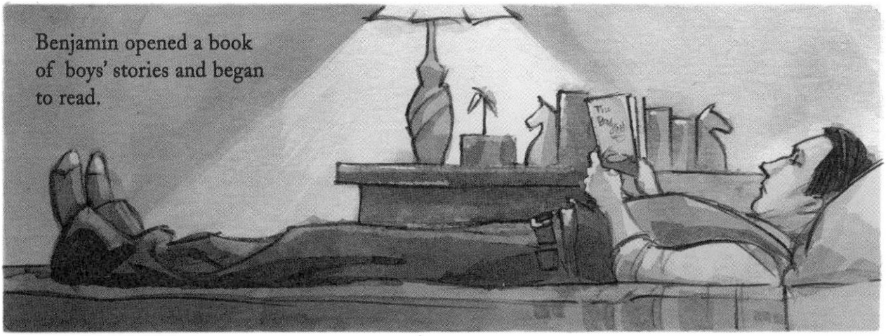
Benjamin opened a book of boys' stories and began to read.

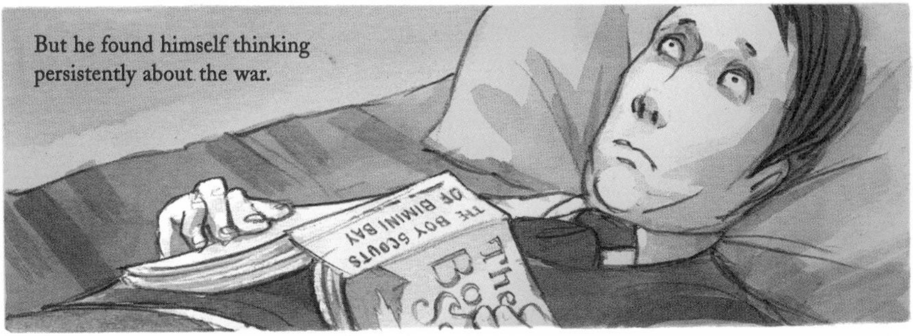
But he found himself thinking persistently about the war.
THE BOY SCOUTS OF BIMINI BAY

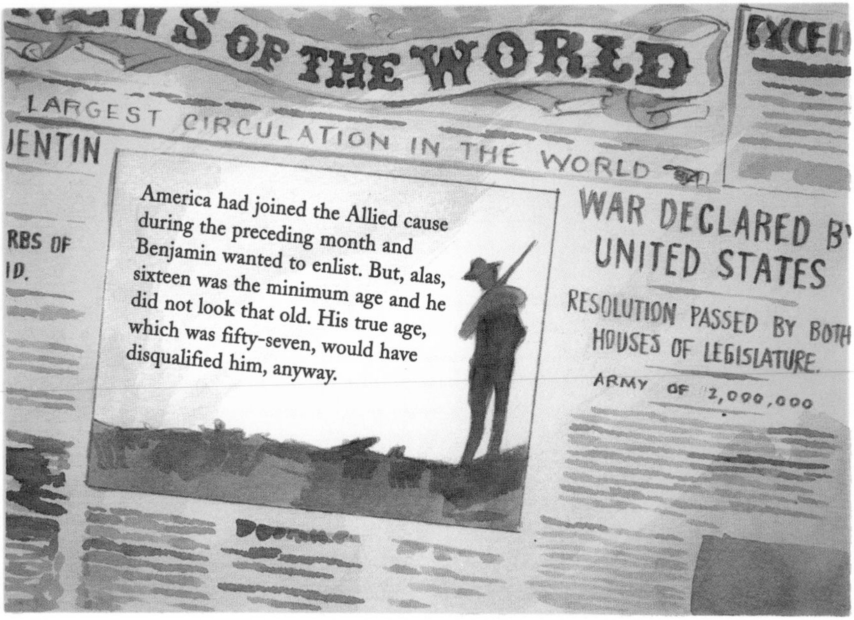
OF THE WORLD
LARGEST CIRCULATION IN THE WORLD
America had joined the Allied cause during the preceding month and Benjamin wanted to enlist. But, alas, sixteen was the minimum age and he did not look that old. His true age, which was fifty-seven, would have disqualified him, anyway.
WAR DECLARED
UNITED STATES
RESOLUTION PASSED BY BOTH HOUSES OF LEGISLATURE.
ARMY OF 2,000,000

There was a knock at his door, and the butler appeared with a letter bearing a large official legend in the corner.

It informed him that many reserve officers who had served in the Spanish-American War were being called back into service at a higher rank.

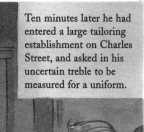

And it enclosed his commission as brigadier-general in the United States Army with orders to report immediately.

Benjamin quivered with enthusiasm. This was what he had wanted.

Ten minutes later he had entered a large tailoring establishment on Charles Street, and asked in his uncertain treble to be measured for a uniform.

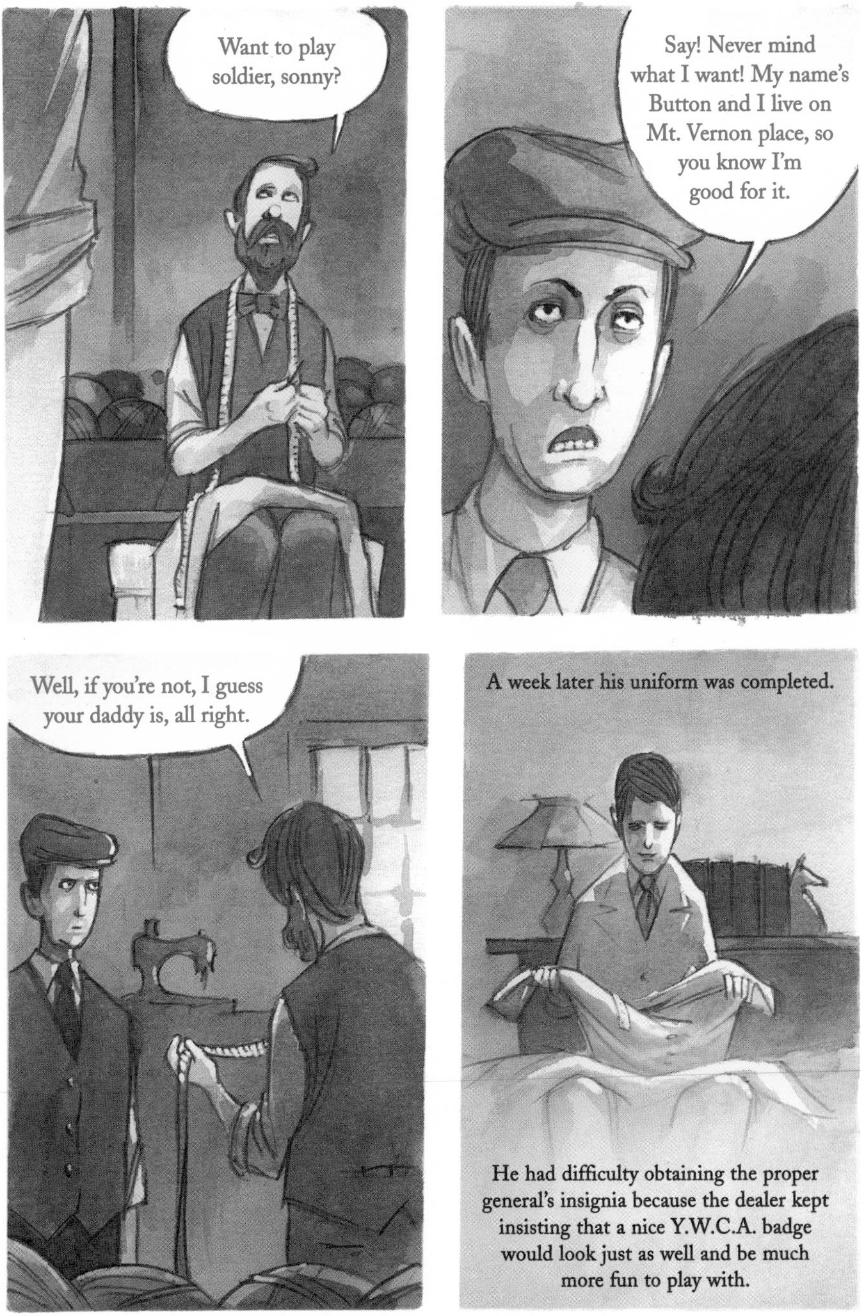
Want to play soldier, sonny?
Say! Never mind what I want! My name's Button and I live on Mt. Vernon place, so you know I'm good for it.
Well, if you're not, I guess your daddy is, all right.
A week later his uniform was completed.
He had difficulty obtaining the proper general's insignia because the dealer kept insisting that a nice Y.W.C.A. badge would look just as well and be much more fun to play with.

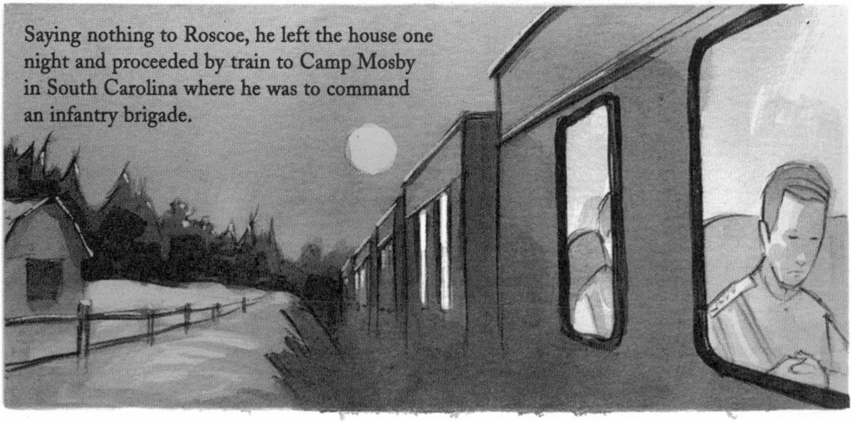
Saying nothing to Roscoe, he left the house one night and proceeded by train to Camp Mosby in South Carolina where he was to command an infantry brigade.

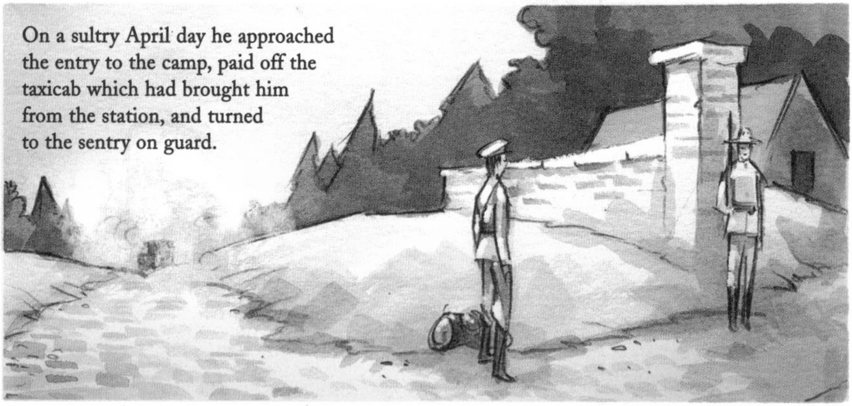
On a sultry April day he approached the entry to the camp, paid off the taxicab which had brought him from the station, and turned to the sentry on guard.

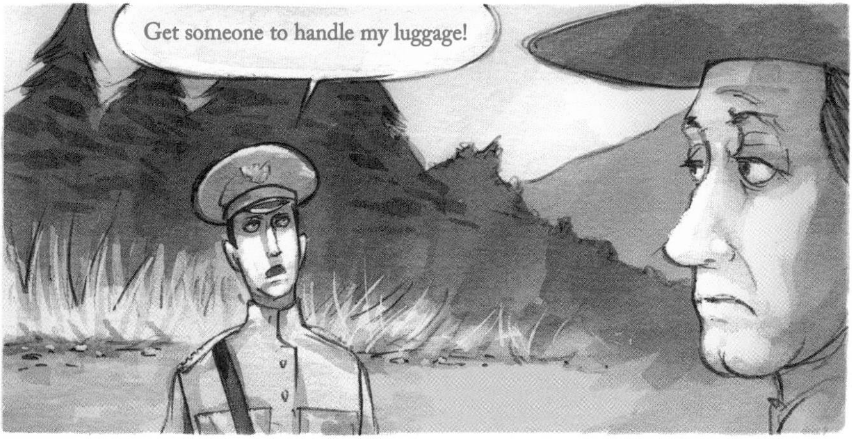
Get someone to handle my luggage!

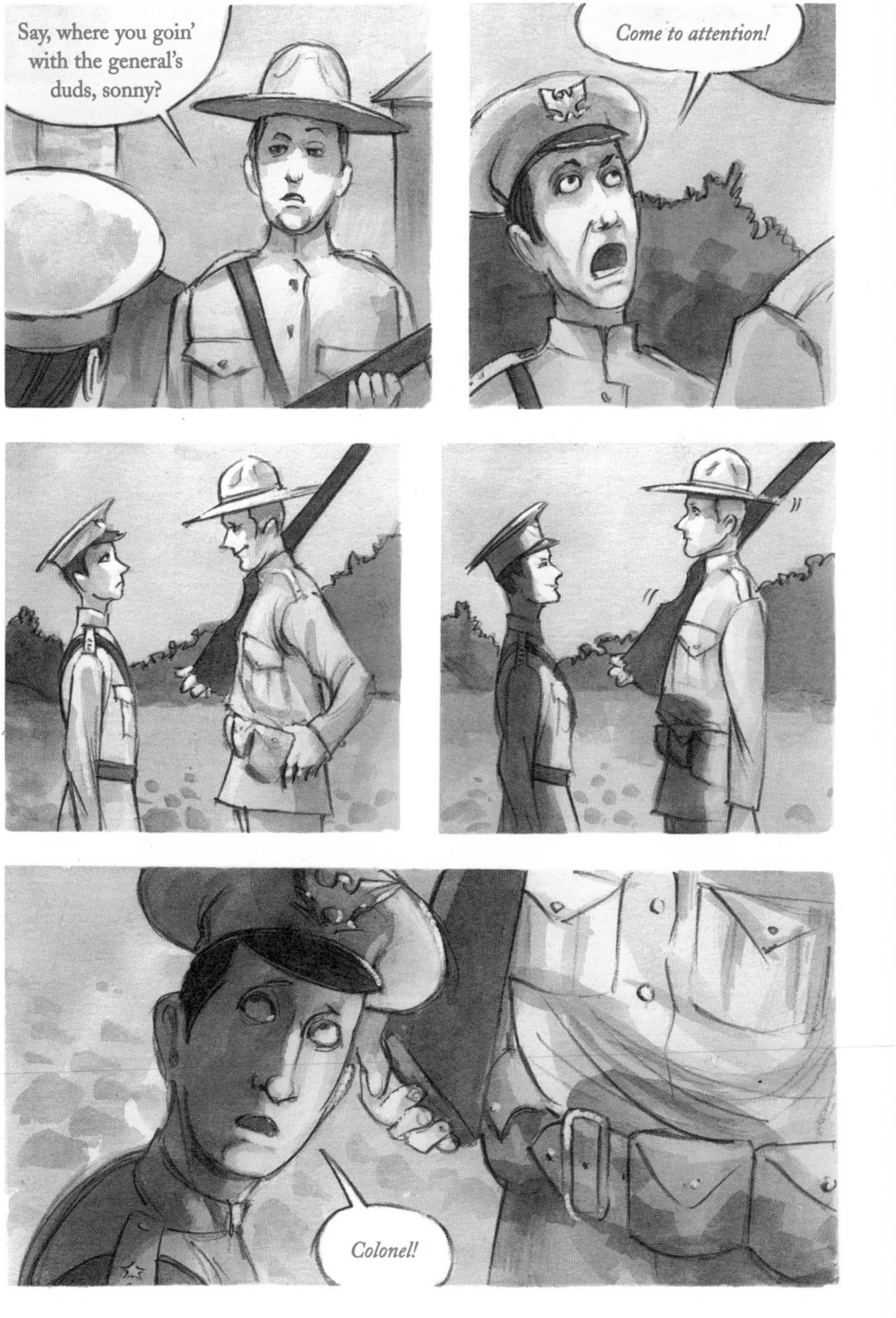
Say, where you goin' with the general's duds, sonny?
Come to attention!
Colonel!

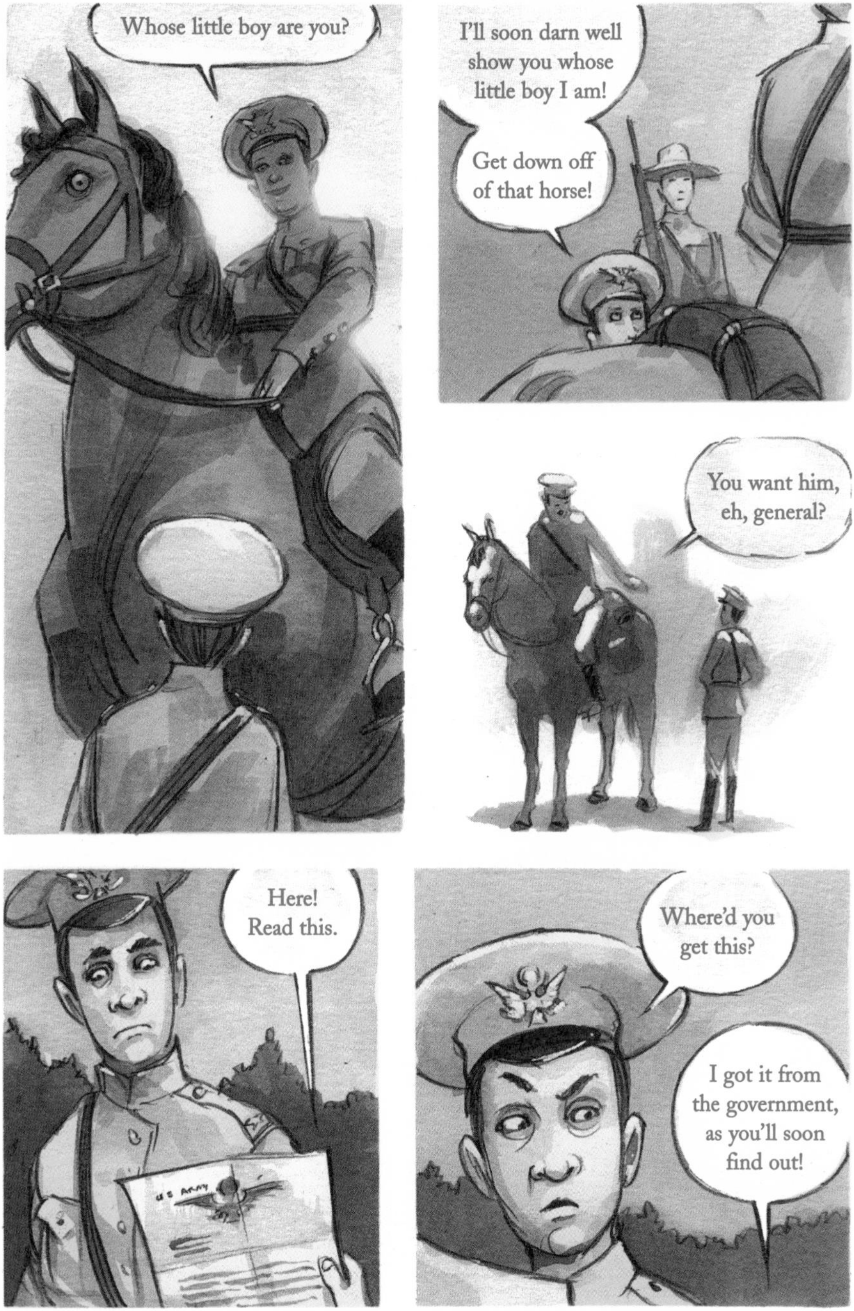
Whose little boy are you?
I'll soon darn well show you whose little boy I am!
Get down off of that horse!
You want him, eh, general?
Here! Read this.
U.S. ARMY
Where'd you get this?
I got it from the government, as you'll soon find out!

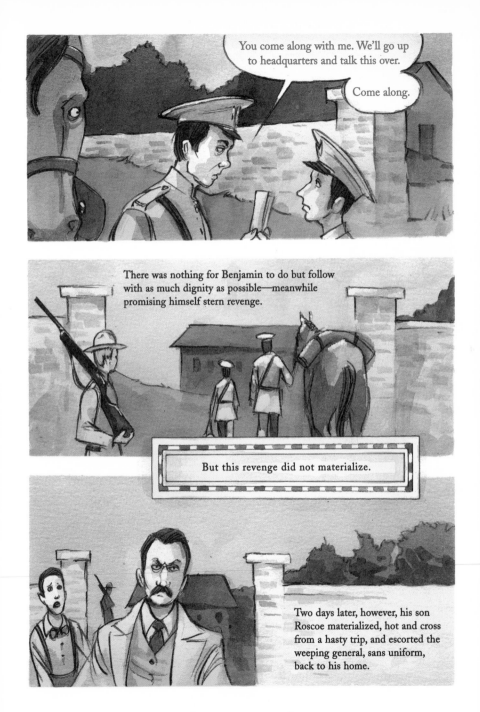

You come along with me. We'll go up to headquarters and talk this over.

Come along.

There was nothing for Benjamin to do but follow with as much dignity as possible—meanwhile promising himself stern revenge.

But this revenge did not materialize.

Two days later, however, his son Roscoe materialized, hot and cross from a hasty trip, and escorted the weeping general, sans uniform, back to his home.

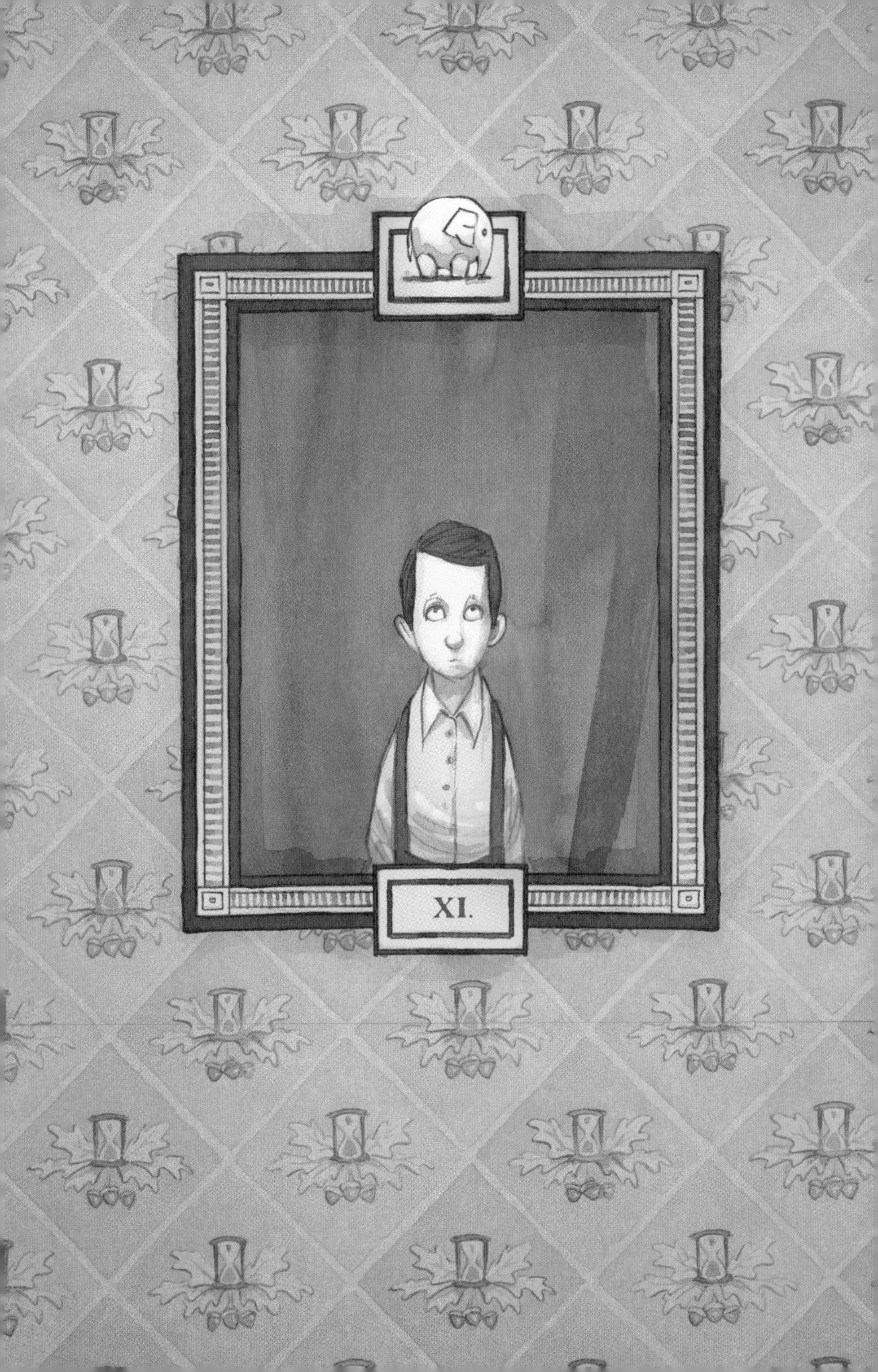
XI.

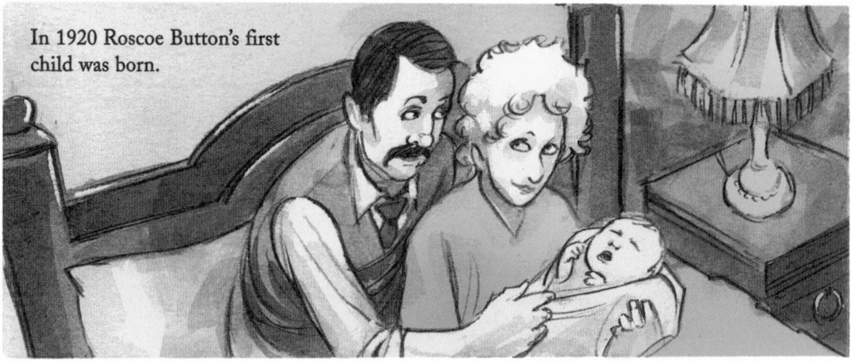
In 1920 Roscoe Button's first child was born.

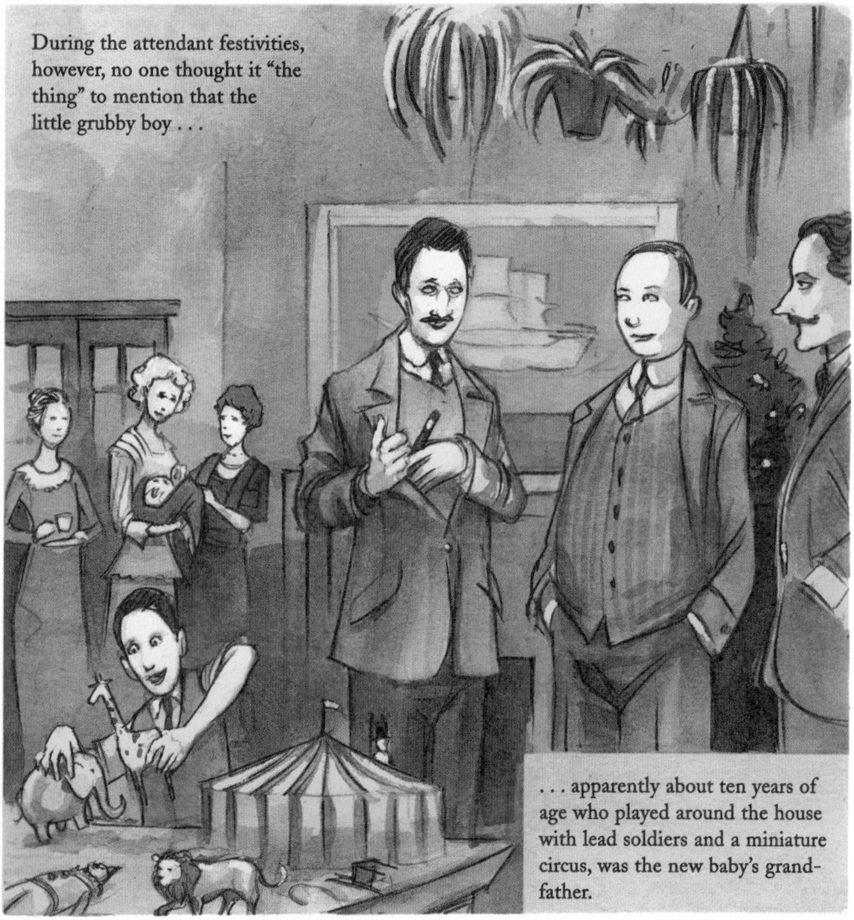
During the attendant festivities, however, no one thought it "the thing" to mention that the little grubby boy . . .
. . . apparently about ten years of age who played around the house with lead soldiers and a miniature circus, was the new baby's grandfather.

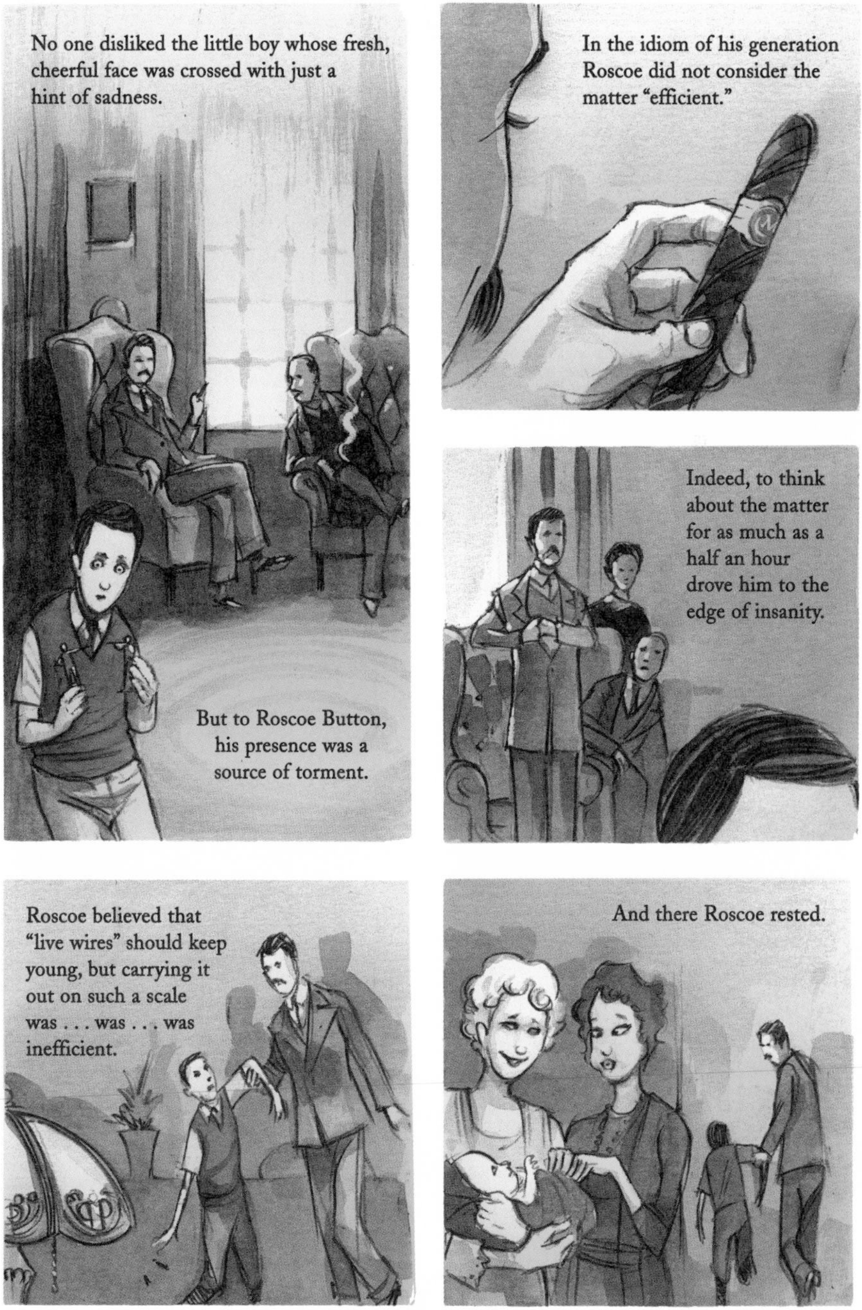
No one disliked the little boy whose fresh, cheerful face was crossed with just a hint of sadness.
But to Roscoe Button, his presence was a source of torment.
In the idiom of his generation Roscoe did not consider the matter "efficient."
Indeed, to think about the matter for as much as a half an hour drove him to the edge of insanity.
Roscoe believed that "live wires" should keep young, but carrying it out on such a scale was . . . was . . . was inefficient.
And there Roscoe rested.

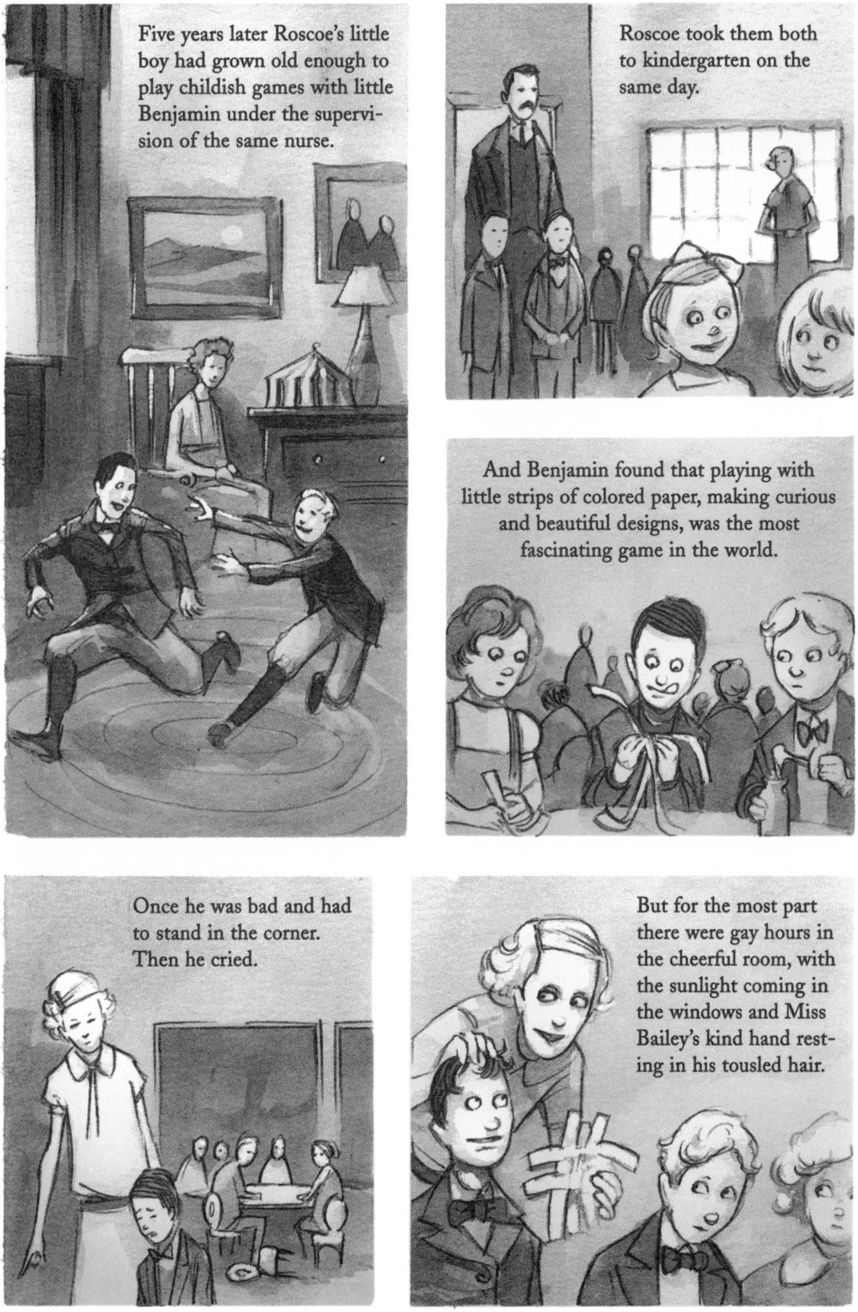
Five years later Roscoe's little boy had grown old enough to play childish games with little Benjamin under the supervision of the same nurse.
Roscoe took them both to kindergarten on the same day.
And Benjamin found that playing with little strips of colored paper, making curious and beautiful designs, was the most fascinating game in the world.
Once he was bad and had to stand in the corner. Then he cried.
But for the most part there were gay hours in the cheerful room, with the sunlight coming in the windows and Miss Bailey's kind hand resting in his tousled hair.

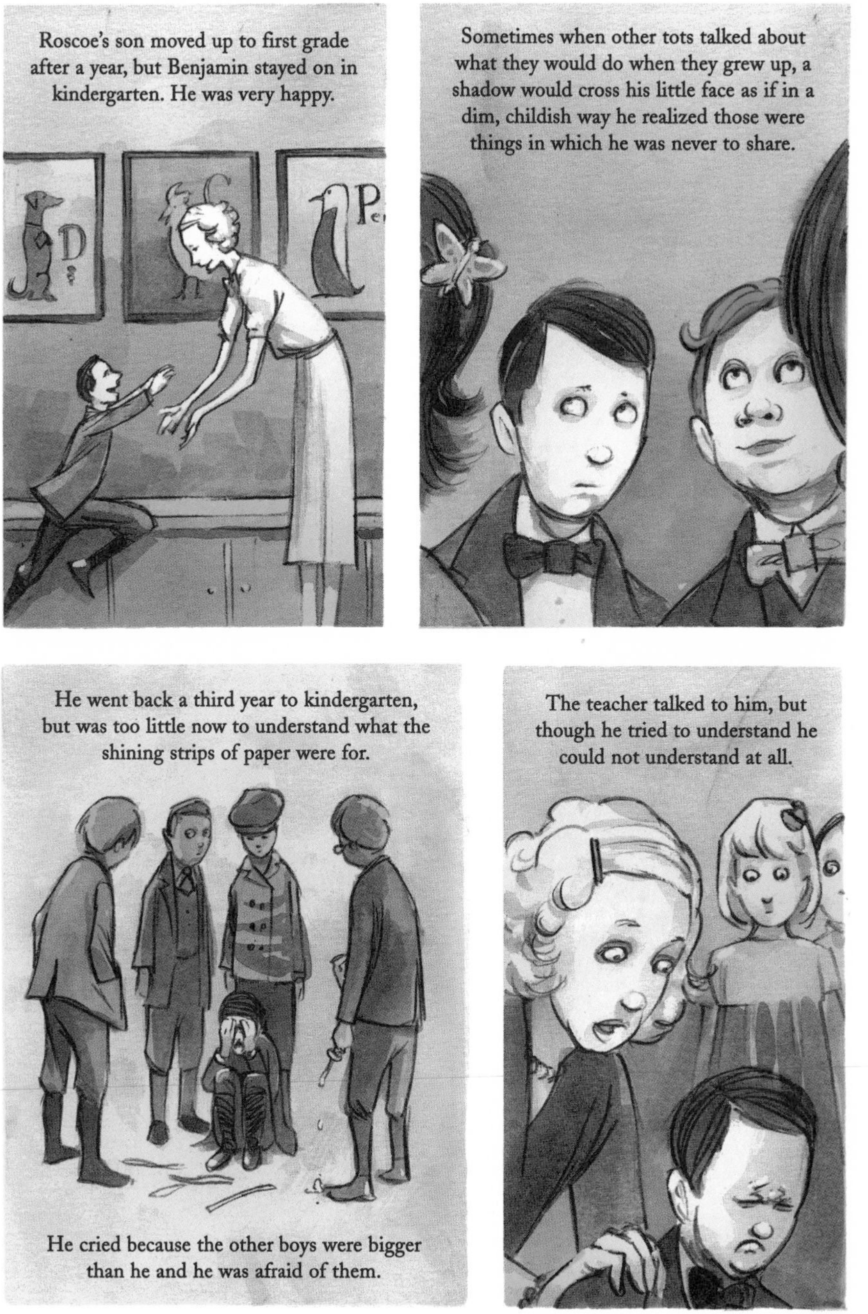
Roscoe's son moved up to first grade after a year, but Benjamin stayed on in kindergarten. He was very happy.
Sometimes when other tots talked about what they would do when they grew up, a shadow would cross his little face as if in a dim, childish way he realized those were things in which he was never to share.
He went back a third year to kindergarten, but was too little now to understand what the shining strips of paper were for.
He cried because the other boys were bigger than he and he was afraid of them.
The teacher talked to him, but though he tried to understand he could not understand at all.

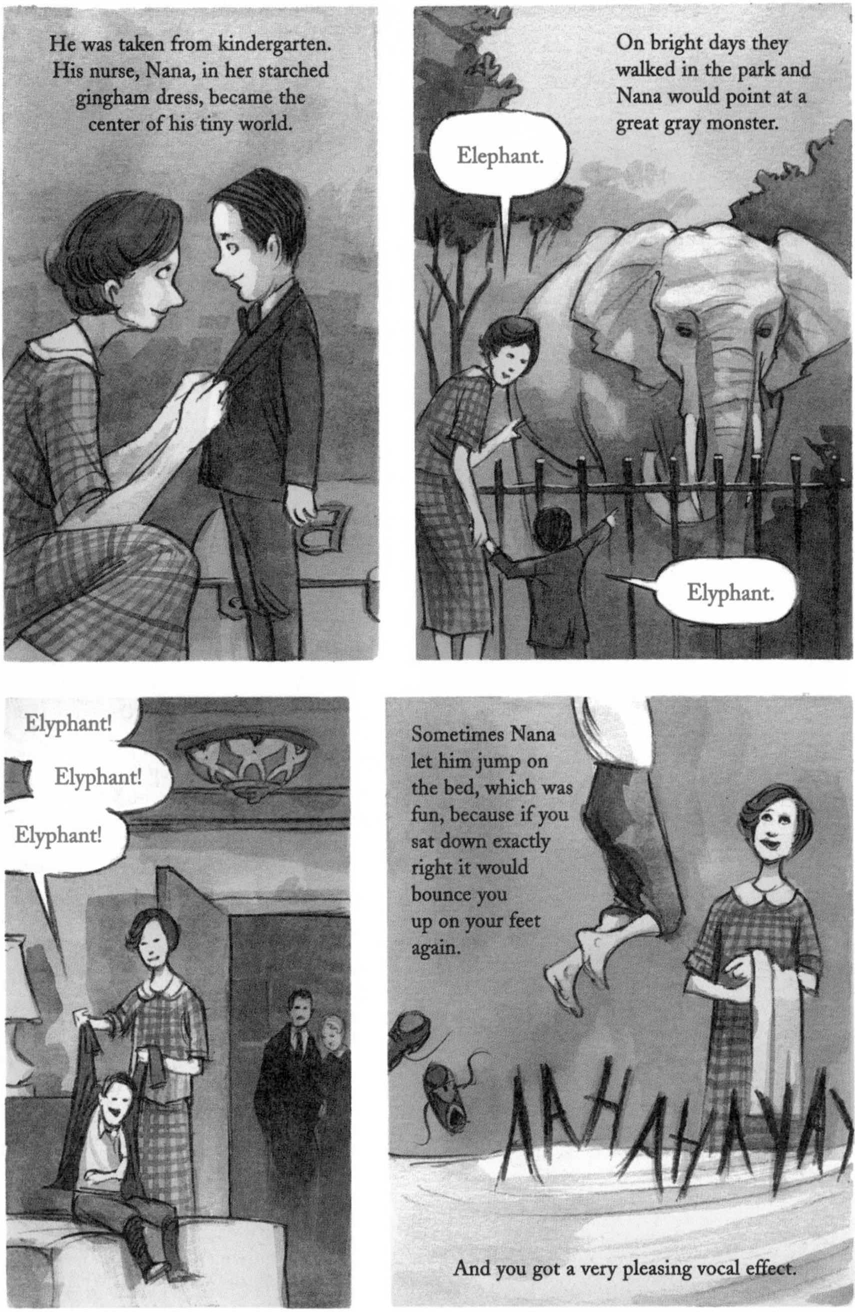
He was taken from kindergarten. His nurse, Nana, in her starched gingham dress, became the center of his tiny world.
On bright days they walked in the park and Nana would point at a great gray monster.
Elephant.
Elyphant.
Elyphant!
Elyphant!
Elyphant!
Sometimes Nana let him jump on the bed, which was fun, because if you sat down exactly right it would bounce you up on your feet again.
AAHAHAYAY
And you got a very pleasing vocal effect.

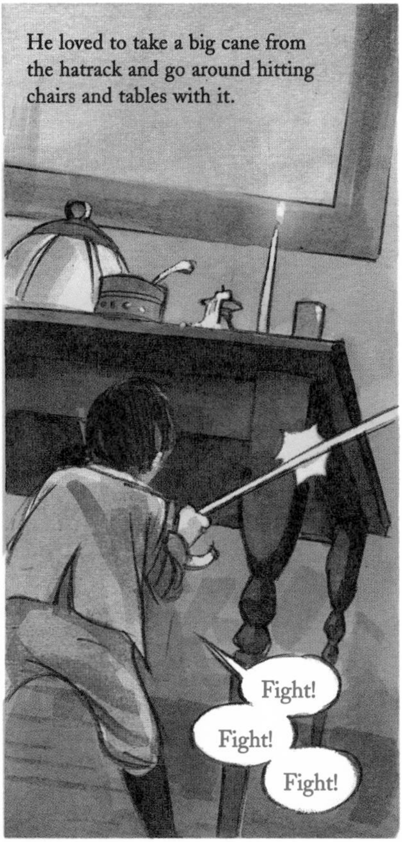
He loved to take a big cane from the hatrack and go around hitting chairs and tables with it.
Fight!
Fight!
Fight!

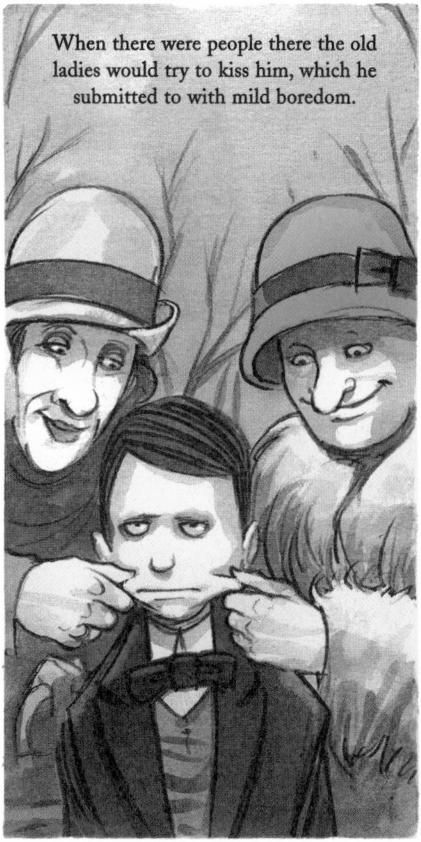
When there were people there the old ladies would try to kiss him, which he submitted to with mild boredom.

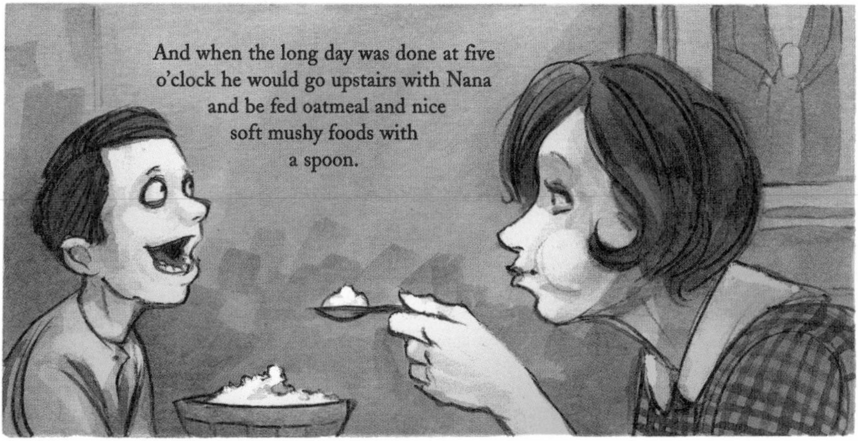
And when the long day was done at five o'clock he would go upstairs with Nana and be fed oatmeal and nice soft mushy foods with a spoon.

There were no troublesome memories in his childish sleep; no token came to him of his brave days at college, of the glittering years when he flustered the hearts of many girls.

There were only the white, safe walls of his crib and Nana and a man who came to see him sometimes.

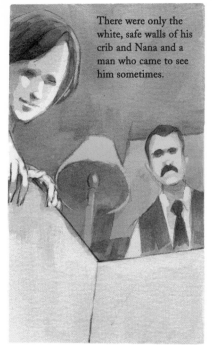

And a great big orange ball that Nana pointed at just before his twilight bed hour and called "sun."

When the sun went, his eyes were sleepy—there were no dreams, no dreams to haunt him.

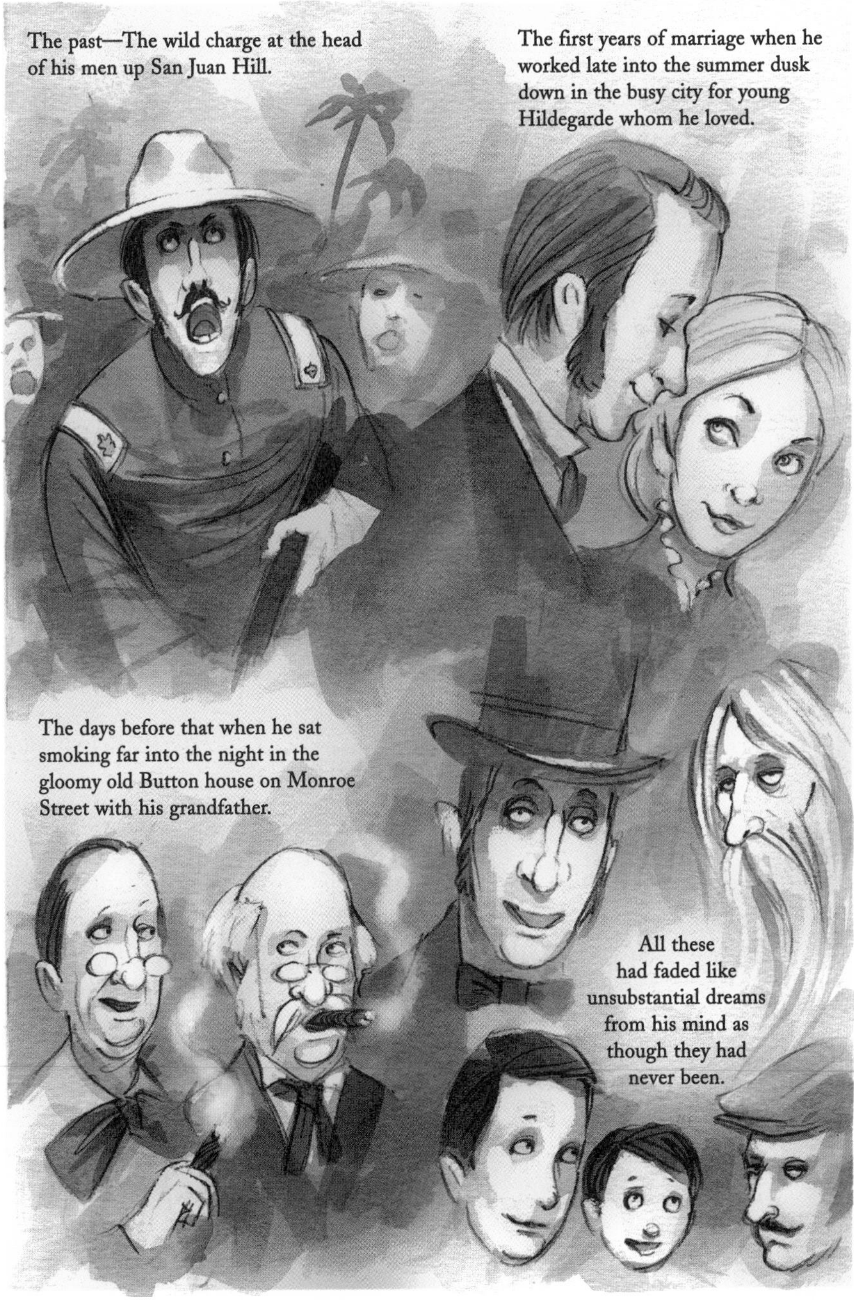
The past—The wild charge at the head of his men up San Juan Hill.
The first years of marriage when he worked late into the summer dusk down in the busy city for young Hildegarde whom he loved.
The days before that when he sat smoking far into the night in the gloomy old Button house on Monroe Street with his grandfather.
All these had faded like unsubstantial dreams from his mind as though they had never been.

He did not remember.

He did not remember clearly whether the milk was warm or cool at his last feeding or how the days passed.

There was only his crib and Nana's familiar presence.

And then he remembered nothing.

When he was hungry, he cried—that was all.

Through the noons and nights he breathed, and over him there were soft mumblings and murmurings that he scarcely heard, and faintly differential smells, and light and darkness.

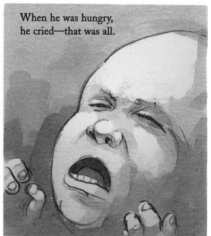

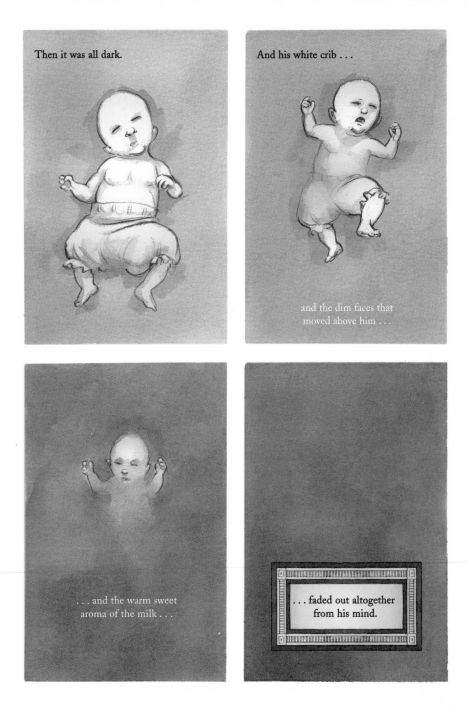

Then it was all dark.

And his white crib . . .

and the dim faces that
moved above him . . .

. . . and the warm sweet
aroma of the milk . . .

. . . faded out altogether
from his mind.

Afterword

CURIOUSER AND CURIOUSER: THE CASE OF BENJAMIN BUTTON

In May 1922, F. Scott Fitzgerald wrote to his literary agent, Harold Ober, with a plan for making money. Impatient with publishing the old-fashioned way—writing stories and then waiting and hoping while Ober shopped them around and negotiated payments with magazine editors—Fitzgerald looked to streamline the process. He proposed forming a contract with David O. Selznick, then at the beginning of his own legendary career, whereby he would send a 1,500-word *synopsis* of a story to the producer for evaluation. If Selznick liked the idea, he would pay the author $2,500, and a complete story of some eight thousand words would then be delivered. "If this works out," Fitzgerald enthused to Ober, "I'm going to do more of the same, as it means just about twice as much money per story, and as it seems unlikely that the satyrical stories I feel moved to write at present (Ben Button + The Diamond in the Sky, for instance) will *ever* bring me any movie money."[1] It didn't work out; Selznick returned the sketch. But unlikely as it may have seemed to Fitzgerald at the time, "Ben Button"—now eighty-six years old—will be reborn as a major motion picture. "Ever" turned out to be an awfully long time.

---

[1] Bruccoli, Matthew J., ed., *As Ever, Scott Fitz: Letters between F. Scott Fitzgerald and His Literary Agent Harold Ober*, 1919–1940 (Philadelphia: Lippincott, 1972), p. 40.

For a brief but anxious period it appeared that "The Curious Case of Benjamin Button" would yield Fitzgerald no financial return whatsoever. He had finished it with great enthusiasm early in 1922, calling it "the funniest story ever written." He acknowledged it to be a "weird thing" but nonetheless declared it "one of his two favorite stories." Along with "The Diamond as Big as the Ritz," it represented, he believed, a significant new phase in his development as a writer. Just a few years earlier, Fitzgerald had arrived on the American literary scene with a flourish. In 1919, he had published his first story in *The Smart Set*, H. L. Mencken's literary monthly, and shortly thereafter made his first sale to the *Saturday Evening Post*, a popular weekly magazine with the highest payment rates in the industry. The following year would be Fitzgerald's *annus mirabilis*: In addition to publishing his first novel, *This Side of Paradise*, and his first collection of stories, *Flappers and Philosophers*, with Scribner, he published five more stories in *The Smart Set* and five more stories in the *Post*. Awash in success, Fitzgerald had already begun to distrust its complications and to make distinctions that would figure centrally in all evaluations of his career. He inscribed a copy of *Flappers and Philosophers* to Mencken with a note dividing the stories into three categories: "Worth reading," "Amusing," and "Trash." The troubling fact, however, was that categorizing the stories by earnings would have produced an order nearly inverse. The kinds of stories upon which his income would come to depend were also those that he would find least rewarding to write.[2]

---

[2] Bruccoli, *As Ever*, pp. 32–33. In 1929 Fitzgerald's royalties on seven books totaled $31.77; eight *Saturday Evening Post* stories brought him $31,000 (Bruccoli, Matthew J., and Judith S. Baughman, *F. Scott Fitzgerald on Authorship* [Columbia: University of South Carolina Press, 1996], p. 13).

At this early, critical juncture in his career, Fitzgerald began experimenting with what he called a "second manner"—satirical fantasy. As Lawrence Buell has noted, Fitzgerald saw himself as developing into a nonrealistic writer and was genuinely enthusiastic about the artistic and commercial possibilities of the fantasy form. He hinted that his next novel would forswear realism, and he worked tirelessly on an intriguingly experimental, but commercially disastrous, stage drama entitled *The Vegetable; or, From President to Postman*. As he planned his second collection of stories, *Tales of the Jazz Age*, he decided to group them into three sections: "My Last Flappers," "Fantasies," and "Unclassified Masterpieces." The strength of the collection, in Fitzgerald's estimation, would be the second section, for "the fantasies are something new & the critics will fall for them." But they didn't, and neither did editors. Ober struggled to sell both "The Diamond as Big as the Ritz" and "The Curious Case of Benjamin Button." Having reluctantly agreed to place the former with the reliably literary but cash-strapped *Smart Set*, Fitzgerald wrote to his agent about "Button": "I was on the point of trying to raise some money to repay your very kind advance, having despaired of selling Benjamin Button to anyone except the *Smart Set*." *Collier's* had finally bought "Button" for a respectable sum, but Fitzgerald had gotten the message. "I know that the magazines only want flapper stories from me," he wrote to Ober soon after, "the trouble you had in disposing of Benjamin Button + The Diamond as Big as the Ritz showed that."[3]

[3] Kuehl, John, and Jackson R. Bryer, eds., *Dear Scott/Dear Max: The Fitzgerald-Perkins Correspondence* (New York: Scribner's, 1971), p. 55. Bruccoli, *As Ever*, pp. 40, 48.

Fitzgerald's career as a fantasist was short-lived, though elements of satirical fantasy would recur in his later work—most notably, perhaps, in the "Valley of Ashes" in *The Great Gatsby*, an apocalyptic wasteland brooded over by the inscrutable, disembodied eyes of Dr. T. J. Eckleberg. As was true of his short fiction in general, Fitzgerald's fantastic tales received scant attention in the decades following his untimely death in 1940. Dismissed as hack work or viewed, at best, as marginal to his career as a novelist, Fitzgerald's stories languished in the obscurity of scholarly neglect until a quickening of interest in the late 1970s began the process of establishing them as essential not only to his oeuvre but also, in a few instances ("Winter Dreams," "May Day," "The Diamond as Big as the Ritz," "Babylon Revisited"), to the canon of modern American literature. "Benjamin Button" has been the subject of only a handful of evaluations and explications.[4]

---

[4] These include Bruccoli, *As Ever*; Bruccoli and Baughman, *Fitzgerald on Authorship*; Buell, Lawrence, "The Significance of Fantasy in Fitzgerald's Short Fiction," in Jackson R. Bryer, ed., *The Short Stories of F. Scott Fitzgerald: New Approaches* (Madison: University of Wisconsin Press, 1982), pp. 23–38; Churchwell, Sarah, "'$4000 a screw': The Prostituted Art of F. Scott Fitzgerald and Ernest Hemingway," *European Journal of American Culture*, vol. 24, no. 2 (2005):105–30; Crosland, Andrew, "Sources for Fitzgerald's 'The Curious Case of Benjamin Button,'" *Fitzgerald/Hemingway Annual* 11 (1979):135–39; Fitzgerald, F. Scott, *Tales of the Jazz Age* (New York: Scribner's, 1922); Gery, John, "The Curious Grace of Benjamin Button," *Studies in Short Fiction* 17 (Fall 1980): 495–97; Gillin, Edward, "Fitzgerald's Twain," in Jackson R. Bryer, Alan Margolies, and Ruth Prigozy, eds., *F. Scott Fitzgerald: New Perspectives* (Athens: University of Georgia Press, 2000), pp. 253–67; Kuehl, John, and Jackson R. Bryer, eds., *Dear Scott/Dear Max*; Petry, Alice Hall, *Fitzgerald's Craft of Short Fiction* (Ann Arbor: University of Michigan Press, 1989).

Long cold, but never closed, his curious case has now been reopened for review. Not since Robert Redford donned white flannels for the 1974 film adaptation of *The Great Gatsby* has Fitzgerald's work enjoyed such attention as that generated by Brad Pitt's star turn as the chronologically-challenged hero of director David Fincher's forthcoming *The Curious Case of Benjamin Button*. Spurred by this popular interest, publishers have sought ways to deliver Fitzgerald's story to a new generation of readers. In addition to the stylishly reconceived and strikingly rendered graphic novel you've just completed, "Button" has been recorded as the title story in a recent audio book (Blackstone Audiobooks) and reissued in a variety of paperback editions. In a development that would no doubt amuse a writer who was deeply versed in the workings of gossip, all things Benjamin Button are also the focus of a variety of blogs, posts, and archives.

In a seriously tongue-in-cheek table of contents to *Tales of the Jazz Age*, Fitzgerald addressed the origins of Benjamin Button's age-reversed existence:

> This story was inspired by a remark of Mark Twain's to the effect that it was a pity that the best part of life came at the beginning and the worst part at the end. By trying the experiment upon only one man in a perfectly normal world I have scarcely given his idea a fair trial.

As Andrew Crosland has documented through reference to letters of the period, Fitzgerald had encountered Twain's observation in reading Albert Bigelow Paine's *Mark Twain: A Biography* (1912):

[Twain] regarded the decrepitude of old age as an unnecessary part of life. Often he said, "If I had been helping the Almighty when he created man, I would have had him begin at the other end, and start human beings with old age. How much better it would have been to start old and have all the bitterness and blindness of age in the beginning! One would not mind then if he were looking forward to a joyful youth. Think of the joyous prospect of growing young instead of old! Think of looking forward to eighteen instead of eighty! Yes, the Almighty made a poor job of it. I wish He had invited my assistance."

Although the Almighty had foregone Twain's assistance, Fitzgerald recognized a good storyline when he heard one, and "Benjamin Button" can be read as an extended "think" on whether the experience of growing young instead of old would be as joyous as Twain suggests. But the story is a conversation with Twain on broader and more substantial issues as well. Much like Twain, Fitzgerald uses fantasy not as a means of escape but as a method of engagement. Exploiting the exaggerations and incongruities inherent in a realistic presentation of fantastical circumstances, Fitzgerald uses humor to grease the gears of satire. Much like Twain, Fitzgerald is a moralist and idealist at heart, and his account of Benjamin Button's progress through America's Gilded Age subtly excoriates its moral hypocrisies and social corruptions even as it admires its evident vitality, strength, and industry.

Much to the shame of his parents and the consternation of polite Southern society, Benjamin is born in 1860 at age seventy and dies as an infant in 1930. What is most strik-

ing about his backward progress through life, however, is not the extent to which others fear he sticks out, but the thoroughness with which he succeeds in making himself fit in. As John Gery has insightfully observed, Benjamin Button's life is imbued with a "curious grace." The consequence of his "difference" is not alienation. Benjamin succeeds quite nicely in life because "rather than opposing the mores of his world, [he] in fact more exactly than any other character in the story adheres to and lives by those mores":

> During the Golden Age of capitalism, he turns the family hardware concern into a thriving business, receives a medal for heroism at San Juan Hill in 1898, perfects all the fashionable dance steps at the turn of the century, and scores seven touchdowns and fourteen field goals *against* Yale as he stars for the 1910 Harvard football team—all the while to the aggravation of his normally aging contemporaries.[5]

From this perspective, "Benjamin Button" is a distinctly American fable about the power of individualism, for it not only demonstrates the error of shunning the extraordinary man but also confirms the ideal that it is the "curious" individual who shapes the course of history.

For all of the weighty historical and philosophical ideas with which it may be loaded, "The Curious Case of Benjamin Button" remains first and foremost a jaunty and marvelous tale, a curiosity in the very best sense. Surely one source of its considerable charm is the refusal of its protagonist to always take himself, or his problems, too seriously. It is a winsome character trait that he shared

[5] Gery, "Curious Grace," pp. 495–97.

with his author, who concluded the preface to the story in *Tales of the Jazz Age* with a bit of fan mail from an anonymous admirer in Cincinnati:

Sir–
I have read the story Benjamin Button in Colliers and I wish to say that as a short story writer you would make a good lunatic. I have seen many peices of cheese in my life but of all the peices of cheese I have ever seen you are the biggest peice. I hate to waste a peice of stationary on you but I will.

Curiouser and curiouser.

DONALD G. SHEEHY
Edinboro University of Pennsylvania

Biographies

F. Scott Fitzgerald is widely regarded as one of the twentieth century's greatest writers. He was born in St. Paul, Minnesota, in 1896 and published his first novel, *This Side of Paradise*, in 1920. His other novels include *The Beautiful and the Damned*, *The Great Gatsby*, and *Tender Is the Night*. He died of a heart attack in 1940 at the age of forty-four.

Nunzio DeFilippis and Christina Weir are the authors of several original graphic novels, including *Skinwalker*, *Three Strikes*, *Maria's Wedding*, and *Past Lies* (all from Oni Press). They've also worked extensively in superhero comics and have written for *Wonder Woman*, *New X-Men*, *Adventures of Superman*, and *Hellions*. They live in Los Angeles and also work in film and television.

Kevin Cornell is an illustrator and designer from Philadelphia, Pennsylvania. He maintains the Web Site www.bearskinrug.co.uk, which he frequently updates with sketches, comics, and mildly amusing prose. Although doctors confirm that he's aging forward in a normal fashion, they agree his maturity level is still rather stunted.

A scholar, poet, and avid nature photographer, Donald Sheehy is a Professor of English at Edinboro University of Pennsylvania, where he teaches American literature and writing courses in the Department of English and Theatre Arts. He has published extensively on the life and work of Robert Frost and is an editor of *The Letters of Robert Frost*, forthcoming from Harvard University Press.